FOR THE LOVE
OF CAKE

Acclaim for Erin Dutton's Work

"*Designed for Love* is …rich in love, romance, and sex. Dutton gives her readers a roller coaster ride filled with sexual thrills and chills. *Designed for Love* is the perfect book to curl up with on a cold winter's day."—*Just About Write*

"*Sequestered Hearts* is packed with raw emotion, but filled with tender moments too. The author writes with sophistication that one would expect from a veteran author. …A romance is about more than just plot and character development. It's about passion, physical intimacy, and connection between the characters. The reader should have a visceral reaction to what is going on within the pages for the novel to succeed. Dutton's words match perfectly with the emotion she has created. *Sequestered Hearts* is one book that cannot be overlooked. It is romance at its finest."—*L-word Literature.com*

"*Sequestered Hearts* by first time novelist, Erin Dutton, is everything a romance should be. It is teeming with longing, heartbreak, and of course, love. …As pure romances go, it is one of the best in print today."—*Just About Write*

In *Fully Involved* "…Dutton's studied evocation of the macho world of firefighting gives the story extra oomph—and happily ever after is what a good romance is all about, right?"—*Q Syndicate*

With *Point of Ignition*… "Erin Dutton has given her fans another fast paced story of fire, with both buildings and emotions burning hotly. …Dutton has done an excellent job of portraying two women who are each fighting for their own dignity and learning to trust again. The delicate tug of war between the characters is well done as is the dichotomy of boredom and drama faced daily by the firefighters. *Point of Ignition* is a story told well that will touch its readers."
—*Just About Write*

Visit us at www.boldstrokesbooks.com

By the Author

Sequestered Hearts

Fully Involved

A Place to Rest

Designed for Love

Point of Ignition

A Perfect Match

Reluctant Hope

More Than Friends

For the Love of Cake

FOR THE LOVE OF CAKE

by

Erin Dutton

2015

ISBN 13: 978-1-62639-241-0

This Trade Paperback Original Is Published By
Bold Strokes Books, Inc.
P.O. Box 249
Valley Falls, NY 12185

First Edition: February 2015

Credits
Editor: Shelley Thrasher
Production Design: Susan Ramundo
Cover Design By Sheri (graphicartist2020@hotmail.com)

Acknowledgments

With every new book, I learn new things from my editor, Dr. Shelley Thrasher. Shelley, you make every book even better and you make me a stronger writer. Thanks also to everyone at Bold Strokes Books who does their part to produce a library that I'm incredibly proud to be a part of.

With this book, I also got the opportunity to explore another interest. I was honored to have Sheri include one of my photographs in her awesome cover design. Thanks to Marcia and Lana at Hermitage Bakery for your friendship and for allowing me to watch you work. And for your petit-fours. They are truly amazing.

Thanks to fellow BSB author Rebekah Weatherspoon for sharing your knowledge of reality television. Any errors or liberties I've taken are mine alone.

Thanks to D. Jackson Leigh, Donna K. Ford, Yolanda Wallace, and VK Powell for including me in the Southeast Pride Tour these past couple of years. Meeting up with these talented authors inspires me to work harder and write more. And to everyone who's come out to visit our booths and chat with us about books. It's so cool to talk to fellow readers and share the excitement.

As always, I'm grateful for my friends and family who love and support me in everything I do. I'm so blessed. This book wouldn't have been possible without the help of my partner, Christina. She is always there when I need to talk about the story. And, when necessary, she takes care of everything else, so I have time to get the words on the page.

Dedication

To dessert...because you inspire me and I love you.

Chapter One

Y ou're the most well-known openly bisexual chef on
television today."

Maya Vaughn canted her head and regarded Charlie Sutter with
an expression she knew conveyed amusement. "Is that a question?"

She refused to open up completely, even though she'd agreed to
the interview. Well-known for gaining access to the most exclusive
celebrity stories, Charlie pretty much expected full disclosure. But
Maya had a rebellious reputation to uphold. And she'd managed to
maintain control by insisting the interview take place in her NoLita
apartment. In fact, these days, she sometimes only felt in control
while ensconced in the light, modern interior of her place in the
trendy neighborhood of Manhattan.

She gave Charlie credit for holding her gaze steadily. "I'm
looking for confirmation."

"That I'm the most well-known? Or that I label myself as
bisexual?" Maya deliberately drew out the question. She leaned back
in the black wingback chair, concentrating on the feel of cool leather
against her bare shoulders. She'd chosen her loose-fitting, sleeveless
top in order to project the same casual air she was currently faking.
"I don't need a label. I love who I love."

"Isn't that just a line?"

She shrugged. "It works." She stopped short of giving Charlie
a flirtatious wink, but judging by the slight narrowing of his eyes,
he'd received the message.

"In the past few years, you've been linked with a number of men and women."

She raised a pierced brow and let the statement hang in the air, forcing Charlie to go on.

"Have you loved them all?"

"Have you loved everyone you've dated?"

"We're talking about *your* escapades."

"Escapades?"

"What else would you call sleeping with," Charlie glanced down, flipping through his index cards though Maya guessed he only did so for effect, "six women and four men in the past year?"

"Wow, exact numbers. So, you were just being politely vague a moment ago?" Inwardly, she winced at the reference to the past year, but on the outside she remained unruffled.

This time, Charlie waited.

"I haven't slept with everyone I've been photographed with, not that it's anyone's business." She hated the defensiveness in her voice. And she resented the focus of this interview. Despite her many accomplishments, including an upcoming stint as a mentor on a food-competition show, her sexuality remained forefront on everyone's mind. Because she identified as unapologetically bi, she was automatically promiscuous.

"I'm not judging you, Maya." Charlie's suddenly low tone set off a tingle of apprehension. "In fact, after last year I would say you've earned a little recreation."

She fought to keep her expression neutral, knowing only the twitch of tiny muscles around her eyes gave away her growing irritation as they trod dangerously close to a topic she considered completely off-limits. She shifted in her chair and crossed her legs in order to cover the instinctive squirm. The silence grew uncomfortable as each waited for the other to speak. Charlie leaned forward as if he meant to touch her arm, but he never closed the distance between them. His sympathetic smile contradicted the predatory gleam in his eyes, and she tensed for flight. She could throw them out right now. Though she'd allowed the cameras into the spacious living room, thanks to the open floor plan, it was only fifteen steps across the gleaming, mahogany hardwood to the door.

"Now you've got a new project coming up."

She relaxed only slightly, uncertain if he'd dropped the subject or if he wanted to lure her into complacency. "Yes. I'm very excited to be taking a turn as one of the mentors on *For the Love of Cake*." The well-known reality show responsible for her own fame was about to begin its seventh season. The producers worried the format had become stale so they'd offered her a contract as a mentor in an attempt to boost the ratings.

"You're the first former alum to become a mentor. To date, you're still the most popular competitor."

"That's a matter of opinion."

"One that many people share."

Now she was certain she was being buttered up.

"I understand they've moved this year's competition out of New York City. Nashville, is it?" He continued to lead her onto safe ground.

"That's right. The producers hope bringing the show closer to the roots of the country might connect with the audience." Most people assumed the South was only good for barbeque and the meat-and-three joints known for their country cooking. But Nashville's food scene was evolving in every forum, from food-truck fare to upscale dining.

"You must welcome the change of venue. Another chance to get out from under the microscope and all."

She braced her hands against the arms of her chair and shifted forward. "I don't have a need to escape."

"No? In less than a year, you've taped three television specials, written a cookbook, and made the rounds of talk shows and magazine covers. I'd say you've set an impossible pace lately."

"Apparently not. Since, as you so aptly pointed out, I've had plenty of time for socializing." She surged to her feet, pulled off her mic, and dropped it in her chair.

"Maya—"

"This interview is over."

"Wait."

"No." Maya strode toward the bedroom, desperate to put a wall between them. Charlie followed, his shoes heavy on the hardwood floors.

"I only meant—"

Maya whirled around quickly, bringing them face-to-face. "I know exactly what you meant. And you know you overstepped. Edit what you have so far however you wish. But we're done now."

❖

"Jori?" Sawyer Drake called as she walked through the front door of Drake's Desserts. "We don't have any customers out here. We could flip the closed sign, lock the door, and—"

Shannon Hayes hurried through the swinging door from the kitchen, hoping to make her presence known before Sawyer embarrassed herself.

"Not going to finish the sentence?" Shannon asked with an easy grin. She wheeled a rack of baked goods close to the display case and began arranging pastries inside.

"No. I don't think I will." Sawyer stepped closer, obviously drawn by the smell of chocolate permeating the entire shop.

"Too bad. It would be the most action I've had in a long time." In the twelve months that Shannon had worked at the bakery, she'd become friends with Sawyer and her partner Jori Diamantina, chef-owner of Drake's Desserts.

"To be fair, you've been working pretty hard."

"Yeah, I should ask my boss for a day off so I can get laid." Shannon winked and tilted her head toward the kitchen.

She wouldn't have the energy for a social life even if she wanted one. Though she'd been hired primarily as a cake decorator, she had a knack for assisting customers at the front counter as well, allowing Jori to spend more time in the kitchen where she was happiest, anyway.

Then, by the grace of God and Facebook, the cake orders had increased steadily with her growing reputation. Last week, Jori had hired a college student to work the counter for summer during peak times in order to free Shannon up for decorating.

"Is this what you two talk about when I'm not around?" Jori asked as she pushed through the swinging door.

Sawyer shrugged. "What could be more important?"

"For Shannon? Her new career."

"I think we've proved you can have sex and a career." Sawyer inched closer to Jori and touched her waist. "Though it certainly is a lot more work when you throw in two careers."

"Thank you, for describing sex with me as *work*."

Sawyer kissed Jori's cheek, then leaned around her to eye the fresh chocolate-chip cookies on the bakery rack. She'd only taken one step when Jori grasped her wrist.

"Stay away from my cookies."

"You know you're going to give them up. You always do." Sawyer squeezed Jori's hip, then smiled, reached around, and snagged a cookie. "I've never been able to resist them."

Jori laughed. "If your name wasn't on the sign I'd never let you get away with that."

Sawyer pulled a five-dollar bill from her pocket and dropped it on the counter. "Worth every penny. And you had your chance to have *your* name up there."

Jori pulled out the same comment about the name of the bakery at least once a month. And every time Sawyer's response was the same. It didn't matter to Shannon what name was on the sign, as long as she got to come to work there every morning. She loved Jori's confidence in her and the creative freedom she granted, and she also enjoyed the familial feel of the small shop and its proprietors.

Jori punched a button on the register and slid the five in the drawer, then pushed it closed. "I wish all of our customers tipped like you do."

"Ah—of course. I'm glad I didn't give you the twenty. So, Shannon, have you been practicing?"

"What?"

Sawyer drew an envelope from her back pocket and turned it to reveal the return address. Then she held it up as if pretending to read the contents against the sunlight from the front window. "Well, I happened to grab the mail on my way in here. Why did you use the bakery address for your application anyway?"

A month ago, Shannon had confessed that she'd applied for a spot on the reality show *For the Love of Cake*. She'd apologized for her poor timing and assured them that she probably wouldn't get it anyway.

"No way," Jori said, reaching for the envelope.

"Whoa, this is Shannon's." Sawyer jerked it away as Jori made one more grab for it, then handed it to Shannon.

"I hope you don't mind that I used the address here. My mailman keeps putting my mail in my neighbor's box, and I'm not certain it's all making its way across the hall." Shannon slipped a finger under the loose edge of the flap and paused. "I don't know if I can open it."

"Sure you can."

"No, I can't. I've been telling myself and everyone else that the show didn't matter that much, but now that I'm holding this—"

"Oh, for heaven's sake, give me that." Jori snatched it away and ripped it open. She began reading to herself while still talking. "You've had us waiting for weeks. I just have to know if—"

"What does it say?" Shannon demanded.

"You got it."

"What?"

"You. Got. It."

"No."

Jori laughed and handed over the paper. "Yes."

"Oh my God." Shannon shook her head, shock making it difficult to read the words on the page.

"So, I'll ask you again." Sawyer wrapped her arm around Jori's waist and smiled at Shannon. "Have you been practicing?"

"I've been dreaming about cake, but I don't know that I'll ever feel completely prepared."

"Why not?" Sawyer asked as she took her turn reading the letter.

"It's not just the cake. I'm looking forward to being challenged and inspired. But—it's national television. I feel a little queasy just thinking about it."

"I know what you mean," Jori said.

"Yeah, Jori would have thrown up already."

"Okay, maybe I would have." Jori pushed Sawyer away playfully. "But you don't have to sound so smug about it." To Shannon, she said, "You'd better get ready. You'll be representing Drake's."

"Oh, believe me. I'm aware of how much pressure I'm under to perform."

"Hey, I was teasing, sort of. I know how hard you've worked for this. I can't say we won't miss you, but we're proud of you."

"Even if I'm eliminated early and return after a day begging for my job back?"

"Absolutely. You'll have a job here as long as you want. But I don't think you'll need it. You're going to be great."

"So, when do you start?" Sawyer asked.

"Two weeks. Not quite long enough to get things in order. But luckily the taping has been moved to Nashville this year so I won't be too far away."

"So close, but not near enough. Even if the producers would allow it, I doubt you'll have time to be here. I don't know how we'll find someone to fill your shoes that quickly," Jori said.

"I went to school with a talented woman named Mackenzie."

"Emphasis on decorating?"

"Well, she's not as good as me, but—yeah, she's a great decorator." She winked. "I can pass on that you'll be looking for someone, if you'd like."

"Absolutely. Tell her to drop by sometime."

Shannon scanned the letter once more, then folded the pages. She got her bag from under the counter and shoved them inside, her fingers brushing the magazine she'd put there earlier and forgotten about.

"Have you seen this?" She slapped the magazine on the counter between her and Jori. Sawyer started to lean in, but Jori snatched it.

"It was waiting in my mailbox yesterday."

"Yum," Jori murmured as she gazed at the cover. "Thank God your mailman didn't give this away."

"What is it, some kind of cooking magazine?" Sawyer asked.

"Sort of." Shannon blushed. "There's an article on Maya Vaughn in there."

Jori flipped the pages until she found the story.

"Who's Maya Vaughn?" Sawyer narrowed her eyes at Jori.

"The hottest pastry chef on the planet." Jori tossed Sawyer a sexy smile, obviously knowing she could get away with that type of comment.

"I thought *you* were the hottest pastry chef on the planet." Sawyer moved closer, surveyed the full-page photo opposite the feature story, and whistled.

From where Shannon stood, she could see the photo clearly, though she didn't need to. She'd already read the article several times and studied the picture for longer than she was willing to admit. In fact, she'd read every article she'd found featuring Maya since she first appeared on the very show she would now be a part of. Though she hated to admit it, she even read those trashy rags at the supermarket checkout if she saw Maya Vaughn on the cover.

Though not as vocal, Shannon's own reaction to the photo had been as instant as Sawyer's. In the shot, Maya stood in front of a stainless-steel worktable with a row of pots hanging on an overhead rack behind her. Her platinum-blond hair, nearly shaved on the sides and longer on top, featured a fuchsia streak in the front and swirled above her head in a style that surely defied gravity. In one fist, she grasped a whisk, raised in the air as if poised to fight. Her white chef coat hung open, revealing a black T-shirt with bright-pink lettering on the front. The swirls and lines of several tattoos began around her wrists and disappeared under her coat sleeves, which were shoved halfway up her forearms.

The rips in her jeans seemed strategically placed to make Shannon's heart and other places pound with lust.

"Shannon?"

She tore her eyes from a hint of inner thigh. Damn, if that rip were two inches higher Maya could be arrested for indecent exposure. "What?"

"I know that look."

A hot blush spread over her face and she couldn't meet Sawyer's eyes. "Her work is amazing. I admire her talent."

"Yeah? Where exactly do you see her talent in that picture?" Sawyer laughed. "Hey, I don't blame you, she's sexy. But I didn't know you went for that type."

"What type? Young enough to be my daughter? I don't."

"She's not quite that young, is she? But I wouldn't blame you," Jori said, grinning when she earned a scowl from Sawyer. "I may be practically married, but I'm not dead. Look at that face, she's gorgeous. And her style—hot in an edgy, unstable sort of way."

Maya's oval face, creamy skin, and high cheekbones could have been called classically beautiful if not for the ring piercing one perfectly arched eyebrow. Shannon had seen photos in which Maya appeared serene, her features smooth and graceful. But in this picture, her eyes flashed, her nose wrinkled, and her mouth curled slightly as if the photographer had caught the beginning of an aggressive growl. Piercings and tattoos—she'd never imagined that at forty-two years old she would find herself so attracted to a much-younger woman who looked more like a rock star than a chef. Was this some type of mid-life crisis?

"So, seriously, you're both that impressed by this chick?" Sawyer asked, glancing between them.

"She's a rock star, professionally, of course," Shannon said, stumbling to cover up the direction her thoughts had just taken. Her stomach had been knotted ever since Sawyer had brought that envelope. Now, worry that she'd be insanely outmatched and get sent home the first day would keep her up at night for the next two weeks. She didn't need to deal with nerves about meeting a chef of Maya Vaughn's caliber as well. She just hoped she could stick around long enough to exchange more than a few words with her.

"Well, you'll get to find out soon enough. She's the newest mentor on the show," Jori said.

Shannon nodded. "I know."

"So how does this thing work, anyway?" Sawyer asked.

"The contestants are split into three groups, and each group works with a mentor. Every show, someone gets put up for elimination."

"So there's like a thirty-three percent chance you could be working pretty closely with her for the next several weeks?"

Shannon nodded.

"Oh, man, I can't wait to watch this show."

❖

"Hey, turn on channel five. It's about to start," Maya called from the kitchen. She stacked a few brownies onto a plate, picked up two glasses of skim milk, and headed for the living room. Her assistant and often taste-tester, Wendy, sat on one end of the sofa, legs folded beneath her, bare feet peeking out of the flared legs of designer sweatpants. Maya handed her the plate. "Try these."

Wendy took a bite and chewed slowly. "Nice. Peanut butter?"

Maya nodded.

"Very good. But the ratio is off a little. It's almost too much peanut butter."

Maya tasted one and agreed. Next time, she'd cut back a bit on the peanut butter and the sugar as well. "Too sweet" didn't belong in Wendy's vocabulary, but Maya wanted a bit more of the nuttiness to come through.

She shifted her attention to the television as her face flashed on-screen, followed by Charlie's. With his strong jaw, the cleft in his chin, and a sexy, perpetual five-o'clock shadow, she could easily imagine how he was able to charm the truth out of so many interview subjects. Seriously, the man didn't have a line on his mocha skin, not even around his striking green eyes.

"Why do you watch these interviews?" Wendy gestured at the screen with a brownie and grinned when a piece flew onto the coffee table in front of her. "Sorry."

Maya faked a stern look, grabbed a napkin, and picked up the crumbs. She hated messiness. At home or in the kitchen, she liked her surroundings clean and organized. Wendy, however, was only so fastidious when it came to her appearance. She liked every perfectly arranged ebony hair in place to accentuate her angular features, and she shadowed the lids of her almond-shaped eyes just so. But when it came to her surroundings, she could thrive in chaos just as well.

"It's amusing to see how far off my story gets once they chop it up in editing."

"I don't think I could stomach it." Wendy winced as Charlie brought up Maya's troubles from the previous year. "You know you could clear all of that up."

"Full disclosure? Why should I?"

"Look. I know they haven't earned it—"

"I don't owe anyone an explanation about the decisions I make."

"I would hardly call it—"

"Since when are you so big on coming clean? Are you going to come out to your grandmother?"

"One does not just come out to one's very traditional Chinese grandmother. It's not even the same thing." Having raised Wendy, her grandmother was more like a parent, but in many ways, the two-generation gap was very apparent. Wendy had endured far too many speeches about how her father's American blood made her lazy and disrespectful. She didn't want to add deviant to the list.

"It doesn't matter. I'm not giving away what little privacy I have. That's it. He signed off on the rules, didn't he?" Maya jabbed her finger toward the television, though the interview had concluded. She didn't insist on controlling every interview she did, so when she asked for a topic to be off-limits, she expected to be respected. Wendy had spoken with Charlie prior to the interview and had assured Maya that he understood the limitations.

"Yes."

"He's lucky I let him use what he already had."

"Are you ready for Nashville?"

"No. Is there even anything to do there?" Maya accepted the subject change as an admission that she was right about Charlie. She and Wendy had worked together for seven years, since just after Maya won her season of *For the Love of Cake*. And she could count on one hand the number of times either of them had ever admitted the other was right. Apologies after a disagreement were even scarcer. But it worked for them.

"Hell if I know. But you already agreed."

"Okay, but they downplayed that whole moving the show from New York to the damn Bible belt until after the ink dried on my contract. I mean, look at me. How am I going to fit in down in Hicktown?"

"I don't think Nashville's like that. I've heard it's fairly progressive—"

"If you finish that sentence with 'for the South,' so help me—"

"Well, it's too late to back out so you'll have to make the best of it."

"Fine. Find me some cool places to hang out while I'm there. Please tell me there's at least one gay bar."

"Don't you mean a bi-bar?"

"Very funny. Is there one or not?"

Wendy gestured to Maya's phone on the coffee table. "You've got Internet on that thing."

Maya shook her head. "Research is in your job description."

"Are you even aware that there should be a line between professional and personal?"

"Then why do I keep you around?"

"Because I'm the only person willing to have absolutely no life except accommodating your insane schedule."

"That's right." Maya snapped her fingers. She gave Wendy a hard time, but she would never truly let her think she didn't appreciate her sacrifice and hard work. She paid her very well and offered as many perks as she could. Over the years, Wendy had become a friend and the only person Maya trusted completely.

Despite her words, Wendy picked up her own phone and began tapping the touchscreen. Within a few seconds, she flipped the display around and showed Maya the website of one such establishment in Nashville.

"Was that so hard?" Maya stood and retrieved a manila envelope from the backpack she'd dropped by the door when she came in earlier. "These are the files on this season's cast."

"Gimme." Wendy grabbed them and scanned several papers. "Are you sure you didn't have anything to do with choosing these?"

"Yeah, why?"

"Because so far, they're all gorgeous."

"You think I'm that superficial?" Maya picked up the sheets as Wendy set them aside. A young, athletic-looking brunette, fresh from culinary school, a slim African-American man with broad shoulders, and a preppy baby dyke with the collar of her polo shirt standing up. While Maya's gaydar pinged, her libido remained silent. Too butch. And by the fresh-faced look, too innocent.

"Oh, here she is." Wendy held up a photograph. "Middle-aged—what do you think? Washed up wannabe-chef or soccer mom with a cake-decorating hobby? Not bad looking, though."

Prepared to play along, Maya snatched the picture out of her hand while Wendy flipped to the bio page. Unlike the usual airbrushed headshot, this photo appeared to be a cropped version of a snapshot. It depicted a woman seemingly mid-smile, as if the grin hadn't completely formed yet, but her full lips definitely teased upward. The tiny lines that creased the corners of her eyes hinted that her humor often reflected in the light-brown irises.

"Oh, Soccer Mom it is." Wendy tapped a finger against the page. "In order to fulfill a lifelong dream, she went to culinary school after her daughter graduated high school." She tossed the bio on the sofa cushion between them and picked up the next contestant's information.

Maya scanned the soccer mom's sheet. According to the bio, Shannon Hayes was forty-two years old, but she listed only one job in the culinary field—at a bakery in Nashville. With so little experience, she'd likely be one of the first eliminated, which would be a shame, because Wendy was right. She was good-looking. She glanced at Shannon's picture once more, then laid the paper on the pile and reached for another one.

CHAPTER TWO

I t's just how I imagined it would be."

Shannon glanced at the woman seated next to her whose already high voice was driven up an octave with excitement. Then she turned her attention back to the buildings passing by outside the window of the sleek black SUV. Less than an hour ago, she'd left her home for an undetermined amount of time. The email she'd received from the producers indicated a tentative timeline for filming all but the finale episode. Depending on when she got eliminated, she might be gone a day or, if she was lucky and made it to the end, almost three weeks. She'd secured her apartment and arranged for her daughter and son-in-law to check on it, hoping for the latter. The SUV picked her up at her front door, then swung by the airport to retrieve the other three occupants. Now, as they rode through downtown Nashville, she tried to imagine it through the eyes of a visitor. She drove past these bars, restaurants, and souvenir shops lining Broadway every day on her way to Drake's, and though she certainly felt different today, the storefronts appeared disappointingly familiar.

"I just love country music." The woman practically crawled into Shannon's lap while trying to see out the window on her side. "Look, do you think he's a singer?" When she turned her head to follow the retreating back of a man in a cowboy hat on the sidewalk, her face was uncomfortably close to Shannon's.

The man could be a street performer or an aspiring recording artist. In this woman's field of vision the cowboy stood out among the crowd. She didn't see that the majority of the people were either tourists or everyday businessmen and women who worked in one of the many multistory buildings lining the streets. In fact, if one looked past the honky-tonks, downtown Nashville wasn't much different from many American cities of its size. Within a few blocks, the skyscrapers gave way to a mix of strip-style business complexes, several universities, and residential areas made up of everything from turn-of-the-century architecture to newly constructed condo complexes.

Shannon pressed her head into the headrest, trying to restore a degree of personal space. The woman grinned and settled back in her seat with a toss of her long blond hair.

"Sorry, I'm Alice." She grabbed Shannon's hand from where it had rested on the seat between them and shook it vigorously. She glanced around as if including the other man and woman in the vehicle in her introduction. They both nodded politely, but neither engaged in conversation. "I'm so excited to be here. But I'm real nervous because I left my cupcake shop with my second cousin looking after it, and she's not very dependable. But how could I turn down an opportunity like this? I mean, I'd probably sell my soul, let alone my store just to make it on this show."

"Shannon," she said when Alice took a breath. But she didn't have time for anything more before Alice began again with a running commentary on the height of the buildings around them. Apparently, the only building in her South Georgia town with more than two stories was the courthouse and that was just "on account of being the county jail as well."

The SUV stopped in front of a brick building. While the place looked old, the façade didn't give many hints about the occupants. Large multipaned windows spanned the side of the long rectangular building.

"Where are we?" Alice asked as they climbed out of the SUV.

As Shannon stepped out, the smell of fresh asphalt stung her nose. She imagined that not long ago, before the location was reclaimed for the show, a map of weed-filled cracks had tracked across this parking lot. "I don't know the exact building, but it probably used to be a warehouse for a manufacturing company back in the early 1900s. They built a bunch of them close to the railroad lines."

"So we have a local?" the neatly dressed African-American man asked as he too exited the vehicle. With one finger, he pushed his black-framed glasses up his nose.

She nodded. "Born and raised."

"Mason." He clasped Shannon's hand in a quick, yet firm shake. "Shannon."

"Yeah, I caught that. You know, in between." They shared a smile as he gestured toward Alice, who had shifted the target of her one-sided conversation to the remaining member of their group.

The petite young woman, who looked barely out of her teens, seemed adept at ignoring Alice's ramblings. She tugged down the hem of her tailored button-down shirt and pulled at the waistband of her skinny jeans, which rode a bit low for Shannon's taste. Shannon hardly kept up with the latest fashion trends, but she had seen some of her daughter Regan's friends dress similarly. The young woman effectively shut them out with a look that said she thought she was much too hip to converse with them.

Two other vehicles pulled up and unloaded, but before Shannon could assess the new members, they were all ushered toward the building. They ambled along like a flock of sheep, crowding together as they reached the door, then filing through one by one. The same sense of nervousness that kept Shannon quiet seemed to pervade the group as well.

Their guide called out as they walked, identifying a locker room, hair and makeup, and craft service. Walls had been constructed and painted beige in order to differentiate the various areas, but the soaring ceilings of the warehouse had been left open above them. They entered a conference room that smelled of fresh paint and new office furniture, and were directed into the chairs around a large rectangular table.

"Everyone please get settled so we can begin," a man called as he entered the room. "I'd like to welcome you all to the show. I'm

Hugh, one of the associate producers. You may hear me referred to as an 'AP,' and I'll be around a lot. Before we put you guys in front of the cameras I want to go over a few things." He scanned the group, making eye contact briefly with each of them.

For the next thirty minutes Hugh paced the front of the room, tugging at the brim of his faded ball cap, and explained what they should expect from the experience. They'd already signed confidentiality agreements detailing these rules. But he reiterated that they would have no access to television or Internet. Also, during any telephone calls with family and friends they weren't allowed to discuss details regarding the show.

She wasn't thrilled about having only limited communication with her daughter, especially considering Regan was currently thirty-seven weeks pregnant. She could go into labor during the taping of the show. Shannon had already discussed the situation with the producers, who'd agreed to give her time to go to the hospital when the time came, but they couldn't guarantee how long she'd be granted. She'd balked when they asked to send a cameraman along with her, knowing Regan wouldn't want cameras anywhere near her hospital room. In the end, Shannon had consented to talk about the experience in an interview afterward.

"I hope you're all well rested, because we'll be filming every day. After filming is over, please remember the details of your contracts—complete confidentiality regarding the results of the show. You'll resume your normal lives for eight weeks while the episodes continue to run, and then the top three will move on to the live finale. You must wait until after the finale airs to discuss the results with *anyone*, including and especially the press."

Shannon glanced around, still trying to gauge the personalities of the others in the group. Hugh continued talking about the importance of being aware of the cameras while also ignoring them. The contestants should know where the cameramen were so as not to block an important shot, but shouldn't appear to be looking into the lenses.

When he was finished, he brought in two other producers, who began another spiel about expectations, much of which overlapped what Hugh had already said. The group spent the first half of the day sitting in the conference room reviewing legal necessities.

During downtime, Shannon tried to check out the competition. In addition to the three from her SUV, there were eight more contestants. She didn't catch all of the names, but she absorbed a few details. There was Ned, whose boring name didn't fit his ostentatious appearance at all. A strip of bright-blue hair ran down the center of his otherwise shaved head, and she would be surprised if he had an inch of untattooed skin below his neck. He carried himself with the bravado and swagger Shannon had come across often in chefs who felt they had something to prove. Sometimes they had the talent to back it up, and sometimes they didn't.

In direct contradiction, Lucia, a petite Hispanic woman, conducted herself with quiet confidence. She held her posture, even while seemingly at rest, as if attempting to offset her short stature. The firm set of her jaw and the alertness shining in her dark eyes indicated she could be a formidable opponent.

"So, are you ready to see where you'll be spending most of your time for the next several weeks?" Hugh clapped his hands together, and the contestants jumped in their chairs. He moved toward the door, his movements slightly twitchy. His nervous energy probably burned enough calories to keep his frame that lean. Shannon put him in his mid-forties, and he'd mentioned earlier that he'd been involved in the show from early on.

They wouldn't meet the mentors or the host until filming began. The producers wanted their authentic reactions to those introductions on film. They would see them for the first time that afternoon in the kitchen.

The chorus of yeses sounded both excited and hesitant. As they made their way through the building, the backstage feel of the warehouse gave way to more polished sets, decorated walls, and strategic lighting. The cameras around them multiplied until every time Shannon tried to turn away from one, she came face-to-face with another. And being told not to look at them only made her want to more. Judging by the way the others jerked their heads back and forth, they were all experiencing the same problem. The sheer number of people running around the set surprised her. Hugh passed most of them up without an introduction, and Shannon guessed they were the many production assistants and crew that actually kept the set up and ready for filming. Much of the ingredients, supplies, fondant, and even, in some cases, layers of cake would be prepared in advance. Everything had to be available the moment it was needed so no time was wasted when they could be filming.

She followed the other contestants into the kitchen, quietly agreeing with the awed exclamations around her. She didn't know a chef whose heart didn't quicken at the sight of stainless-steel counters and top-of-the-line commercial appliances. While the area looked spacious enough, the twelve chefs filled it quickly. And soon, when they were working to complete timed challenges, the area would seem even more cramped. Shannon hoped the trembling anticipation she felt inside wasn't visible to the others. She felt like a racehorse waiting for the gate to open.

"Okay, ladies and gentlemen, take a few minutes to look around. After lunch we'll start filming, and your access to the kitchen will be limited to challenge time only."

They all moved quickly, eager to memorize the kitchen. As a fan and past viewer, Shannon assumed her ability to efficiently locate tools and ingredients could mean victory or defeat. She only hoped the layout would be the same every day. Each workstation included a two-burner stovetop, a cutting surface, a small workspace, and a folded nylon case that probably held a set of knives.

As she circled the tables, she noted the location of mixers, pots and pans, and accessories on her way to the pantry. Metal racks, five shelves high, contained various flours, sugars, and, among other things, a larger variety of spices than she'd ever had the luxury of working with.

An array of colorful fruits graced one long table. She'd read somewhere that the show regularly donated unused perishable food to local shelters and food banks. She counted herself lucky to have been selected for the show, but just thinking about what she could do in this kitchen made her even more determined to stick around as long as possible.

Before she could spend any more time plotting how to make that happen, Hugh called them out of the kitchen. He directed the group to a large space where they would spend much of their downtime between shots. Comfortable-looking sofas and stylish chairs clustered on one side of the room, and several round tables and chairs spread out over the other side.

He left them to enjoy lunch—a variety of gourmet salads and sandwiches. After they ate, someone would return to take them, in groups, to hair and makeup. That afternoon they would be on camera for the first time.

As they settled around the tables, Shannon found herself once again grouped with Alice and Mason. She ate slowly, nerves chewing away at her appetite. Alice dominated the conversation once more, but Mason and Shannon were just as content to let her prattle on. Alice seemed like a sweet girl, but Shannon couldn't fathom how much energy it took to stay so wound up. She shared an understanding smile with Mason and forced down another bite. She didn't know what time they would get dinner and didn't want hunger slowing her down later.

CHAPTER THREE

Chefs, welcome to your kitchen. Today, you will begin the competition that may change your life, or at the very least the trajectory of your career. So, would you like to meet this year's mentors?" The show's host, Eric Wetzel, smiled wider than Shannon thought possible, as if his contract demanded that, while on air, he show off his too-straight, too-white teeth as often as he could. Eric had hosted since the second season after replacing an annoyingly perky blonde. His dark hair was styled in a smooth wave across his forehead, and his navy suit and bright-pink tie seemed out of place in a kitchen.

This time the affirmative responses sounded more excited, as if each contestant aspired to be heard over the others. Shannon's nerves had ratcheted up with each step toward this moment. The idea that she was about to meet three legends in the field, particularly Maya Vaughn, had her arms and legs going weak.

"Chefs, welcome an award-winning pastry chef whose mastery of spun sugar is unmatched, Wayne Neighbors." Eric waved his arm in a sweeping arc toward the swinging kitchen door.

Wayne pushed through like a prizefighter headed for the ring, and the contestants greeted him with the appropriate amount of applause and cheers. In fact, he was built like a fighter, not the world-renowned chef Shannon knew him to be. Even taller than he appeared on television, he towered over most of them. His broad shoulders, round and firm as cantaloupes, strained against the gray fabric of his chef's coat. His boxy jacket hid his waist but stretched taut again around the tops of his thick thighs.

Shannon didn't need an introduction as the next mentor entered. Jacques Babineaux was known as the grandfather of modern pastry. His forty-plus years of experience in the business had garnered him a James Beard Award and countless Food and Wine "Bests." He had his hands in more restaurants than even he could probably count.

"And of course, fans of the show will remember our next mentor as the winner of season one, Maya Vaughn."

Just hearing Maya's name sent a shot of adrenaline through Shannon, accelerating her heart rate. She curled her fingers into suddenly damp palms and mentally chastised herself for responding like a teenage girl.

Maya waved at the contestants as she entered, but her gaze never settled on them. She shook hands with the other mentors and smiled at Eric. Shannon continued watching Maya even when Eric began to speak again. When Maya widened her stance and crossed her arms over her chest, her chef coat gaped open at the bottom and her white T-shirt pulled up, revealing a swath of tight skin. Shannon tried to force herself to look away, at least that was her intention, but instead she followed the sexy chasms bisecting defined abdominals and the ridge of each hipbone visible above her low-slung pants. In the years since Maya had first appeared on the show, she'd gotten in better shape, and every magazine cover seemed to show more skin than the last. But having enough money to hire a personal trainer probably helped.

One of the cameramen crept closer, focusing on Maya. If he got the shot, Shannon certainly wouldn't be the only lesbian lusting after Maya once again this season. In her peripheral vision, she caught sight of a camera panning the contestants and forced her attention to Eric. If she didn't get busted by one of the dozen other contestants, certainly viewers at home would catch her staring.

"I hope you're all ready to compete, because we're going to jump right in with your first challenge." Once again, Eric kept things moving, and Shannon was grateful she didn't have too much time to think. "The mentors need a baseline for your individual skills so they can choose teams. Here on the table in front of me, we have a two-layer round cake, decorated using eight classic techniques. Everyone take your place behind a blank cake. You'll have ten minutes to duplicate as much of the design as possible. Starting now."

Shannon jostled against Alice and bounced off another man's shoulder as everyone rushed forward to claim a table. She mumbled a quick "excuse me," slid her cake toward her, and immediately went to work. She began with one of the simpler applications, copying the piping around the bottom of the cake. At first, the movements of the many crewmembers just out of camera range distracted her, and twice she had to clean off a line of piping that went astray as she involuntarily lifted her eyes from her work. She bent her head more intently toward her cake to block out her surroundings.

Between tasks, she did steal glances at the others. She wasn't the fastest in the group, but not the slowest either. When it became clear that she wasn't likely to finish all of the decorations on the sample cake, she switched tactics and began working on some of the more difficult portions. Perhaps she could impress the mentors if she balanced solid technique with the risk of the more demanding tasks.

As the clock counted down toward zero, the contestants glanced at its digital display even more often and their pace increased. Maya evaluated them one by one, making mental notes about who she might want on her team. She'd studied the bios extensively and knew the various chefs and their backgrounds, but that research couldn't replace seeing their skills in person. In her head, she referred to them by the nicknames she and Wendy had given them: Baby Dyke, Hotshot, and Hot Tamale. Okay, some of them were less politically correct than others.

When time expired and Eric called for them to stop their work, they stepped back and seemed to exhale as one. Eric invited the mentors to get a closer look. Maya filed in behind Wayne, both deferring to Jacques as a respected elder in their field. She didn't listen to the comments from the two men, preferring to make her own assessment.

While she inspected the first cake, the corresponding decorator studied her with as much intensity. She could feel his eyes on her as she slowly turned the piece and looked closely at his piping.

"Nice ink." He winked at her.

She glanced at the tattoos decorating his arms and emerging from his collar to cover his neck but didn't comment. If he thought the shared bond of tattoos was enough to win her over, he was mistaken. She refused to respond as well to his quick head nod and flirtatious grin. He obviously believed he was the badass his appearance projected him to be. He'd completed most of the design in the time allotted, his lines smooth and clean. Apparently, he possessed the skills to back up his cockiness.

"Nicely done, Ned." She didn't wait for his response before taking two steps to her right and sizing up the next cake. "Alice, solid work."

"Thank you, Chef. I didn't have time to finish, but I did my best on what I got done."

Maya nodded and moved on. "Sloppy, Damien." She shook her head as she continued to move down the row. "Rushing won't get you to the end of this competition."

She stopped in front of Soccer Mom, recalling Wendy's quick assessment and dismissal of her. Shannon's chestnut hair was pinned into a smooth, secure bun, and despite Maya's affinity for order, she suddenly found she wanted to pull it down. She imagined it falling against Shannon's shoulders in shining waves. Shannon's posture was tense and as buttoned-up as her charcoal chef coat bearing the show's logo.

The honey-brown eyes that had nearly danced in her application photo were now sharply focused on her own cake, and somehow Maya knew from her expression that she judged herself harshly as well. The patterns she'd completed were flawless, but she'd finished only about three-quarters of the design.

"Middle of the pack? Is that good enough for you?" She purposely injected a bite into her tone to see how Shannon responded.

"No, Chef."

Something flashed in her eyes, but her tone was flat and too accepting. Maya expected much more fire from the contestants when challenged. But more than that, she very much wanted to see if she could rile *this* chef. Typically, the meek didn't last the first three eliminations on this show. She couldn't waste a team pick on someone who might be the first to leave.

"So what are you going to do about it?" She waited only a beat, since Shannon obviously wasn't going to rise up, and continued to the next contestant. "Mason, your piping is good, but you need to practice the more difficult techniques. You have stiff competition here and it'll take all you have."

After she'd evaluated the remaining chefs, Maya joined Jacques and Wayne at the front of the room. Eric lined the competitors up opposite them. He explained once again that the three mentors would select their teams. Going forward, they would work with those groups, coaching them through challenges that would pit them against the other teams and sometimes among each other.

Maya scanned the faces before her. Seven years after she'd stood in their place, she could clearly recall how nervous she'd been. Fresh off the high of rocking through culinary school, she'd projected an air of confidence in the face of some stiff competition. She'd used every bit of her training and natural talent to reach the finale. The final challenge that year had been a celebrity wedding cake and a groom's cake. She'd nailed them, leaving no doubt she deserved to win.

Back then, she'd counted only on herself to succeed. Now, she wanted the bragging rights that went with coaching a winning team in her first attempt as a mentor. Her choices for her team would be instrumental in making that happen. Unfortunately, at best she would probably get her third-ranked competitor as both Jacques and Wayne got to choose before her.

Jacques took Ned and Wayne picked the young butch. Maya selected Lucia because her skills proved as solid as her training and extensive experience. After the guys chose again, Maya selected Alice, then smiled politely as Alice talked during the entire time it took to walk the length of the room and join her team. Hopefully she wouldn't regret that decision.

Of the six remaining competitors, she needed to select two more. She wanted Shannon. She lacked experience, but her sample cake showed promise. Shannon hadn't finished, but she had duplicated some of the more intricate patterns while some of the others had tackled only the easiest. Maya had been tough during her critique and mostly Shannon's reaction disappointed her, but Maya had detected something—a spark just before Shannon seemed to shut it down that intrigued her. She wanted to know what it would take to bring out that fight.

When it was her turn, she called out Shannon's name without hesitation. Shannon met her eyes with an expression of pure happiness, her broad smile lifting her cheeks and causing a slight crinkle at the corners of her eyes. As she passed Maya, she mouthed the words *thank you*, then took her place next to the other two team members. Maya tried to ignore the surge of pleasure at Shannon's reaction; instead, she focused on Damien, her final competitor.

"Look at the other chefs in your group, because you'll be spending a lot of time with them in the coming weeks, if you're lucky," Eric said with a wink. "You'll be bunking according to your teams. The cars are waiting outside to take you to the hotel where you'll be directed to your suites."

As the larger cameras on set stopped rolling, the guys carrying the handhelds emerged and surrounded the chattering contestants. Before her team could head for the door, Maya called them together.

"Take a minute to enjoy your new accommodations, but then get settled and get some rest. Tomorrow will be another long day. Don't let the excitement get the best of you, or you'll find yourself out of the competition before you have time to shine."

"One of us has to live with a guy?" Clearly, Alice couldn't imagine anything more inappropriate.

The newly formed team stood just inside their hotel suite, all of them taking in the generous living room complete with a large flat-screen television and wet bar. A cameraman with a handheld circled, capturing their expressions. They'd been told that cameras would be allowed in their suites to film at various times, but they wouldn't be under twenty-four-hour surveillance. Any phone calls they made would be monitored to ensure they didn't discuss the progress of the show, but their conversations would not be used on air. They had all turned in their cell phones for the duration of filming.

"I'll share with him." Shannon figured bunking with Damien had to be more peaceful than with Alice. She saw a flicker of disappointment in Lucia's expression. Ideally, she'd much rather share with Lucia and stick Alice with Damien, but she clearly couldn't arrange that now.

In the modest kitchen, really no more than a kitchenette, Lucia opened cabinets and the refrigerator. "It's stocked with the basics."

They probably wouldn't need much more. Though Shannon liked to cook, she couldn't imagine any of them wanting to prepare a gourmet meal after spending all day in the kitchen.

"There's always room service." Alice indicated a menu on the counter.

The cameraman followed Alice as she walked into the next room, exclaiming aloud with every step about the plush surroundings. Shannon crossed the living area to the room she and Damien would share. She'd always wondered what the inside of this hotel looked like but had never had occasion to stay here. The only time she'd ever stayed in a local hotel had been with her husband for their five-year anniversary, and the chain establishment on West End Avenue hadn't been anywhere near this nice.

The bedroom boasted a floor-to-ceiling window along one wall and a door leading to the en suite opposite it. The black-and-beige paisley-printed accent pillows on the two queen beds broke up the solid beige of the bedspreads and the walls. Identical black dressers faced the foot of each bed.

Damien had staked out the bed near the bathroom, leaving her next to the window. He'd already started putting his clothes into one of the dressers. She wheeled her suitcase close to her bed and left it to unpack later.

"I hope you don't mind that we'll be sharing a room," she said.

He shrugged. "Like they said, we'll be spending a lot of time together."

Well, it wasn't a ringing endorsement, but what did she expect from a man stuck on a team with all women? She went to the window to check out the view. To the left, between two buildings, she caught a glimpse of the river. Across the street, another high-rise blocked her view of anything south of Broadway, but she knew the converted warehouse where they would be working wasn't far away. She couldn't see Drake's, but reminding herself that Jori and Sawyer believed in her helped ease her nerves.

❖

"I wonder how Shannon's first day went." Jori leaned against her pillow and stretched her legs out on the king-sized bed. Usually, she'd already fallen asleep by the time Sawyer got home. But today, she'd stayed awake, nervous for Shannon. Though she might regret it when her alarm went off at four a.m., right now she very much enjoyed watching Sawyer go through her nightly ritual of readying for bed, especially when she stepped out of her pants and tossed them in the hamper. She stripped off her dress shirt and bra and pulled a T-shirt on. No matter how many times they went to bed together, the sight of Sawyer in a T-shirt and panties always made Jori's heartbeat accelerate a little.

"Well, she hasn't called yet asking for her job back, so that has to be a good sign." Sawyer slipped between the sheets next to her and extended her arm, waiting for Jori to move closer.

"Very funny." Jori set aside her book, curled against her side, and rested her head on her chest. "I can't replace her."

"You don't have a choice."

"I spoke with her friend from culinary school. She seems nice enough."

"But she's not Shannon. I know you connected with her right away, but you need to move forward as if she won't be coming back. Even if she doesn't win, this show will open new doors for her. What if she wants to pursue one of those leads?"

"I'll be happy for her, of course."

"You need to work on your sincerity before you try that one on Shannon."

Jori sighed. "I know you think it's silly. We've only worked together for a year, and—"

"And you so rarely let anyone close to you."

"I was going to say, it typically takes me a while to warm up to new people."

"Yeah, that too." Sawyer kissed Jori's temple.

"My point is, though I know it's selfish, I'll miss Shannon's work. But I'll miss her company as well. We've gotten to be friends."

"Oh, honey, you two aren't breaking up. You'll still be friends. You just may have to work a little harder at keeping in touch."

Jori smiled when Sawyer wrapped her other arm around her and held her close. She was overreacting to Shannon's absence from the bakery. But knowing Sawyer understood why helped ease her anxiety. From the time Jori was young and in foster care, nearly everyone in her life had been transient. The families she was forced to live with never treated her like one of their own, so she became accustomed to being on the outside. Until she met Sawyer and the rest of the Drake family, Jori hadn't known how warm and welcoming family could be. Though she'd opened up considerably since then, Shannon was still one of a handful of people she called a friend.

"Sweetheart, I know you don't like change, but you took a chance leaving the restaurant and opening the bakery. Shannon needs to take her chance as well." Sawyer lifted Jori's chin with her fingers and kissed her softly on the mouth.

Jori melted into the kiss, immersing herself in the familiar feel of Sawyer's lips caressing hers. When Sawyer shifted and moved over her, she embraced Sawyer's hips with her legs. They'd been so busy lately, it had been longer than she wanted to admit since they'd made time for this intimacy. Just the feel of Sawyer's weight against her was enough to arouse her. Sawyer kissed her neck, then nipped gently at her ear.

"It's late," Sawyer murmured. "Should I let you go to sleep?" Her warm breath against Jori's neck and the rasp of need already coloring her voice made Jori's response easy.

"I can be quick."

Sawyer smiled and moved lower. She pushed up Jori's shirt and closed her teeth on one nipple. Jori gasped at the spear of pleasure and lifted her hips. Knowing exactly what she needed, Sawyer slid inside her.

"I love you." The truth of those words shone in Sawyer's eyes as she stroked Jori in firm, deep strokes, filling her when she sank all the way in, then pulling back slowly.

Jori matched her, pressing against Sawyer's hand in an increasing rhythm. "Oh, God, yes."

Minutes later, as her orgasm swept over her in a deep, pulsing wave, she panted, emotion bringing her voice nearly to a sob. She wrapped her arms around Sawyer and held her tight until the sharp edge of pleasure smoothed.

"You always know just what I need." She sighed and settled at Sawyer's side, fully sated and pleasantly languid.

"And I always will."

She trusted those words more than she ever had before. Her upbringing had taught her that change was a bad thing, but since meeting Sawyer, she'd learned to fear new things less.

❖

The others had all gone to bed, but Shannon still felt too keyed up to sleep. She'd grabbed the throw from the foot of her bed, left Damien already snoring away, and headed for the living room. She pulled the sheer drapes across the big windows but left the heavier pair open, letting in enough light from the city outside that she didn't need to turn on any lamps. She nestled into an armchair in the corner.

Though she'd spent the two weeks since getting her acceptance trying to mentally prepare for the experience, she couldn't have anticipated just how overwhelming it would be. Today had been a whirlwind, and she still hadn't fully sorted the events in her head. Meeting the mentors had been surreal—icons of the industry had evaluated her work—and found it lacking, she reminded herself, thinking of Maya's comment about being in the middle of the pack.

Wayne had offered an unconvincing "Well done." Jacques hadn't commented, merely nodding politely, which Shannon could only assume meant he hadn't been impressed either.

Though she'd told Jori and Sawyer she was keeping her expectations low, she now realized a part of her had thought she would go in and rock it, blowing away Eric and the mentors with her skills. But based on today, the other competitors were good, some of them *really* good, and she was no longer so sure of herself. Maybe she should simply be hoping she didn't suffer the embarrassment of being the first sent home.

"No," she said aloud. "They picked you for a reason. *Someone* must have thought you had potential." She pushed aside the internal voice that said reality-show contestants weren't always chosen for their skill. She'd watched enough television to guess that sometimes a big personality or a volatile temper would probably get a person cast on a show.

But she hadn't been flashy or over-exuberant in her audition tape. The subsequent Skype interview had been more detailed, and she'd cringed a little as they delved into her past. But her story wasn't exciting or out of the ordinary. She'd been a sophomore in college when her boyfriend of two years, a newly graduated law student, proposed. She accepted because he was a catch and her parents and her friends loved him. In fact, a couple of her friends joked that if she ever broke it off with him, they'd snap him up.

So she let herself fall into marriage, not knowing at the time she wasn't old enough, or wise enough, or secure enough in herself to demand what she really wanted. When he passed the bar and landed a job with a prestigious firm and asked her to stay at home, she agreed. He wanted the big house, the fancy car, the obedient wife, and the two-point-five kids. She foolishly thought she was the luckiest woman in the world. He expected to start on the kids right away and she complied. Nine years later, after exhausting every method, they sat side by side while a doctor dispassionately told them she'd never bear children. He waited barely three months before he left her.

Shannon shook her head, remembering how uncomfortable she'd been in the interview for the show as she detailed that failure and the subsequent ten years it had taken her to get back to culinary school. Years filled with raising a daughter she first fostered then adopted as a single mother, years of discovering that what she really wanted had nothing to do with men at all. She'd lifted her chin as she told the show's producer that she was a lesbian, having come too far to hide that fact just to get on television.

Suddenly needing to ground herself against the roller coaster of the past two weeks, she picked up the hotel phone and dialed her daughter's number.

"Hey, Mom." Regan answered just when Shannon thought her voice mail might come on.

"Hi, sweetie, you sound tired. Did I wake you?"

"No. I can't get comfortable and I feel like a whale."

"I'm sorry. I wish I was there." She'd enjoyed being with her daughter for every step of her pregnancy. The decision to leave only weeks before her due date had been difficult.

"Don't even say it. This was a once-in-a-lifetime chance for you."

"So is being there for the birth of my granddaughter, unless you're planning to have a bunch more."

"Let's just get through this one first. If I don't kill my husband, maybe we'll have another one."

Shannon laughed. "Just think of it as practice for the next eighteen years of parenting together. Your marriage is strong, you'll be fine."

"Mom—"

"I know. It was a long time ago." Regan had never even met Shannon's ex-husband, but she knew the backstory. Now, as her daughter was about to become a mother herself, that time in her life felt so far away. "You're almost through it. You've only got a few weeks left, honey."

"Easy for you to say. Your feet still fit in your shoes."

"Too many more of these long days and they won't."

"How's it going?"

"Eh—I'm not really supposed to talk about it." Though she felt lonely and nervous, she wasn't about to break the rules on the first day.

"Then I'll just guess from the enthusiasm in your voice," Regan teased her. "So, shake off whatever's going on and step it up, Mom. You're not missing my kid's birth to come in second place."

"Thank you. That's just what I need right now."

"Time for tough love?"

"Yep." Shannon had doled out plenty of tough love in the early years of their relationship. Regan had been taken from her birth mother by the Department of Children's Services when she was five years old. She'd spent the next six years in foster care, until coming to live with Shannon. At eleven, she'd carried more resentment toward both her mother and the system that took her away than any one child should ever have. That resentment manifested as mistrust of everyone, especially those who seemed to want to help her. Back then, Regan hadn't believed that Shannon, or anyone, would treat her well without wanting something in return.

"Okay, kid, go lie down and let my granddaughter go to sleep."

"Sure, but she's the one keeping me awake at night with all the dancing around in there."

Shannon could hear the smile in Regan's voice and she closed her eyes, trying to see her—to soak in the familiar and lock it away to call upon later.

"Good luck, Mom. Give 'em hell."

CHAPTER FOUR

This is a decorating-only immunity challenge. After taking turns consulting with a very special client, you'll each have two hours to construct a cake using the premade sponge cake on the racks behind you." Eric gestured widely, encompassing them all. "You should be quite familiar with today's clients. It seems that all three of our mentors have a birthday coming up. Each team member will be decorating a cake for your respective mentor. You'll each have five minutes to consult with your client and will be judged today on your consultation as well as your decorating. The top cake will receive immunity for today's elimination."

Shannon's heart raced at the thought of a one-on-one consultation with Maya Vaughn. Only two weeks ago, she'd nervously hoped to exchange a few words with Maya, and now on the second day she'd have a full five minutes with her. She'd already been keyed up this morning, and now she felt as if everyone could see how she trembled. She'd lain awake last night thinking about the previous day and planning ways to improve, which was difficult without knowing what the challenges would be.

"Okay, who's first," Maya said as she gathered their team near one end of the room.

Shannon's brain screamed at her to step forward, to show initiative, but her legs wouldn't cooperate. Instead, Lucia raised her hand and Maya led her to a pair of chairs nearby. Shannon couldn't hear what they said, but she stole glances at them anyway. Even sitting, Lucia held herself erect, her posture professional, but her smile projected openness. The five minutes passed quickly, and Lucia took her place behind one of the worktables.

Alice lurched forward and flung herself into the chair opposite Maya. While they talked, Alice kept leaning into the space between them and touching Maya's forearm. Maya angled back as if she wanted to scoot her chair back, her expression tight as she responded to whatever Alice was asking. When Alice stood, Shannon jerked into action, finally managing to unglue her feet from the floor.

"Shannon, have a seat," Maya said as Shannon practically stumbled into the chair.

She inhaled slowly, then let her breath out, trying to concentrate. She could feel Maya's eyes on her, but she couldn't seem to drag her own gaze off the floor. *Focus, damn it. Act like you've done this before.* She'd had tons of customer consults for Drake's, but none had made her this nervous.

She looked at Maya's feet, clad in heavy, well-worn brown boots, then her legs, encased in soft denim. She slid past the fashionable belt and over a flat stomach, but froze when she reached her breasts, high and firm and wearing a trendy T-shirt like it was stitched just for them. Certainly, she'd admired them in magazine photos, but up close and in 3D, they were pretty amazing breasts. Maya crossed her arms over her chest, and Shannon had the impression of strong forearms before she forced her attention up. When she locked on Maya's blue-gray eyes, she knew she'd been caught checking her out. One side of Maya's mouth quirked, and Shannon swore she read interest in the returned gaze.

"Is there something you want to know?" If she had any doubt about being busted, the sultry tone in Maya's voice confirmed it.

"Yes." Shannon took a breath, unable to think of one appropriate, professional query. She almost laughed out loud at the thought of asking Maya on national television if the short hair at the nape of her neck was as soft as it looked or if her currently smirking mouth was as kissable as she imagined. "I'm—uh—a little nervous." She cursed the slight stutter in her words. She felt the cameraman's presence beside her and fought the urge to look at him.

"You only have a few minutes left." Maya's amused tone let on that she was aware Shannon probably had no idea how much of her time she'd wasted.

Shannon stared at her, trying desperately to grasp a question, any question as her time fizzled away. "Do you have any hobbies?"

"Hobbies?" Maya chuckled. "I don't have time for hobbies."

"You're not all work, are you?" Maya's casual manner relaxed Shannon slightly, and she managed an almost conversational tone.

"Lately, I am. I suppose based on how my time is spent these days my hobbies include making small talk with people I don't know, dodging paparazzi, and primping and posing for photo shoots." She wrinkled her nose. "That makes me sound horribly ungrateful, doesn't it?"

"If you had free time, let's say for your upcoming birthday—"

"My birthday is nine months away."

"I'm trying to play along."

"Well, then by all means," Maya said, gesturing for her to continue.

"What would your ideal birthday celebration be?"

"A lavish party, perhaps? That's what I'm supposed to say, right?" Maya answered sarcastically, and then her expression softened. "I think maybe a quiet dinner, then live music at an intimate club somewhere. And no cake."

"No cake? Is that a trick? Should I leave my counter empty and say I gave the client what she wanted?"

"I suppose not."

"That would have made this challenge a whole lot easier."

"We're not here to make it easy on you. Our time is up. I hope you got everything you need."

"Not even close," Shannon mumbled as she stood, not looking back to see if Maya heard her.

She went to her table, already feeling defeated. She knew more about Maya going into the interview than she'd actually been able to get out of the conversation. She thought about the only question she'd managed to ask. Maya didn't want a big, extravagant party. She wanted intimacy and live music at a small club. That's where Shannon's certainty stopped and the guesswork began. She studied Maya as she talked to Damien. Today, she looked edgy and fashionable without trying too hard. Shannon had seen red-carpet photos. Maya Vaughn in a designer gown was a sight to behold. She tended toward dresses with smooth, sleek lines, and her hair and makeup often had a classic old-Hollywood feel.

Seeing Damien go to his counter spurred Shannon into action. Not only had she wasted her own interview time, but she'd apparently burned through another five minutes and still had no concrete plan. But she set about gathering supplies anyway.

For the remainder of the two hours, Shannon worked steadily, glancing up only to check the clock. And when Eric called time, she stepped back, feeling more confident. She finally looked at the other three cakes around her, and her hopes waned. They'd all done flashy designs bursting with color. One even had a layer with a leopard-print pattern painted on it. Her own creation didn't even look like it was for the same client. She'd decided on an understated version of an old-school pin-up feel. She kept the colors clean and classy, black and white with accents the same deep red as Maya's lipstick.

The mentors began examining the cakes one by one, sometimes offering feedback and sometimes moving on with very little comment. Since Shannon couldn't change her choices now, she might as well take pride in the work she'd done. She forced her shoulders back and lifted her chin.

Jacques was the first to arrive at her table. He leaned in and turned her cake. "Good smooth fondant, solid technique. Nicely done."

"I agree. And your selective use of color here makes the design pop," Wayne said as he came to stand next to Jacques.

"Thank you, Chefs." Shannon allowed herself a small smile.

As they both moved on, Maya stopped in front of her cake. With no other clues, Shannon didn't know her well enough to interpret her raised brow. Hell, she hadn't even known her well enough to make her a cake. Shannon slowly inhaled, trying to combat the nerves that left her slightly breathless. She wanted to be brave, wanted to prod Maya for some kind of comment. But she ended up just staring at her and wishing she knew what Maya was thinking. When she moved on to the next cake without comment, Shannon suppressed a groan of frustration.

❖

"You produced some great cakes today. But only one of you can win immunity. Your performance was judged both on your creation and by the mentor feedback regarding your interview." Eric paused, clearly for effect, while he scanned all the contestants. Maya barely managed to not roll her eyes. She'd forgotten how dramatic he could be, but the viewing audience ate up his antics. And he knew how to capitalize on his success. In the six years he'd hosted the show, he'd launched a clothing line and a cologne brand. She'd heard somewhere that he invested heavily in real estate as well. As he let the tension build, a nervous chuckle and an impatient sigh from the contestants broke the deliberate silence. "And today, immunity goes to Ned."

Ned let out a triumphant grunt and pumped his fist. Several of his peers nodded as if expecting his win, while others shook their head in self-recrimination. Maya's team's response was varied as well. Alice looked genuinely happy for Ned, and Maya could almost hear the string of congratulatory remarks she was itching to spew. Lucia's expression was stony and unreadable. Though quiet, she would likely prove stiff competition for the others. Damien glared at Ned and then at Eric, clearly displeased with the result. His cake had been so far out of the running that any jealousy on his part was clearly unwarranted. Though Shannon was somewhat more guarded, the tiny twitches around her eyes and the bunching of her jaw indicated she too was unhappy. However, judging from her downcast gaze and the concave posture of her shoulders, she seemed to be directing her criticism inward.

The cameras had stopped rolling, and Eric announced a break for lunch before the afternoon's elimination challenge. He instructed them to be back in the kitchen in thirty minutes. Wayne and Jacques immediately headed for their dressing rooms, expecting a production assistant to bring their lunch to them. But Maya didn't feel like being closed up in four walls. So when the PA tried to steer her toward her own room, she dismissed her. The PA's brows drew together. Obviously no one had ever resisted the usual order of things.

But Maya brushed her off and followed the contestants to catering. During her own season, Maya's time had seemed to pass in a blur of nerves, excitement, and competition. But now, as a mentor, she spent much more time waiting—for the chefs to receive instructions from Hugh, for them to complete challenges, or for cameras to set up for another shot. Boxing herself in during the breaks would only amplify the restlessness of that inactivity.

For the sake of efficiency, a spread of sandwiches, deli-style sides, bags of chips, and a variety of fresh fruit had been laid out on a long table. She hung back and let the others go first, then shuffled along behind, gathering a sandwich, a scoop of cold pasta salad, and a bottle of apple juice.

She found most of her team seated together. Damien had settled with a group of the guys, but her women had claimed a table with one remaining chair.

"Mind if I join you guys?"

"Of course not." Alice jumped in and answered for the group. "Do you mind if we pick your brain? There's obviously so much we can learn from you, and it seems like we have so little time. I mean, it's only three weeks until the break. And that's if we get all the way to the end, which would be amazing."

Maya had paused halfway through Alice's rambling answer, still holding her lunch, and instantly regretted her decision.

"Alice, let's not talk about work right now. This is supposed to be a break from the madness to regroup before we start again." Shannon jumped in so quickly that Maya gave her an appreciative look, then let her gaze linger as an adorable flush colored her cheeks.

Maya pulled out the chair next to Shannon, which unfortunately put her directly across from Alice. She nodded at Lucia and received a warm smile.

"Sure, okay. What should we talk about then? Perhaps we could share some stories about our hometowns. Since we're all from such different backgrounds."

Beside her, Shannon sighed, then seemed to try to cover it with a cough.

Undeterred, Alice continued. "I imagine my rural Georgia upbringing was very different from yours in New York City."

"Actually, she's from Albany," Shannon muttered, then blushed even deeper.

"That's right." Maya met Shannon's eyes and smiled, hoping to ease whatever was making her uncomfortable. Maya's bio was quite accessible on the Internet or any number of interviews she'd done over the years. She'd grown used to fans of the show talking to her about childhood, her education, and even her personal life. For some, nothing was off-limits. While Maya was quick to shut down inquiries that became too personal, she'd learned to accept a degree of curiosity. Shannon's knowledge of where she was raised wasn't nearly as surprising as Alice's obvious ignorance of it. She recalled from Shannon's application that she'd grown up in the Nashville area. "I suppose that makes you the big-city girl at this table."

"Hardly. Despite where we were born, anyone could look at us and tell who has more life experience." Shannon scoffed. "I got cast on a national television show and still couldn't get out of this town."

"Is it weird living in a hotel in your own hometown?"

"A little. But I'm sure it'll give me a different perspective on the city. I typically only come downtown to go to work, then go back to my apartment in the suburbs. I don't like crowds."

"There sure weren't many crowds where I'm from," Alice said, obviously eager to get back into the conversation.

"Mmm hmm." Maya angled her chair slightly away from Alice and spoke to Shannon. "You seemed uncomfortable during the challenge today."

"I was nervous. And out of my element. The cameras and lights don't simulate my usual environment for being creative."

"And what would that be?"

"Well, these days I work in a little bakery about seven blocks from here. When we don't have any customers in the shop, I like listening to music while I decorate. I try to pick songs that set the mood I'm trying to convey." Shannon's voice lifted with passion for her work, and her eyes lit up as if she could actually hear the music in her head.

"Your theme today centered around me. So what songs would you pick?"

"I thought you didn't want to talk about work?"

"Actually, those were your words." She'd initially thought avoiding shoptalk was a good idea but found she was interested in hearing more about Shannon's work. After culinary school, Maya had worked in restaurants for a very short time, then landed the spot on the show. Since then, she'd done cookbooks, and press, and appearances, never again needing a full-time gig. Sometimes all of the traveling made her weary, and the idea of working in a quaint little shop appealed to her. But she'd had experiences so many young chefs could only dream of, and fame didn't last forever. She'd have plenty of time to settle down later.

"I got the sense you agreed."

"I did, in theory. But," she shrugged, "we're chefs. It's what we do. Besides, don't you think the differences in creative process are interesting?"

"I'm definitely interested in your process." Shannon's voice dropped and her immediate shocked expression indicated she hadn't intended to sound so flirtatious. "I mean—I hope to learn as much as I can from you."

Maya still wanted to know what imaginary playlist Shannon had heard while she decorated a cake for her. But she couldn't find a way to bring the conversation back to the subject. Instead, to test Shannon's reaction to brutal honesty, she said, "Look, your cake was good, spot-on for my personality. And I don't know how you did it because your consultation was a mess. That's what really hurt you today."

"I know." No excuses. Maya gave her points for that. Shannon's eyes betrayed her worry despite the lift of her chin. She had skills, no doubt. Maya searched her memory for something in Shannon's bio that explained her lack of confidence, but nothing stood out. She'd have to get to know her better before she figured it out, but that meant Shannon had to stick around.

"So, do better." Maya's voice came out more rough than she intended. Realizing she'd leaned even closer as she spoke, she shoved her chair back abruptly, causing the legs to scrape harshly against the floor. She shouldn't appear to pay Shannon more attention than the others, so she looked at Lucia and Alice before her next statement. "I don't like to lose."

Before anyone could respond, Hugh appeared near their table.

"Maya, can I have a minute, please?"

"Sure." Maya gathered her trash and followed him away from the table.

"What a bitch." Alice huffed as soon as they were out of earshot.

"What? I think she was perfectly pleasant," Shannon said.

"Ha. She's not very friendly. Frankly, not what I expected at all." Alice shook her head. "Very disappointing."

Lucia shrugged. "I didn't see Wayne or Jacques eating lunch with their teams."

"She's got a point." Shannon balled up her napkin and tossed it on her plate on top of the remnants of her lunch. Any appetite she had left after her performance that morning had disappeared when Maya joined them. She still hadn't fully wrapped her head around the idea that she'd just shared lunch with Maya Vaughn.

When Maya had lowered her voice and spoken only to her, Shannon's stomach had flipped nervously. First, she'd met Maya's eyes, but that only intensified the flutter, so, instead, she studied the tattoos on Maya's arms. Maya had shed her chef's coat during the break, and Shannon was able to make out some of the designs. The amazingly detailed depiction of an old-fashioned hand mixer that spanned the inside of her left forearm was particularly impressive.

A flowing script wrapped around her right wrist, but she hadn't been able to read the message.

"It doesn't matter. I guess we're stuck with her," Alice grumbled.

Alice's sudden negativity surprised Shannon, considering her otherwise bubbly personality. She could certainly think of worse fates than being mentored by an amazing chef. The fact that Maya was gorgeous and oozed sex appeal didn't hurt either.

Despite Sawyer spelling out the exact odds that she'd end up on Maya's team, Shannon hadn't let herself hope too much. Given her luck, she'd expected to be mentored by one of the other guys and left to watch Maya from afar. Granted, her concentration might have fared a little better. She'd completely embarrassed herself during that interview, and worse, Maya seemed to know exactly why. She'd probably gotten a good laugh about the pathetic, star-struck lesbian blundering around.

"You're not a contestant this time, Maya," Hugh said over his shoulder as he strode toward the kitchen set. "You can't eat lunch with them."

"Why not?" Maya stretched her legs to keep up with him. During Maya's season, Hugh had been an assistant to one of the producers. And in the ensuing seasons he'd worked his way up to associate producer. As a past winner, her association with the show had never really ended. She'd returned several times for challenges when the show brought back all-stars to compete against the newbies. And in all of those years, he hadn't slowed down a bit.

"We have a special lunch catered for you and the guys."

"If I choose to—"

He stopped short and pulled his cell phone from his pocket, apparently in response to a vibrating alert. He touched the screen, his eyes glued to the display. "You'll have an unfair advantage if you spend more time with your team."

Maya shrugged. "Wayne and Jacques are free to do the same, aren't they?"

"Just don't do it, okay? You're a mentor—a star—and we want you set apart from the competitors."

"Okay." She still didn't understand what the big deal was, but she'd comply. Of course, none of the mentors on her season had eaten lunch with her team. In fact, they'd pretty much looked at her like she didn't deserve to be there. Perhaps that's why she sympathized with the wide-eyed chefs.

CHAPTER FIVE

D amn it," Maya muttered to herself as she watched her team bickering.

"What was that?" Wayne asked smugly.

"Nothing."

Thirty minutes into the elimination challenge and her group had already fallen noticeably behind. The contestants had to work within their teams to design and decorate a cake for a client's retirement party. Two representatives from each team had met with the client and taken the ideas back to the others. While Lucia and Alice had handled that task, Shannon and Damien had begun gathering balls of fondant, layers of cake for carving, and other supplies.

The problem for Team Vaughn began when the four of them got behind one worktable. They disagreed drastically over design, taking up far too much time deciding what to do. Then when they finally started work, they were too rushed. Damien's fondant work was sloppy, and the faster he tried to go the worse it got. Alice tried to micro-manage the team and as a result didn't seem to be getting any of her own tasks done. Shannon let Alice walk all over her, first in the design phase and then while implementing the idea. Lucia worked consistently on her items, but she didn't participate much with the team.

By the time Eric called time, Maya's team had already been beaten. Maya almost felt more exhausted than if she'd been the one up there under the lights working. She mostly remained silent during the judging of each cake, letting Wayne and Jacques give the critiques.

Wayne's team was awarded the win, and he puffed up with pride, leaving the judges' table to give them all high fives.

"Maya, since your team came in last, one of them will go home."

Eric dismissed the other two teams and they headed back to the hotel. He sent Maya's team to the lounge area to await their fate. While the crew reset to shoot the elimination, Maya took her place behind the long, elevated desk designated for judging. Wayne and Jacques joined her.

"Okay, let's hear it." She turned to them with a resigned sigh.

"They're kind of a mess." Wayne furrowed his brows as if to soften his words.

Maya nodded, biting her lower lip.

"*A mess* would have been preferable." The slight French lilt to Jacques' tone made him sound haughty no matter what he said.

Maya tamped down the irrational urge to defend her team. Their performance this afternoon didn't merit the effort. "Who would you send home?"

"Looking at both challenges?"

"Sure."

Wayne considered the question for an uncomfortably long moment. Maya's stomach twisted nervously. "Damien and Shannon are your weakest links. But I think she edged him out this time."

Jacques nodded in agreement.

"That's what I figured." She relaxed a bit. She didn't want to send Shannon home today.

"Okay, guys, I'm going to bring them in." Hugh leaned against the edge of the counter and met Maya's eyes. "Since this is your first time doing this, let me go over a couple of things. These guys can talk it through with you, but we want you to make the final announcement. I know you all probably already know what you want to do. But we want you to play it up. Talk to them, see if you can make them fight it out a little. It makes for good drama that way."

He didn't wait for her answer before he headed back to the lounge, presumably to brief the contestants on how the first elimination would go—where to stand, what they should do once Maya announced the chef they would be sending home.

Hugh led the chefs into the room and they stood in a line in front of the mentors. Maya leaned forward, resting her elbows on the table, and gave them her best look of disappointment. Alice fidgeted. Hugh turned control over to Eric, who gave a practiced speech for the cameras about the elimination process, providing essentially the same information Hugh had just given the chefs for the viewers.

"You all earned a place on the show, but today, we're not really sure why," Jacques said as soon as Eric handed control to the judges. "As a team you worked horribly together."

"Your inability to come together on a design put you behind from the start, and you never recovered." Wayne eyed each of them individually. "Unfortunately we can send only one chef home, so three of you get a pass this week. But don't walk out of here triumphant, because none of you should be proud to be standing here right now."

Shannon searched the three mentors' faces, wondering what the odds were that she would stay another day. She'd joked with Jori about being booted from the show and crawling back to her job, but she'd actually thought she'd last at least a little longer. She found no answers in Jacques' stony expression. Wayne, too, seemed to be putting up a tough front. And Maya was looking at everyone but her. Oh God, could she really be going home today?

"Lucia." Maya paused until Lucia stepped forward. "You're safe and going on to the next show."

Lucia nodded, a small smile of relief touching her lips as she backed up several steps, then turned and hurried from the room.

"Alice, you're also safe."

"Thank you so much. I—" Alice caught Maya's stern look and cut off whatever she was about to say.

"Damien, Shannon, you're both up for elimination." Maya met Shannon's eyes only briefly before she looked at the other mentors.

Shannon couldn't keep from watching Maya. Though Maya's hands were tucked under the table in front of her, the rhythmic flexing of her bicep muscles seemed to indicate a nervous gesture, such as clenching and unclenching her fists. The three mentors began detailing the strengths and weaknesses each of them had shown during the two challenges. Shannon forced her racing mind to absorb the words, hoping maybe later she could make sense of them.

"Shannon." She flinched when Maya barked her name. Had she missed a question? "Why should you stay instead of Damien?"

She nodded and purposefully straightened her posture. "I'm not ready to leave." Damien's expression reflected the same desperation that stirred inside of her. None of them wanted to leave. If she hoped to convince the mentors to keep her, she had to do better than that. She took a deep breath and made eye contact with each mentor in turn as she spoke. "I failed in the consultation this morning. I can't sugarcoat that. And I'm not proud of my team's work this afternoon either. In fact, in our shop, I wouldn't even have shown that cake to a client. We didn't work well together, and I should have done more to fix that problem." She locked eyes with Maya and felt as if she were speaking only to her. Maybe the decision was already made, but if she had any hope of affecting her fate, she needed Maya to hear her, to understand how badly she needed more time. "But I haven't shown you everything I have yet."

Maya narrowed her eyes and jerked her gaze from Shannon's face to Damien's. "Damien, why should you stay?"

"Between the two of us, I'm the better decorator. I'm more creative and more experienced."

Shannon stared at him, but he didn't look at her. Her face heated with embarrassment and anger. While she'd tried to be diplomatic and focus on herself, he apparently wasn't pulling his punches.

"That's a bold statement," Wayne said. "Shannon, do you have a response to that?"

"He doesn't know me well enough to judge my creativity or my talent. As for experience—well, you aren't looking for 'America's most experienced pastry chef,' are you?"

"We are not." Wayne looked impressed with her answer. But when he and Jacques both looked to Maya, Shannon's suspicion that Maya alone controlled her fate was confirmed.

"Damien, I'm sorry, but you won't be continuing in the competition," Maya said.

He looked like he wanted to say something else, but her tone left no doubt the decision was final.

Shannon exhaled slowly, trying to ease the adrenaline jitters. Her knees felt weak, and she shoved her hands in her pants pockets to hide any visible shaking. She'd survived. For one more day, at least. She didn't look at Damien.

"Shannon, you may join the rest of your team. A car is waiting to take you back to the hotel." Eric's statement signaled an end to filming for the day. The crew immediately began bustling around, everyone seeming to know exactly what they needed to do before leaving. Shannon tried to stay out of the way as she headed toward the lounge.

When she stepped through the door, Alice cheered and jumped up to give her a hug.

"I was hoping it was you. Now it's just us girls."

"I am not so happy about this," Lucia said. Then when Alice gave her a look, she said, "I'm also glad you returned. But I do not want to be up for elimination again."

"I agree. We can and will do better. I don't want to be on the bottom again." Shannon herded them toward the door. "Let's go back and get rested. I'm sure tomorrow won't be any easier."

She recalled Maya's question about whether middle of the pack was good enough for her. As it turned out, today, she'd have been quite happy with the middle. But not for long. She'd rearranged her life to be here, given up her job at Drake's, would probably miss her granddaughter's birth, and traded living in her own home for a hotel room. She vowed to work hard enough to make all of that worth the sacrifice.

❖

Maya shoved through the door to her dressing room and closed it quickly behind her. She crossed to the mini-fridge, pulled out a bottle of water, and took a long drink. Then, after recapping the bottle, she squeezed it until the plastic crackled. The excessive talking she'd done these past two days could only partially explain her dry throat. This elimination had worked her up more than she'd expected.

Damien was an easy choice for her today. He lacked the skills and discipline to go to the end. And, based on what little interaction she'd had with him, she didn't like his attitude. But she'd worried that Wayne and Jacques wouldn't agree. If they both found some reason to keep him around and send Shannon home, could Maya, as the newest mentor, really have gone against the advice of two renowned chefs?

Maybe she shouldn't have taken this job. Maybe she should have listened to Wendy when she said it was too big a commitment right now. She just hadn't thought she'd get so invested. She expected to come in, with her on-screen persona, put on an act, and walk away each day unaffected. But seeing Shannon's passion and, alternately, her self-flagellation had touched her. Not only did it make her want to keep Shannon in the competition, but she yearned for the days when her own life was so simple. Lately, the spotlight had been a bit too glaring.

She'd always hated when celebrities acted like fame was such a hardship. But she hadn't understood how completely her privacy could be invaded until she'd seen the headlines full of speculation stamped above the pictures of her leaving her doctor's office. The more outrageous the lies became, the more closely she guarded the truth.

For the past eleven months, she'd worked practically nonstop, trying to keep her mind occupied and her heart from breaking at the thought of the life she'd once had growing inside her.

Suddenly, she didn't feel like going back to her hotel room to sit alone with her thoughts. She shrugged off her chef coat, grabbed her purse, and headed for the door.

Twenty minutes later, she handed cab fare to her driver and climbed out of the car. The glow of blue neon cast a ghostly pallor over the line of people waiting outside the door. She fell in at the end of it, behind a couple of skinny guys who clung to each other like new lovers celebrating the freedom of a night out in a safe place.

The line moved quickly. Within a few minutes she'd handed over the cover charge and was allowed inside. She entered a dark room, lit by various colored lights and laser effects. A haze of artificial fog hung in the air, and club music seemed to vibrate all the way through Maya. She felt like the young girl she'd once been, new to New York City and bursting with newfound freedom. She'd discovered her own sexuality on dance floors just like this one, with liquid courage and the support of her gay friends making her brave enough to explore her desires. She'd toned down the drinking a great deal since then, and, now that she thought about it, she didn't have as many real friends either.

She moved through the crowd of gyrating college-aged kids and older gay guys trying to cling to their dance-music-fueled youth. As she navigated into the large room used for the drag show, she passed the restrooms. The collection of women and men in both lines obviously had little regard for gender-specific facilities.

In the showroom, the dozen or so tables near the stage had already been claimed, and people had jammed into the area behind them. Maya fell in with the people passing through the crowd like a tiny stream cutting its way through a forest. As she moved, she brushed bodies on both sides, sometimes turning sideways and shuffling along to avoid an errant elbow, drink, or hand holding a cigarette. Several times, she nearly crashed into the girl in front of her when traffic halted abruptly.

She finally made it to the back of the room where a bar stretched across one wall and a duo of bartenders managed the flow of alcohol like air-traffic controllers. No one seemed to recognize her. Over the years she'd learned to distinguish between an interested look due to her appearance and one born of recognition. Then, of course, there was the expression of the person who had figured out that they'd seen her somewhere but hadn't yet placed just where.

She'd just squeezed into a space at the bar and was still waiting to catch the attention of the bartender when she felt someone press close behind her. She turned her head, coming eye-to-eye with an attractive brunette. Pretty—yes, but her hair was too light, not the deep, rich brown of Shannon's.

Maya shook her head. Why should she suddenly be comparing other women to Shannon? She barely knew her, and all she'd done so far was aggravate Maya with her lack of confidence. Sure, she was attractive, in a humble, accessible, down-to-earth sort of way. But women like that rarely caught Maya's eye. She tended to notice women who were different—who stood out in a crowd, not only the classically beautiful, but also flamboyant and super-confident women of all shapes and sizes.

"Can I buy you a drink?" The woman leaned in and spoke near Maya's ear in order to be heard. Her hair smelled like cigarette smoke, and the sting of alcohol on her breath said it wouldn't be her first drink of the night. Maya had no idea what Shannon's hair smelled like.

"Sure, thanks."

When the bartender came over, she ordered rum and Diet Coke.

"I haven't seen you here before."

She managed to suppress an eye roll at the obvious line. "I don't know how you'd tell with all of these people."

"I come here a lot." The woman winked and grinned as if she'd just revealed some impressive tidbit about herself.

"I'm just passing through." *In more ways than one.* She glanced in the direction of the door, but she couldn't see it through the crowd.

"A tourist, huh? Business or pleasure?"

"A little of each, I hope." Before she could stop herself, she flirted, more as an automatic response to the interest in the woman's voice than anything else. She sipped from her drink, then replaced it on the bar, careful to keep it close. She wouldn't have more than the one. When she visited a new city, she didn't seek out the bars for alcohol. She did so because they were the easiest place to blend into the crowd—an accepting crowd—and not be alone for a little while.

She didn't have to be Maya Vaughn; she could become just another body in the throng.

The lights went down even further and a spotlight focused on the center of the stage. Over the house speakers, an announcer introduced the emcee for the show. Maya turned, finding that if she tilted her head just right she could see most of the stage. She was grateful for the entertainment that would keep her from having to make any more small talk for a while.

❖

"So, did you meet her?" Even through the phone, excitement colored Jori's voice.

Shannon laughed. "Is that really your first question?" She'd been the first of the roommates to get up and showered this morning. So she took a few minutes while the others were getting ready to make a phone call.

"Yep. You can't talk about the show, and you're not allowed to do anything else. So is there something else new you have to catch me up on?"

"Fair enough. Okay. Yes, I met her."

"Is she as hot in person?"

"Hotter." Shannon whispered, glancing around to make sure none of her roommates were within earshot. They'd gathered in the kitchen eating the breakfast Alice had prepared. Shannon couldn't eat a thing until she'd had at least two cups of coffee. "Insanely hot. And confident. And so focused you can just see it in her eyes. But I don't think I made a very good first impression."

"You sound smitten."

"Maybe I have a little crush. But it's purely professional."

Jori laughed. "You have a professional crush?"

"You know what I mean. Okay, so it's physical, too. But think about what we know about her. She's a player, a *bisexual* player at that."

"Sounds like Sawyer when I met her. Except for the bisexual part."

"Yeah? I don't remember hearing any rumors about Sawyer having an abortion last year."

"Wow. That sounded a little cold. I didn't know you were such a fan of the tabloids."

"I can hardly miss them. I remember every headline screaming about it. I've told you what my ex-husband and I went through trying to have a baby. I wouldn't trade Regan for anything, but I wanted a baby of my own so badly. I can't respect anyone's decision to terminate a life because pregnancy is inconvenient." As she heard the bitterness in her voice, Shannon became aware that her phone calls were being monitored. They hadn't been given the details about who would be listening, but she could guess, and she didn't want some production assistant spreading gossip about her opinions on Maya Vaughn's life choices. "I gotta go, Jori. We're due to leave soon and I have to get downstairs. Tell Sawyer I said hello."

"I would if I ever saw her. It seems like the only time we have together is when I make a delivery to the restaurant or if she stops by the bakery."

"Maybe once things settle down there—"

"Well, I'm counting on business picking up after you make us famous on that show."

"Sure. I'll drop the name Drake's as often as I can."

"I know you can't tell me. But however things are going, we're proud of you."

"That helps, thanks."

"So stop lusting after your mentor and get to work changing that first impression, huh?"

She smiled at Jori's teasing tone. "Absolutely." Jori's advice was sounder than she knew. Shannon should be thinking about Maya only in a professional capacity. She obviously couldn't afford any more distractions. So far, she hadn't put forward the image she wanted the mentors to see. Any further lack of focus might blow what could be the biggest boost possible in her career.

CHAPTER SIX

Maya slumped into a chair, pulled off her sunglasses, and winced against the lights. Thankful for the silence signaling that she was one of the first to arrive, she closed her eyes and turned her scrubbed-clean face toward the woman who came at her with a makeup brush.

She'd stayed at the bar too late, given her early call this morning. After nursing the same drink through the entire drag show, she'd rebuffed the advances of her drunken companion and put her in a cab. Then she got a separate taxi for herself, preferring the inside of her own hotel room to the invitation to her new friend's apartment. She'd dragged herself out of bed only a few hours later and called for a car to drive her to the set. When she knew she had only a short time to sleep, she always slept lightly, disturbed by the slightest sound, as if her body feared she wouldn't wake in time otherwise. So she'd tossed and turned, waking from weird dreams to look at the clock and engage in a negotiation with her body about how many hours she could still manage if she went to sleep *right now*.

The sound of distant voices growing louder signaled the end of her solitude. She drew in a deep breath and opened her eyes. The contestants were arriving for hair and makeup. They all seemed annoyingly well rested and perky this morning. Never good on little sleep, she became sensitive to sound when she was tired. One guy incessantly stirred his coffee, and the sound of the plastic spoon scraping his foam cup nearly drove her insane. Why couldn't he use one of those little plastic straws? They were so much quieter.

The three women on her team had entered together and moved toward the chairs at the opposite end of the row. She caught a couple of curious glances, as if they weren't sure whether they should approach her. She sent them a glare to let them know that though her anger from yesterday's performance had cooled slightly, they'd still better keep their distance.

Remembering her attempt at distraction last night, Maya looked surreptitiously at Shannon. Once again, the chestnut hair that she'd compared to that of the brunette in the bar was pulled back into a neat bun, but a strand near her temple had escaped and caressed the side of her face, curling at the end to just touch her jawbone. She carried her chef coat slung across her arm, and without its boxy shape, Maya could see that she had a nice figure, curvy in all the right places. Attractive—yes, but she still didn't stand out in a crowd, not even this crowd. Maya's eyes should have gravitated to a number of the other women first, but for some reason even as she scanned them, she came back to Shannon.

"Chef Hayes," she called out, her voice sharper than she'd intended. Her fascination with Shannon irritated her, and, though she knew it was irrational, she wanted to blame her.

"Yes, Chef." Shannon strode over and stopped beside her chair. Maya kept her face directed to the woman applying her makeup, but she shifted her body toward Shannon.

"Damien threw you under the bus yesterday for his own benefit. I'm not a fan of that. But he never would have had the chance if you hadn't given it to him. I know you can be a stronger competitor than this. I wouldn't have chosen you for my team otherwise."

"Yes, Chef."

"Damn it. Where's your backbone?"

"I'm sorry?" Shannon glanced at the makeup girl, who seemed to be trying to look like she wasn't listening in.

"Why do you want to be here?"

"To learn, to compete—"

"Don't give me the television-interview answer. I want brutal honesty."

Shannon frowned. She took a step back as if she wanted to leave, but one of the guys from makeup grabbed her shoulders and steered her into the chair next to Maya.

"Honey, if you're just going to stand there, at least let me do you."

She sighed and tilted her face toward him.

"You put your whole life on hold to be here. Surely something deeper than education drives you?" Maya wouldn't let the topic go until she better understood Shannon's motivation. Aside from her own competitiveness, Maya genuinely wanted to see her succeed. She'd obviously fought to follow her dream, not letting the fact that she was older than most other aspiring chefs deter her. So where was that determination now?

"I put my whole life on hold a long time ago. I'm finally living it now," Shannon snapped.

"Now we're getting somewhere. What do you mean?"

Shannon started to shake her head, but the makeup guy grasped her chin and held her still, so she waved a hand in the air dismissively instead.

Maya turned in her chair and touched her forearm. Shannon blinked, her eyes shining with anger and a well of unshed tears. The contact suddenly felt too intimate and Maya pulled her hand back. "Tell me."

"I was married and, for nine years, I did what he wanted me to do. Then—well, then there was my daughter. For the first time in my life, I'm making decisions while only thinking of myself."

The makeup guy gave her a tissue and a stern look, indicating he did not intend to redo her eyes. She dabbed carefully under her lids.

"So, then—why do you want to be here?"

Shannon didn't answer.

"I'm trying to help you." Maya met her eyes in the mirror and held them, wanting to make sure Shannon saw her sincerity. "Please."

"Because I have to know if I'm good enough."

Maya stared at her for a long moment, surprised by the ache in her heart at Shannon's words. "Well, let me put that question to rest for you. You are most definitely good enough."

"You have to say that since you picked me for your team. Admitting I wasn't would be admitting a mistake on your part."

"I don't make mistakes." Maya winked, trying to lighten the mood. "You deserve to be here."

"I'm not that naive. I know how these reality shows work, and it isn't all about talent. I fit a demographic. I'm the oldest person on the show. I'm the generation past, trying desperately to keep up with the young hotshots."

Maya shrugged. "Does it matter why you were cast?"

"What do you mean?"

"You're here now. So, the way I see it, you have two outcomes. Either you're the old lady who can't keep up or you rise to the challenge and beat them. That's the only part you can control." Maya grinned at the hard glint in Shannon's eyes when she said "old lady." Maybe she could ignite that fire yet.

❖

"Oh my God, I need coffee," Sawyer called as she let herself in the back door at the bakery. Jori crossed the kitchen and met her with a mug before she'd taken two more steps. "Yes, this is why I love you." She carefully took a sip, then gave an exaggerated moan.

Jori pressed close to her and kissed the side of her neck. "Yeah? If I'd known coffee was all I had to give you to earn your love, I wouldn't have bothered wooing you so hard in the beginning."

Sawyer laughed. "You? I distinctly recall being the one doing the wooing. You, my love, wanted nothing to do with me."

"The first of many mistakes I made where you're concerned." She smiled as she remembered the first few months, four years ago, when both Jori's apprehension and Sawyer's own family had conspired to keep them apart.

"No worries, it's all sorted now."

"Good." Jori slapped her ass lightly. "Now go make nice with the new girl. Her name is Mackenzie and I told her you'd be stopping by this morning."

"Certainly." Still cradling her warm mug, she headed for the front of the shop.

Jori followed more slowly, content to observe as Sawyer greeted Mackenzie and slipped into comfortable conversation with her.

Though not quite as skilled as Shannon, so far Mackenzie had impressed Jori. The willowy blonde piling baked goods into the display case wasn't what Jori had expected. Perhaps because Shannon had said she went to pastry school with her, Jori had mistakenly imagined someone older. Though she'd have to be at least in her twenties to have graduated already, this girl didn't look it. Her wavy hair fell in a loose braid down the center of her back. She wore a fitted T-shirt and the skinny jeans that seemed so popular these days, though Jori thought they usually made the wearer appear oddly disproportionate. But as long as Mackenzie continued working as hard as she had, Jori wouldn't hold her fashion choices against her.

"Welcome to Drake's. I'm sure you'll have no trouble fitting in." Sawyer lifted her coffee cup in salutation.

Jori leaned against the counter and pointed at Sawyer's mug. "In case you didn't catch it, that gesture was a hint. First thing in the morning, keep Sawyer's coffee full and she'll be happy."

"Very funny."

"Actually, it's a joke. Because she's so rarely here first thing in the morning," Jori half-teased. She hoped if they worked hard enough now, they might someday be in a position to adjust their staggered schedules.

"That's because while you're already nestled in bed at night, I'm still at the restaurant."

"Oh, yeah, I've been meaning to stop by there and check out Drake's. Now that I'm working downtown it won't be such a headache with parking and all," Mackenzie said.

"Sure. Be sure to do that. The food's great. And I'm not just saying that because my brother and sister are the chefs. Speaking of which, I better go keep them in line." She kissed Jori's cheek as she passed. "Nice to meet you, Mackenzie. Any time you want to try out our lunch menu, just get your boss here to text me an order."

❖

"A great cake is not just about appearance. Even the most elaborate showpiece should still taste good. In fact, one could argue it should taste even better. But too often decorating trumps the palate. Today, you'll each be bringing us a tasting of your best three flavor profiles. The winner will be safe from elimination in the next challenge."

They'd been given the same instructions earlier that morning, then had to provide Hugh with a list of their tasting menu so the appropriate ingredients could be assembled before taping began. Now, Eric delivered the rules for the cameras with a dramatic flair, and they were supposed to react as if it were the first time they'd heard them. As he signaled the start of time, they rushed to their stations. As a viewer, Shannon had often wondered how the contestants came up with their ideas in those few seconds before beginning work. Now she knew they often had more preparation time than she'd thought. Apparently, reality shows often had less reality than they portrayed.

"You've got this," she mumbled as she gathered what she needed to mix her three batters. She'd selected flavor combinations she had done before at Drake's. Her recipes were proven, and she was confident she could create a great sampling.

She quickly prepared her batters, filled layer pans, and put them in the oven. While they baked, she made icings and fillings. She worked steadily without a moment of downtime, glancing often at the clock. It seemed as if the producers had calculated time for baking, cooling, and assembly, then cut five minutes off that time in order to frame the limit on this challenge. Then again, every challenge felt that way. She put her head down and worked faster, intent on making up the difference.

"Tell me about your flavors."

She jerked her eyes up at the words and found Maya leaning over the counter to peer into the saucepan she intently stirred. She'd been focused on keeping her caramel filling from burning and hadn't heard her approach. Now, their faces were only inches apart, and Shannon couldn't tear her eyes from Maya's. This close, she discovered Maya's irises were a deep blue at the center that lightened to steely gray around the outside edges.

"Are you really going to keep it a secret until the judging?" Maya's lips twitched into a half smile.

"Um, no—I—this is a caramel filling for my chocolate cake, which will also have a caramel buttercream icing." Shannon's face burned as she heard the tremor in her own voice. If Maya would just back up a step, she might be able to regain her composure. She glanced at the cameraman shooting over Maya's shoulder, then flicked her eyes away. But then she thought, *Maybe they won't be able to use this part since I looked at the camera.* She debated whether to give it another good, long look just to be certain.

Around them, Wayne and Jacques visited the counters of their team members as well, offering suggestions and advice.

"Can I taste it?" Maya's words brought Shannon's attention squarely back to her. The anticipation on her face as she asked made Shannon's mind spin up all kinds of inappropriate thoughts. Coupled with Maya's quiet tone and their physical proximity, she could almost convince herself Maya had something other than a culinary sampling in mind. "Chef Hayes?"

Shannon shook her head and cleared her throat. "Of course." She drew a spoon out of a nearby canister and held it out.

When Maya took it, her fingers brushed Shannon's and she drew her lower lip between her teeth, the only outward sign that she might also be affected by their nearness. Shannon stepped back and let Maya dip into the caramel. Once she'd lifted the spoon clear, Shannon slid the pan off the burner, pleased with the consistency of threads that fell away from Maya's spoon.

"Be careful," Shannon warned her, the words *it's hot* stuck in her throat.

While Maya blew lightly across her spoon, Shannon busied herself with extracting her cakes from the pans. The clock wouldn't wait for her to lust after Maya Vaughn. She didn't look up even when she saw Maya raise the spoon higher, partly because she didn't have time and partly because she didn't think she could handle seeing Maya slide that spoon between her lips.

"Nice," Maya murmured, before moving on to the chef to her right.

Shannon kept her head down and tried not to listen to Maya's interaction with Lucia. She didn't want to compare Maya's tone with Lucia to the one she'd used with her. She didn't want to examine the intimacy she'd felt in their exchange. Maybe a small part of her wanted to hold onto the illusion that there was something extra in Maya's voice just for her, which, she admitted, was ridiculous.

When her cakes were still a bit warm for her liking, she placed her first layer down, spread the filling, then set the top layer. She completed each cake this way, hoping they would cool enough before she tried to ice them. She would have trouble assembling an appealing plate if her icing melted into a puddle around her cake.

She had just sliced and plated her final piece of cake when Eric called time. When she raised her hands and stepped back, several other competitors mirrored her pose. She scanned her creations, proud of her work.

One by one the competitors stepped forward as their cakes were presented to the mentors seated at the judges' table facing the chefs. Each of the other chefs seemed to have adopted a similar strategy to Shannon's, making both traditional flavors and more exotic selections as well. She hoped the mentors would find something they liked in the mix. Lucia got the expected praise. But Ned's plate wasn't received quite as favorably. Wayne hated his pineapple cake with cherry filling and coconut icing. And Maya didn't like his chocolate cake with pistachio-crusted ganache. She said his cakes were dry, probably because he tried to do too much and sacrificed quality.

As her turn neared, Shannon's heart pounded and she tried to discreetly wipe her damp palms on the side of her pants. Though this wasn't an elimination challenge, she desperately wanted to do well. To her right Mason moved forward and offered his cakes, but she didn't hear a word he said. She'd already started thinking about what she would say. When Mason returned to his place in line, she raised her eyes to Maya, who was looking back with what seemed to be a mixture of hope and something else she couldn't identify.

"Shannon." Maya's tone was tentative. She waved her hand, inviting Shannon to step up.

"Today, I made my carrot cake with whipped cream-cheese icing. Next, you have a coconut cake with lime buttercream. Finally, chocolate cake with a salted caramel filling and caramel buttercream." She kept her presentation simple. These amazing chefs wouldn't need fancy words to impress their palates; she relied on her flavors to accomplish that.

As they tasted, they glanced at each other, but she couldn't decipher anything from their expressions and wondered if they knew each other well enough to communicate this way.

Wayne was the first to speak. "This carrot cake may be the best I've ever tasted."

Shannon pushed her shoulders back and lifted her chin. She'd just gotten the biggest compliment of her life, and she wanted to bask in it for a moment.

"I agree, it's very good." Jacques' praise felt a bit more reserved, but he gave Shannon a reassuring smile. "All of your cakes are moist. Good flavors. Well done."

Shannon turned to Maya, waiting. She needed her praise even more than that of the other two, and she couldn't stand another of her silent evaluations.

"Your caramel filling is incredible. I could eat it with a spoon. Again." Maya smiled. "And your icings are exquisite, sweet yet still light and not at all cloying."

Shannon couldn't hold back her full grin, and she was sure it shone all the way to her eyes. She did manage to stifle the urge to rush forward and grab Maya's hands where they rested on the table in front of her, long fingers stacked together. For the first time since she'd arrived, she felt good about her effort and the results. She didn't know if she'd won immunity, but she definitely wasn't middle of the pack this morning.

❖

"Well?" Maya asked as soon as she was alone with the other mentors. She already knew who she'd vote for. Several of the chefs had standout cakes on their plate, but most had an obviously weak piece as well. For her there were two clear front-runners.

"Looks like your team is the big winner today. It's between Lucia and Shannon for me," Wayne said, echoing Maya's own thoughts.

Jacques nodded and raised his hands in a sign of agreement. "Your chefs, your decision."

Maya nodded. "I agree. But I give Shannon the win this time. I could rave about all three of her cakes, but her chocolate-caramel cake blew me away."

Throughout this challenge, a ferocious competitiveness had shone in Shannon's eyes. But she'd also projected an aura of calm and confidence in her baking. During many of the challenges, when only the decorating mattered, the chefs would use sponge cake premade by bakers who worked prep for the show. But today Shannon had proved she wasn't just a good decorator but a successful pastry chef, in the real world where taste mattered.

Chapter Seven

Shannon rolled over and grabbed one of the many pillows from the other side of the bed. She hugged it close to her chest and tried in vain to get comfortable. She squinted at the clock. It had only been ten minutes since she last looked, and she was no closer to falling asleep. At least since Damien was gone, she wasn't keeping anyone else awake with her restlessness.

At home, when she couldn't sleep, she would get up and bake. When she'd first started at Drake's and was nervous about her new job, she'd discovered several new recipes late at night that had made it into the display case.

She got out of bed and wandered into the darkened living room of the suite. Their tiny kitchen didn't have an oven, only a microwave and a stovetop. Besides, she probably shouldn't be banging around in a kitchen just outside the room where Lucia and Alice slept. Maybe a walk would burn some energy.

She returned to her room and pulled her favorite hoodie over her T-shirt, hoping it would disguise the fact that she hadn't bothered with a bra. She grabbed her hotel key and slipped as quietly as she could into the hallway. In the elevator, she hesitated, then selected the floor for the restaurant, fitness room, and spa. She preferred to avoid the possibility of running into anyone else, but didn't want to chance disturbing anyone by prowling the hallways outside of guest rooms. As the car descended, she tapped her foot. She hated standing in those little boxes and waiting; even in the fastest elevator she got irritated.

Today had been the best day since she'd arrived, and though she should have been exhausted from all the activity and resting up for another long day tomorrow, her mind had been racing. She'd been thrilled when Maya announced that she'd won immunity and had felt much more relaxed during the afternoon's elimination challenge. The three teams were tasked with creating a preteen's birthday cake. They had to consult with an overbearing parent while pleasing the child as well. As it turned out, she didn't need the immunity. Her team's design came in second behind Jacques' team, and Wayne eliminated one of his contestants.

If only her team had come in first, this would have been the kind of day she'd hoped for when she learned she'd made it onto the show. But it was definitely a step in the right direction. She felt inspired by their success today, and judging by the fire she'd seen in Lucia's eyes, the team had some fuel for the next challenge. It was that challenge that had Shannon awake and pacing the hallways of her hotel. As a franchise, the show had several key trials during each season but was otherwise unique from year to year. Ready to tackle the next test, she had been working her way through possible scenarios all night when she should have been sleeping.

The car slowed, then stopped in a motion that made her stomach flip a little. She strode to the other end of the building, walking with purpose, then began to wander back toward the elevators, this time slowing to read the menu displayed on the outside of the darkened restaurant window. Out of habit, she skipped to the end of the page and checked the desserts. Not bad. She noted several that looked like fresh chef specials, but a couple others could easily come out of the freezer. Working at Drake's had spoiled her. Jori still oversaw the dessert menu for the restaurant, and either the restaurant pastry chef or Jori herself made every item fresh.

She'd learned a little about her competitors in the past couple of days. Many of them were just starting out in the business and hoped to launch a stellar career. Some of them came from families who didn't help them out, and they had a ton of loans to pay back.

Regardless of what motivated them, they all wanted to win. She was no different. Just because she had a great job she could return to, she didn't want to go backward. For so many years, she'd set aside her own ambitions to make a home for her and Regan. And, when things were difficult, she consoled herself with the idea that her sacrifice was noble. Now that she'd finally gotten her own chance, she desperately needed to prove that she'd had the talent to succeed all along. But only in an empty hotel hallway in the middle of the night would she willingly admit, solely to herself, that she could be that shallow.

She halted as she passed the fitness center, staring through the glass-paned door. Holy hell, speaking of shallow—Maya Vaughn, barely clad, ran smoothly on the treadmill belt, and Shannon's reaction was completely physical.

Maya wore only a sports bra and brightly colored running shorts, the tiny ones that Shannon hadn't thought anyone actually wore for running. If she had an ounce of body fat around her toned muscles, Shannon couldn't find it. A blue bandana concealed her hair. The cord from her earbuds led to a small pouch strapped around one bicep. But the device in the strap was a blur as she pumped her arms to keep up with the speeding belt of the treadmill.

Shannon tried to keep in shape by power-walking her neighborhood several times a week. But she hated running. Maybe she'd never done it long enough to obtain the high that kept people doing it, and she actually had no desire to. However, while watching Maya's muscles bunch, Shannon thought she might run if that's what she was chasing.

Just as she was about to turn away, Maya glanced at the door. Damn. Maya smiled and waved. She couldn't leave now without looking like some kind of creepy stalker. Maybe if she acted like she intended to work out, she wouldn't seem so crazy. As she stepped inside, Maya slowed the treadmill and removed her earbuds.

"Hi. I don't want to interrupt your workout."

Maya hopped off the machine and trotted closer to Shannon. "I'll take any excuse to quit a little early."

Shannon managed a nod, but she couldn't tear her eyes from the drops of sweat that traced down the side of Maya's face and neck. They pooled in the hollow between her collarbones, then streamed into the cleavage just above the edge of her neon-green sports bra. Her mouth went dry, and she had the crazy thought that licking the only moisture in sight would only increase her thirst. Realizing she was staring at Maya's breasts, she jerked her eyes lower, searching for safer ground. But there she found tight abs also glistening with perspiration. She drew in a shaky breath as she imagined pressing herself to Maya's damp skin and feeling the muscles twitch under her hands. Before she could control her brain, she said, "It doesn't look like you quit early very often."

"I guess I don't." Maya laughed and picked up a towel from a shelf by the door. "So, did you come to work out?" She glanced down at Shannon's pajama pants and her bright-green Crocs, a small smile teasing her beautiful lips.

Shannon matched the expression. "What? They're very comfortable."

"Sure, for twelve hours standing in a kitchen. Not for cardio." Maya's gaze shifted to Shannon's sweatshirt, lingering on her chest.

Shannon's nipples were proudly announcing their opinion of her perusal of Maya's body a few moments ago as well as her lack of bra—sports bra or otherwise. She folded her arms over her chest. Well, so much for pretending she intended to use the gym as well.

"I—uh—couldn't sleep. I figured a walk might help. I'm not brave or crazy enough to stroll around downtown Nashville in the middle of the night. So I've been pacing the hotel hallways."

"Wow, they should put that on the tourism posters." Maya painted her hand across the air in front of her. "Nashville—come pace our hotel hallways."

"It's got a ring to it, doesn't it? A certain appeal?"

"I suppose that depends on who I'm pacing next to."

Shannon chuckled nervously. "I'm guessing your fantasy fellow hallway stroller isn't wearing pajamas and Crocs."

Maya shook her head slowly. "I can't say that he or she would have—before today."

"He *or* she?"

Maya lifted her chin as if to say, *so what.*

Shannon opted for straightforward honesty. "I'll admit, I don't understand it."

"And by 'it' you mean?" Maya picked up a T-shirt from a nearby weight bench and pulled it over her head.

"The whole bisexual thing."

Maya laughed. "The bisexual *thing*?"

"Well, how can you be into both?"

"Because women are clearly so much more attractive?"

"So you've heard that before."

"It's apparently the lesbian platform on bisexuality." Maya grimaced. "You were married once. Can't you appreciate a good-looking man?"

"Sure. But that doesn't mean I want to sleep with one now."

"No going back once you've seen the light?"

"Something like that."

"So we agree that aesthetically, women and men both have the potential to be physically attractive. As a lesbian, *now*—" Maya grinned as she put emphasis on that word—"you might not understand how I can be physically attracted to both, so you'll just have to take that as fact. In the same way you might prefer brunettes to blondes, I have my own physical types, and they aren't limited by gender. We agree so far?"

"I suppose."

"Then let's go beyond the physical. If I were looking for a relationship, I'd seek out the same qualities in both genders: strength, loyalty, sense of humor, beauty, and so on. But in your world, if I find that in a guy instead of a girl, I'm a traitor."

"I didn't say that."

Maya huffed. "You didn't have to. Enough lesbians before you already have."

"Look. It's just a tough thing to swallow. It's bad enough to lose a woman to another woman. But to a man?"

"Love shouldn't be a competition. And being bisexual doesn't make me less reliable or more promiscuous. If I'm in a relationship, I'm loyal—I'm committed."

"When was the last time you were in one?"

"It's been awhile."

"Trouble getting dates?" Shannon tried to lighten the mood, partly to avoid admitting Maya's logic made sense and partly to keep from imagining the kind of person Maya might be attracted to. She figured she'd have her pick of any one of the gorgeous young men or women who had shared magazine pages with her over the years.

"Something like that." Maya tossed her own phrase back at her sarcastically.

"Come on. I don't imagine you have to work too hard at it."

"What does that mean?"

"Look at you. You're gorgeous and interesting and charismatic."

"Don't forget famous." Now her sarcasm took on a hard edge.

"I didn't forget. Give me a break. I was trying to pay you a compliment."

"Maybe you could tell me just how hard I have to work at it." Maya advanced on her swiftly.

"That's not a good idea." When Shannon pressed her hand to the center of her chest, stopping her, she felt the warmth of Maya's skin through her T-shirt. Her splayed fingertips rested on the edge of Maya's sports bra under her shirt. It wouldn't take much to curl her fingertips into that fabric and pull her closer still.

"There's no one else around."

"That's not the point."

Maya smiled, a slow, almost predatory pull of her beautiful lips. "It's too late to play hard to get. I've seen you looking at me. And I want very much to kiss you right now. What point could be more important than that?"

Shannon laughed, trying to diffuse the arousal that threatened to cloud her judgment and somehow kept her from looking away from Maya's lips. God, she wanted that kiss. She closed her eyes briefly and reminded herself she didn't have the luxury of giving in to such base sensations. And Maya's insistence that nothing else mattered only highlighted the differences between them. "You're so young."

"That's not an answer."

"You said yourself that I needed to focus on the show. That's what I intend to do. I should go. I don't think we're supposed to socialize outside of taping, anyway."

Maya shrugged, seemingly unconcerned with both Shannon's abrupt subject change and their possible violation of the rules.

Shannon let her hand fall away, immediately missing the contact. "Of the two of us, you're obviously more serious about being in the gym than I am. So I'm leaving."

"The camera adds ten pounds." Maya's voice didn't carry the teasing tone it had earlier. She sounded serious.

Shannon wanted to say that she'd seen her on television and she looked gorgeous, that no extra pound, or ten, could change that. Not to mention, she was even more stunning in person. Instead, she said, "I guess I'll head back and try to go to sleep." She backed toward the door.

"You should. You have an early morning tomorrow."

"You don't?"

"Nope. We don't have to be there until the afternoon."

"No challenge judging?"

Maya shrugged. "We don't know much more than you do."

"Damn."

"Why? Were you scheming to extract details of the show from me?" Amusement colored Maya's voice, but the already present spark of heat flared brighter.

"And if I were?" She took another step back, as if she could retreat from the answering flame in her own body. But Maya moved forward, keeping near her.

"I would be interested in your methods."

"Chef Vaughn," she whispered, surprised she wasn't trembling with the effort of holding back.

"If you're going to look at me like that, you'd better call me Maya."

Standing close in the quiet of the gym, Shannon no longer saw the put-on bravado and charisma that Maya displayed around the set. Instead, now, her eyes were full of sincerity and emotion.

Maya held her gaze and pulled in a deep breath, caution infiltrating her expression as if she had to will it there. "You should go."

Shannon nodded slowly and leaned back into the push bar on the door. She made her way to her room with Maya's sexy face still floating in her head. So much for going to sleep. Her mind and body were racing much too fast to settle down now.

❖

Maya picked up a small ceramic bell with the words MUSIC CITY written in fancy script around it. She shook it gently, disappointed in its dull tenor. She returned it to the shelf and meandered through the rest of the store. She'd traveled a lot in the last seven years and had a strange obsession with tacky souvenir shops. She rarely made a purchase, but she loved walking among the shelves lined with coffee mugs, T-shirts, flyswatters, figurines of animals wearing clothes and doing people-things, and those weird tiny spoons. The staples in these shops didn't change, only the names and slogans imprinted on them. Interspersed among them were regional items, as well. In the South, she found a lot of barbeque sauce and various meat rubs, items featuring the word "redneck," and, so far in Nashville, stuff with guitars, boots, and cowboy hats on it.

She pushed through the shop door onto the street, thinking that the tinkling bell hanging from the door sounded better than the ones inside. She'd spent her morning exploring the several blocks that Nashvillians called "downtown." Wandering more than exploring, she kept getting distracted by thoughts of her encounter with Shannon the night before. She would suddenly realize she'd covered two blocks and not seen a damn thing. So she stopped and surveyed the fronts of the buildings behind her to see if she'd missed anything good.

Knowing she didn't have to get up early today, and having already planned this outing, she'd hit the fitness room late last night, confident she'd have the place to herself. Thrilled to find it empty, she'd plugged in her earbuds and jumped on the treadmill, intent on pushing her endurance. She didn't really like to run. She just needed to stay in shape—to be camera ready. Exercise bored her, and running seemed the fastest means to the end—appearance, yes, but also the strength and energy boost that came with being fit. Not a big fan of sweating in public, she didn't run outside, only on a treadmill—preferably in private. The pictures of celebrities in sunglasses trotting down the road with their hair plastered to their heads and sweat rings on their designer workout clothes were not flattering.

So last night when she'd seen movement out of the corner of her eye, she'd hoped it wasn't a photographer or some well-meaning fan. Apparently locals were accustomed to seeing their country stars around town, so they took celebrity sightings mostly in stride. The few times she'd been recognized had been pretty low-key. But last night, she'd just wanted to run off her excitement over her team's win, plus that sampling of spinach dip she'd had at dinner, without being bothered.

When she'd looked over and saw Shannon's face through the door, she'd nearly stumbled off the machine, somehow managing to get it stopped before thoroughly embarrassing herself. She'd never thought she could find someone in pajama pants and an oversized sweatshirt so damn attractive, and she'd seen enough people sporting the outfit in Walmart to have tested the theory. But on Shannon, with her just-out-of-bed tousled hair and her face free of makeup, the look was downright sexy. Good God, the woman was wearing Crocs.

She hadn't meant to flirt with her, but she couldn't seem to help herself. She'd seen the way Shannon looked at her from the first day of competition. Shannon was a fan and obviously a lesbian. So, Maya told herself, flirting with her could be just the result of a habitual response. Sure. It was a purely physical reaction.

She'd honestly tried to make herself stop, but then Shannon had gazed at her like she wanted to push her against the wall and do naughty things to her. Could she really be responsible for her own actions at that point? Who could blame her for blurting out her desire to kiss her? She hadn't imagined the answering look of interest, but, in the moment, Shannon apparently possessed more self-control than she did. She did take pleasure, though, in the rough edge of desire in Shannon's voice as she'd shut her down. She should be thanking Shannon for her common sense instead of wishing she'd capitalized on the hint of weakness she'd detected in her eyes.

She couldn't get involved with a contestant. Not because she didn't think she could be objective, she was certain she could, but Hugh would rupture something if he found out. Besides, Shannon didn't seem like the casual-fling type of woman, and pursuing anything more while trying to hide from television cameras would be dangerous. Maya wasn't interested in that kind of drama. She remained purposely vague with the media regarding her relationships, guarding them like her last precious secret. She didn't know Shannon well enough to trust her to do the same, let alone any of the many other people running around the set of the show at any given time.

Immediately following her own stint on the show, she'd soaked up the popularity, dating often, both men and women. She'd even taken a couple of shots at actual relationships. But when work, her travel, or jealousy got in the way, things ended, sometimes badly and with her reputation trashed in the media. Over the years, she'd gradually stopped trying so hard, and she walked away more easily. Since last year—since the baby—she hadn't seen anyone more than once and, regardless of what the reporters thought, she hadn't slept with anyone. She wouldn't put herself in that situation again.

No, she needed to stick to the plan—focus on the show, ignore any hint of attraction, and get back home to New York with her reputation intact. The vow to do just that had barely passed through her mind when a visual reminder of Shannon hit her.

She stopped in the middle of the sidewalk and stared at the sign for Drake's Desserts. She debated whether going inside could be considered unethical in any way. She was drawn to the door by curiosity about the quaint bakery where Shannon had worked. If she didn't reveal her identity, maybe a quick step inside would be okay.

When she opened the door, a subtle chime announced her presence, and a woman called from the back that she'd be right out. Maya drew in the aromas so familiar to any pastry chef and automatically cataloged them: rich chocolate, coffee, vanilla, something with apple—a pie perhaps—and the sharp, clean scent of lemon.

No matter how much time she spent in television studios, nothing felt more like coming home than walking into a bakery. And this particular shop appealed to her. Sky-blue walls lent an airy feel to what could have been a confined space. The stainless-steel counter bisecting the room doubled as a display case laden with cookies, cupcakes, petit-fours, and other essentials. A chalkboard on the wall behind the counter listed today's specials, which apparently were also the dessert line-up for the restaurant next door. Conveniently, if Maya was interested in lunch as well, a stack of menus for Drake's rested in a stand next to the register.

"Sorry, my assistant isn't here yet," a woman said as she rushed in from the back with her head down. "What can I get for you?"

Maya had been so busy admiring the shop, she hadn't even thought about placing an order. Since it would be rude not to, she said, "What's your best dessert today?"

"Definitely, the lemon cake." The woman looked up as she spoke, and her last word came out with a squeak. Recognition sparked in her beautiful dark eyes, but she cleared her throat and rushed on, "It travels well, too—um—if you're not going to eat it right away."

Maya smiled. "Great. I'll try it. And a couple of your chocolate-chip cookies."

The shopkeeper nodded and began gathering up the order. Maya watched openly, taking a bit of pleasure in catching the curious glances the woman tried to steal. The flush of color that crept up her neck somehow made her already attractive features even more appealing. With her olive skin, slightly exotic bone structure, and trim figure, she was just the type of woman Maya would normally chase. But knowing she was Shannon's boss complicated the situation. And the flash of the ring on her left hand as she worked took the idea completely off the table.

Given that Maya had left the hotel that morning in an olive, military-style jacket to ward off the slight chill in the air and a knit cap that covered her hair, leaving only the fringe of her bangs to lie against her forehead, she had to give the woman credit for recognizing her. Had she not pulled off her over-sized aviators when she entered the shop, maybe she wouldn't have.

When she'd finished, she set the order on the counter and met Maya's eyes. "On the house."

"That's not necessary." Maya reached for her wallet.

"I insist. It's not every day I get a legendary pastry chef in here."

"Legendary is a stretch." A tiny hint of flirtation crept into Maya's voice. Old habits and all.

"Well, extremely talented at the very least." This woman wasn't flirting back. Her tone was friendly but strictly business.

"It seems I'll be a better judge of *your* talent than you of mine." She pointed at the box between them, this time making sure that she sounded warm but not too overt. "You've never tasted anything I've made."

"You may have a point. Perhaps my hero-worship is misplaced."

"Hero-worship?" Maya laughed with her, raising her hands, palms out. "Now you're just being ridiculous."

"Jori Diamantina." She extended her hand.

"Maya Vaughn."

"Yeah, I know." Jori blushed again and Maya wished she could read her thoughts. "I don't suppose you could tell me how she's doing."

Maya shook her head. "I think I'm under contract not to. In fact, I hate to ask, but you probably shouldn't advertise that I was in here. I was nearby and couldn't resist."

"Of course."

"Thanks. You have an adorable shop here." Maya left with her treats, sneaking her hand inside the box for a chocolate-chip cookie as soon as she stepped outside the shop. It was a perfect cookie, crispy on the edge, soft in the middle, with the perfect balance of sweetness and a touch of salt. Too many chefs omitted the salt, but she was a firm believer that just a bit was necessary to enhance the flavor. With Jori and Shannon's combined talent, this little shop had obviously flourished. If the show wasn't such an opportunity for Shannon, Maya might feel sorry that the network had stolen her away.

CHAPTER EIGHT

S o, fill me in." Wendy leaned back and propped her bare feet up on the coffee table in the sitting area of Maya's hotel room. A glass half full of whatever she'd pilfered from the mini-bar was balanced between her thumb and two fingers.

"Haven't you read my daily newsletter emails?" Maya said sarcastically. She stood near the desk and sifted through the mail that Wendy had picked up at her apartment and brought with her. She sorted the envelopes into piles to deal with later.

"Actually, I haven't gotten a single email from you in three days. They must be keeping you busy. No time for sightseeing?"

Maya recalled her stroll through downtown four days before and her visit to Drake's. "Not much."

"Did you find me a good bakery?" If she didn't know Wendy so well, she might have thought she'd read her mind. But Wendy knew she liked to scope out the local shops, so whenever she visited, she took advantage of Maya's expertise to satisfy her sweet tooth.

"Absolutely. Drake's Desserts. Amazing lemon cake. And you'll love her chocolate-chip cookies." She grabbed a bottle of water and sat on the sofa next to Wendy.

"*Her* cookies?"

"Jori Diamantina." She pronounced the last name slowly, though it didn't sound nearly as good as when Jori had said it.

Wendy smiled, obviously picking up on the tone in Maya's voice. "What a great name. Did you hit on her?"

"She's taken. And she also happens to be the boss of one of my team members. So, seriously, no mention of the show if you go in there."

"Oh yeah, which one?"

"Shannon Hayes." At Wendy's questioning look, she expanded. "Soccer Mom."

"She's still around? How's your team doing?"

"You know they don't want us talking about the show."

"Who am I going to tell?"

"Not a word to anyone."

Wendy made a motion as if locking her lips and throwing away the key.

Maya gave her a quick summary of the competition so far, leaving out her encounter in the fitness room with Shannon. Her team had survived three more eliminations since that night and remained intact. Because of an imbalance in the number of competitors on the three teams, during yesterday's team challenge, she'd had to choose someone to sit out. She put Alice on the sideline, relying on Lucia and Shannon. They worked very well together, making solid decisions and completing tasks quickly. Alice chattered at them from the sideline, and from across the room Maya could feel Lucia and Shannon trying to tune her out.

"Do you think you have the winner?"

"Maybe. Ned is a tough competitor, but Lucia has been a contender from the beginning. And Shannon is talented and is really growing in the competition. I think they could be the final three."

"Wow. Go, Soccer Mom. I didn't think she had it in her."

"I didn't either, at first. But she's a strong decorator, has a good feel for flavor and texture, and is a fast learner. If I can keep her motivated, she's got a chance."

"If *you* can keep her motivated?"

"If—ah, if she stays motivated."

Wendy narrowed her eyes. "What are you not telling me?"

"What do you mean?" Maya stood and crossed the room, acting as if she only meant to throw away her empty water bottle.

Though she avoided looking at Wendy, she could feel her stare. Out of the corner of her eye, she saw Wendy sit up straighter with understanding, and she smothered a curse.

"Soccer Mom? Really?"

"She has a name." She went to the window and pretended interest in something outside.

"Okay. But with Hot Tamale and Baby Dyke, and that cute athletic brunette I don't have a nickname for—oh, is Sporty-Spice too dated? With all of that, you're really going with Soccer Mom?"

"I'm not *going* with anyone. I'm here to do a job and that's it. I just—we had a moment several days ago. But she's been avoiding me ever since."

"A moment?"

Maya sighed. She returned to the sofa and flopped down next to Wendy. Wedging her arm against Wendy's, she tilted her head until it rested on her shoulder. "I ran into her in the fitness room late one night and almost kissed her, but she stopped me. That's all." Though she made light of the encounter, even now, days later, whenever she made eye contact with Shannon, she felt like she was back in the gym fighting that almost desperate urge. She could still feel the press of Shannon's hand against her chest, and she swore Shannon had wanted to pull her in at least as much as she'd wanted to push her away. But these days as quickly as their gazes collided, Shannon looked away. Shannon had also avoided even a moment alone with her.

"Maya Vaughn—shot down. Wow."

"Oh, knock it off."

"Well, come on, that *never* happens. According to the media, anyway." Wendy brushed her hand over Maya's hair and cupped her cheek. "You let them make you out to be some kind of player."

"I was."

"Maybe. But you're not anymore. I know the truth. You don't take a chance very often."

"Hey, I date." Maya sat up straighter, breaking the contact. Sometimes she wished Wendy didn't know her so well.

"You do." Wendy nodded. "You date. You get photographed with your companion for the evening at this event or that. But how many times does it lead to a second?" She threaded her arm around Maya's elbow and took her hand as if the soft touch would erase the sting from her words.

"I'm not getting involved with Shannon." She halfheartedly attempted to pull free, but Wendy held on. She couldn't get involved even if she wanted to, with the way Shannon was avoiding her. The fact that Shannon apparently found her so utterly resistible shouldn't have made her irritated with Wendy, but it did.

"And you shouldn't. Especially not while the show's filming. But when you're done down here, you should consider dating someone. Because I would very much like to have a social life myself, and I can't do that if you keep working like a maniac."

Now she jerked away in earnest. "Any time the job is too demanding for you—"

"Don't pick a fight with me just because you're all worked up over Soccer Mom." Wendy's calm tone, combined with the fact that she was right, only stoked Maya's rising irritation.

"I'm not."

"You are. On both counts."

"If you can't do what I need you to do, then I'll find someone who will." She stood, needing a height advantage to make her feel as if she had the upper hand in this conversation. But when Wendy met her eyes evenly, she turned away and strode across the room once again, seeking solace near the window.

"Oh, okay." Wendy's nonchalance challenged Maya's irrational anger.

"Okay? Then you're done," she bit out, giving wheels to her sudden need to do something reckless. She'd used every bit of her restraint in the gym with Shannon, and since then she'd been looking for an excuse to let go. She'd thought that opportunity might come during Wendy's visit, maybe if they went out somewhere together. But this would do, too. "I'll find an assistant who'll do what I ask without backtalk. Someone more professional and competent."

"Be sure she has no life and is willing to devote all her time to protecting your fragile ego and shielding you from the big, bad media so you don't actually have to take any responsibility for your life." Wendy delivered the line without raising her voice at all. She could as easily have been reading Maya the room-service menu. But the truth to her words hit Maya harder than any shouting could have.

"Get the hell out."

"Whatever." Wendy gathered her phone and her purse and headed for the door.

"I'm serious."

"I know." Wendy waved a dismissive hand over her shoulder without even turning around. She pulled open the door and paused. "Call me when you're being rational again."

As the door closed behind her, Maya searched for something to throw at it. She wouldn't actually do it, but the act of looking satisfied the tiniest bit of the urge. Without a sparring partner, the tension drained from her fight. She sighed and sank into the nearest chair.

She rested her elbows on her knees and cradled her head, squeezing her temples in frustration. She might as well run after Wendy right now, because she was going to have to apologize eventually. After the year she'd had, she couldn't handle any more loss. Tears burned as they gathered in her eyes like water pressuring a dam, then spilled all at once over her lids and down her cheek. She managed to smother a sob until it worked its way out as a muffled whimper. But it too was only the beginning of a flood of strangled cries.

She dropped her head farther, lacing her fingers together at the back of her neck and pressing her bent arms against the side of her head as if she could continue to hide from the grief she'd been running from for months. But, alone in a hotel room, having just sent away her one true friend, she had no place left to escape to. So she gave in—to the tears and the shuddering breath. She welcomed the pain because it shut her brain off to any type of rational thought. She stayed curled in a ball on the sofa, no longer trying to hold back, until she had no tears left.

As she began to quiet, her mind came alive again, slashing at her with thoughts of a baby who never had a name, of a year spent running from one corner of the country to the other in a futile attempt to escape, and of the desire she almost never admitted—to have the pure love of someone who didn't care who she was supposed to be, but only who she really was. At her core, she was lonely and had been for a very long time.

After months of telling herself she had everything under control, tonight she'd picked a fight with the one person who'd actually been there through it all. She drew herself up and wiped her eyes. She went to the door, intent on finding Wendy and apologizing, but when she threw it open, Wendy stood on the other side.

"Did that make you feel better?" Wendy asked as she stepped back inside and closed the door.

"Not really. Why couldn't you just yell back at me?"

"Come here." Wendy took her elbow and drew her into a hug.

"Do you really think I have a fragile ego?" she muttered against Wendy's neck.

"Yes, honey." Wendy guided her back across the suite to the sofa and they sat down. Wendy kept her arm around her shoulder. "And I think the fact that that one remark is what you took from our whole argument only reinforces my opinion."

"So, what? You've just been standing out there waiting for me to come after you?"

"I was going to leave, but apparently the walls are thin around here and I heard you crying. I couldn't go, but knocking felt awkward at that point."

Maya chuckled. "So you decided to wait me out?"

Wendy shrugged. "I'll admit it was a risk. You've been bottled up for so long. I wasn't sure how long it would take once you got started."

She pinched Wendy's side, taking pleasure in her quick yelp. But when she tried to wriggle away, Maya held her tighter. "I'm sorry."

"Do you want to talk?"

"It's nothing new. Just everything catching up with me, I guess."

"Maybe you should take a vacation when this show is over."

"If by *vacation* you mean a retreat while we tell everyone I'm recovering from exhaustion, I don't think so." She pulled away long enough to give exaggerated finger quotes.

Wendy laughed. "Not that I don't think a little therapy would do you good, but I meant an actual vacation. Somewhere warm maybe." Wendy met her eyes, and she struggled not to look away from the compassion in them. "What the hell is this weather, anyway? I thought we were in the South. Do you know it was forty-four degrees this morning?"

"It's not Florida."

"I'm sorry I haven't done more for you this year." Wendy brushed her hand over Maya's forehead and smoothed back her hair.

"It's not like I've let you. I'll figure out a way to work through all of this after this show's over." She couldn't process her latent guilt and her growing dissatisfaction with her life while filming the show *and* fighting her attraction to Shannon. It was too much. So she separated all the issues and put them in little boxes in her brain and her heart and made what might be an empty promise to get back to them later.

"Are you okay to finish?"

"I can't back out now. It would only create more drama." And she really didn't want to. Even aside from maintaining her reputation and relationship with the show, she wanted to see someone from her team win. She needed to focus on her competitive side and sort her emotional stuff out later.

She'd no sooner made that vow when it hit her that she would miss Shannon if she left. Despite the distance that had developed between them, the thought of not seeing Shannon every day threatened to release the feelings of loneliness just as she'd managed to get a lid on that particular box.

❖

Jori glanced up at the door chime indicating someone had entered Drake's. She'd left Mackenzie alone in the front while she caught up on paperwork. By her last count there were two customers in the shop. This latest bell meant either one of them had left or a third had entered. She left her desk and went to the doorway between the shop and the kitchen.

Sawyer stood inside the open door, holding it open for a young child and the mother who struggled to watch her child around the large cake box she carried. Sawyer balanced two Styrofoam take-out containers in her left hand, and, as she released the door, she saw Jori and waved.

She rounded the corner of the display case and paused, her shoulders and chest lifting as she subtly drew in a deep breath. Their eyes met, and Jori gave her a smile full of promise. If she resisted the pull of heavenly aromas emanating from the case and came in the back, she'd find more sweets. And with Mackenzie preoccupied with customers, they could sneak a few precious moments alone.

"Come have some lunch when you're through," Jori said to Mackenzie before leading Sawyer through the door.

The door had barely swung shut behind them when Sawyer slid the boxes onto a nearby counter and grabbed Jori around the waist. She pulled her in swiftly and covered her mouth in a searing kiss. Jori fisted her hands in the back of Sawyer's shirt and held on, familiar arousal thrilling through her blood.

When Sawyer lifted her mouth from Jori's she rested their foreheads together, staying close. "I owed you that from last night. You were asleep when I got home."

Longing to reestablish the connection, Jori pressed her lips to Sawyer's again quickly, this time keeping the kiss brief and light. "You owe me more than that. I told you to wake me."

Sawyer slipped her hands down to cup Jori's ass and pull her more snugly against her. "I'll make it up tonight."

Jori growled low in her throat. "See that you do."

Sawyer nodded. "Yes, ma'am."

She released Jori and gestured to the take-out boxes. "Brady made that especially for you. I know you're busy, but try to eat it while it's still warm."

Jori opened one of the boxes and leaned over to smell the contents. "You told him I haven't been eating." She let good-natured accusation color her tone. Brady Drake's chicken Alfredo was legendary. And for Jori, he added not only pasta and grilled chicken to the rich, cheesy sauce, but also an assortment of vegetables—broccoli, cauliflower, zucchini, and whatever else he had fresh. On the side, he placed two thick, crusty slices of her homemade bread, which he'd grilled until the outside was crisp but the inside still soft and yeasty.

"He knows how often you skip lunch."

"Luckily, with the amount of carbs I'm about to consume, I won't have to worry about eating for days." She usually preferred a light lunch. That's what she told herself when she forgot to stop working long enough to eat. Brady had sent enough food for two meals, and she had no doubt that Mackenzie's container was just as full. If she managed to eat even half of it, she'd be ready for a nap, but it would be worth fighting that urge this afternoon.

"That's not a good plan."

"Are you still looking for another part-time server?" Done discussing her diet, she changed the subject. She knew Sawyer worried about her, but it wasn't as if she were wasting away. However, Sawyer wasn't likely to enjoy the new subject any more.

"Yes. I'm doing interviews the day after tomorrow. Why?"

"Mackenzie's cousin is looking for a job." She rushed the sentence out, well aware of the reception it would get. Sawyer hated hiring "friends" of her employees. She didn't want the obligation and guilt if things didn't work out. Having initially taken her current job out of a sense of duty to her family, she now shied away from such complicated relationships among her staff.

"She's waited tables before. She's very prompt and responsible," Mackenzie added as she walked into the kitchen, obviously having overheard. "She's sleeping on my couch and I'm desperate to get her out, so she needs the money."

Sawyer swiped her finger over the screen of her phone a couple of times. "I'll tell you what. See if she can come by Drake's tomorrow at four and I'll talk to her."

"Great. I'll make sure she's there." Mackenzie took a bite of her lunch and moaned. She grasped Sawyer's shoulder. "This is amazing."

"I'm glad you like it but I can't take credit. I'll pass your praise on to my brother. He's the chef."

Jori picked up her own container and grabbed a plastic fork. "Take a break and enjoy your lunch. I'll cover the front." She gestured to Sawyer. "I'll walk you out."

Sawyer nodded and followed her through to the lobby of the shop. As the kitchen door swung shut behind them, she gave Jori a look of irritation.

"Don't say it," Jori whispered. She settled on a stool in the corner, out of view of the sidewalk but where she could still help any customers that came in.

"I shouldn't have to," she said so sharply that Jori winced. "You really put me on the spot there."

"I'm sorry. I tried to ask while we were alone, but I didn't know she'd be back just then."

Sawyer sighed and nodded. "I really do need another server. If the cousin has solid experience, I'll give her a shot."

Jori tried to understand Sawyer's reluctance to tangle business with personal relationships. But in truth, she'd loved the family atmosphere she'd found working at Drake's restaurant, even when that left her in the middle of three squabbling siblings. She hadn't been one of those lucky foster kids who found loving, generous parents to adopt her. She'd been on her own all of her life, until she became a part of the Drake family. She craved the very connection that Sawyer had felt smothered by all of her life, so much so that it had been a point of contention when they first got together. Jori's need for family didn't scare Sawyer so much anymore. In fact, they could even talk about Jori's desire to someday have children without Sawyer having a panic attack.

Sawyer had confessed her doubts about her own value as a parent, but she'd said she had faith in how wonderful a mother Jori would be. Though she hadn't totally committed to the idea of kids yet, she now seemed much more open than during their early discussions.

CHAPTER NINE

"Why on earth are you up so early when we don't have to be?" Alice asked as she shuffled out of the bedroom, her slippers making a whooshing sound against the carpet.

"I'm sorry if I woke you." Shannon set the novel she'd been reading on the arm of the sofa. She picked up her mug from the coffee table and sipped her now-tepid tea. Though they finally had a free day, she woke up at six just as if her alarm had sounded. She formed habits very quickly, and her body had already adjusted to the early wake-up call due to the show's schedule. She'd showered and dressed, then straightened her room before settling in the living room with her book.

Alice pulled the carafe from the coffeemaker. "Only briefly. I heard you out here moving around, but I went right back to sleep. We've been competing nonstop for what—ten days straight now. Aren't you glad to have a break?"

Shannon shrugged. "I just want to keep going and get it over with."

"I agree," Lucia said as she exited the bedroom, her hair still wet from a shower. She'd already dressed in crisp, dark blue jeans and a pale-yellow, flowing blouse.

"I haven't stepped foot out of this hotel unless it was to go to the set. I'm looking forward to exploring the city a bit. I'm meeting some of the others to walk around downtown. You ladies should come with us." Alice practically bubbled, but Shannon couldn't summon the same level of excitement for a city she already knew so well.

"I'm in," Lucia said.

"I think I'll catch up on my laundry and maybe call my daughter."

"I'll get ready." Alice headed for her bedroom, but she paused in the doorway and looked at Shannon. "Laundry can wait. Get your butt off that couch and come with us. We all need a break. You can be our tour guide for the day."

Shannon sighed. The last thing she wanted to do was wander around Nashville with the same people she'd been looking at constantly for the past ten days. But Alice wasn't likely to go quietly—the woman didn't do anything quietly.

Shannon went to her bedroom and checked her appearance in the mirror. She took her time gathering her coat and purse. By the time she returned to the living room, Alice and Lucia were ready and waiting.

"The guys are meeting us downstairs." Alice practically bounced to the elevator.

"What guys?" Lucia asked.

"Mason and Ned." She giggled a little when she said Ned's name.

"Ned, huh?" Shannon teased.

"What? He's kind of hot."

"If you're into tattoos and wild hair." Lucia didn't seem convinced.

Shannon didn't say anything. Ned didn't appeal to her. And she would never have thought she could be into tattoos or outrageous hairstyles. But Maya had both. The similarities ended there. While both were talented chefs, Ned boasted about his work louder than anyone, and Maya conducted herself with a steady, quiet confidence. Personally, Shannon found Maya's bravado sexy because she'd seen the sweet, genuine woman underneath. Unless she'd completely missed something, she didn't think Ned had anything buried under his arrogance.

As they stepped out of the elevator and into the lobby, Alice rushed forward to greet Ned and Mason. Shannon followed more slowly and returned Mason's subdued wave. Two cameramen sprawled in chairs in the lobby, but they jumped up as she and the other women approached.

"Guess we have babysitters," Mason mumbled.

"Apparently." Alice didn't sound pleased that they wouldn't be left alone for the day.

"So where are we off to?" Ned asked as they all headed for the door.

"Let's just start walking and see where we end up."

They exited the hotel, trailed by the two cameramen, one of whom circled them to get a shot from the front as they walked along the street. Other pedestrians gave them curious looks as they passed. Those who didn't seem as fazed by the cameras still took a second look at Ned's bright-blue Mohawk.

"This is inconspicuous," Lucia muttered.

"If you wanted inconspicuous, you shouldn't have signed up to be on national television." Ned preened like a peacock in front of the cameras.

"Isn't your shop around here somewhere?" Alice asked, looking around like she might see it.

"A few blocks over." She glanced in the direction of Drake's. They were so close, she imagined she could feel the heat of the ovens and smell the baking cakes and the sugary tang of icing. She missed her kitchen at the bakery. She missed designing cakes just for the simple joy of pleasing the customer—of making their occasions special. She'd been gone less than two weeks, but the pressure she'd been under in that time made it feel like longer. How would she ever handle the change in her life after the show was over? Could she go back to the kind of work she was doing at Drake's?

"Let's go check it out," Ned said.

"I don't think I should." Shannon stopped in the middle of the sidewalk, causing Mason to almost run into her.

"Come on, we'll just walk by."

"I'm pretty sure one of the many papers we signed said no physical contact with friends and family unless the producers say so. I don't need to give anyone a reason to kick me off the show. But you guys go ahead if you want to. I'll meet up with you later."

"Let's all stay together. We'll find someplace good to eat." Alice looped her arm through Shannon's and tugged her along the sidewalk. "Besides, it's our first day off since we've been here. The last place I want to be is surrounded by cake."

Ned shrugged and charged ahead.

"Thanks," Shannon murmured to Alice.

Alice smiled, then began a running commentary on the sights around them. Shannon followed along, answering the occasional question about this business or that.

Her family had always lived in the suburbs, and unless they were going out for a meal or catching a show at the performing-arts center, they didn't venture into the downtown area. She'd often thought it was because her parents, both attorneys, spent their long working hours in the congested area, and when they finally got home, they didn't want to go back down there. But as a child, those adventures among the tall buildings and crowded streets had been magical.

She called out a few tidbits about the new convention center being built just south of Broadway. Since she'd been at Drake's she'd seen the progress, beginning with the blasting and clearing away of the old buildings through to the nearly finished, modern structure now spanning three city blocks.

They strolled around for a couple of hours, ducking into souvenir shops and Western clothing stores.

"We should all get matching tattoos," Alice exclaimed as they passed a tattoo shop.

"Not a chance," Lucia said quickly.

"Yeah. I only let *my* guy touch a needle to this skin," Ned said.

At Alice's eager look, Shannon shook her head, but she thought about the antique hand mixer inked on Maya's forearm. She'd never considered getting a tattoo but had to admit she found Maya's sexy. And she liked the significance of it. She might think about getting one to commemorate this amazing time in her life. But she wouldn't be choosing it on a whim. She'd have to think about subject matter and placement. Besides, if she got one, she wanted it to be original, not matching anyone else's.

"Okay. How about lunch? I'm starving."

Shannon led the group to her favorite barbeque joint. Since it was well past noon, the lunch crowd had thinned and a hostess led the five of them to a table right away. As soon as they were settled, they ordered a round of beers. When Mason, a native Chicagoan, asked for local flavor, Shannon added a basket of fried pickles and an order of fried green tomatoes as appetizers.

"Man, it feels good to have a break today." Ned leaned back in his chair and laid his arm along the back of Alice's.

"I'm trying to absorb as much relaxation as I can. Who knows when we'll have another day like this," Alice said, her voice high and fast.

Lucia laughed. "So you're stressing yourself out about relaxing."

"I guess I am."

"I know what you mean, though," Shannon said. "I feel like we've been on a roller coaster for days. We never know from one challenge to the next when we might be in danger of elimination."

"Maybe *you* don't. I haven't been nervous yet." Ned finished his beer and waved at the waitress for another one. "But I can see why you ladies would worry."

"Ned," Mason warned him.

"It can't be easy having such an unstable mentor."

Mason sighed.

"What?" Shannon snapped.

Mason tried to smooth things over. "I think what he meant to say—"

"I heard what he said. And I know what he meant."

"Man, you lesbians really do stick together, don't you?"

Shannon laughed, because she couldn't do anything else with the rush of adrenaline currently coursing through her.

"Oh, I'm sorry. Technically, she's bi, isn't she?" Ned's disgusting leer made Shannon want to slap his face. "That's so hot."

"I don't see what any of that has to do with her ability to mentor." She refused to let him bait her into a discussion about his opinions on homosexuality. First, they weren't relevant. And second, she didn't really care what he thought about her lifestyle.

"She's a walking publicity stunt. That's got to be a big distraction from the work. I mean, I don't have to worry about reading about Jacques' sexual exploits in the tabloids tomorrow."

"We can't even read the tabloids while we're here," Lucia said calmly. "And she's never been anything but professional with me."

Mason looked at Shannon. "She's flirted with you, hasn't she? But that's probably because she knows you're a lesbian."

"No, she hasn't." Shannon glared at him. She could distinctly recall her every interaction with Maya, and, yes, there had been some flirtation. But she wouldn't admit that to the other competitors. Besides, she'd barely spoken to Maya in several days unless it had to do with the competition. Every day she stood stiffly in front of Maya while she critiqued her work.

"I've seen the way she looks at you." He hooked his thumb in Ned's direction. "She's never looked at him like that."

Before Shannon had a chance to respond, Ned jumped in again. "Hey, I'm not saying she doesn't have some talent. She won her season, after all. But think about it—why do you think the producers invited her to mentor this year? The show was getting stale. They needed a ratings boost, and Maya Vaughn has always been good for that. From the first day of her season, she's been a sideshow—a gimmick."

"Yeah? Have you looked in the mirror lately?" Alice shot back.

Ned narrowed his eyes and puffed out his chest. "What's that supposed to mean?"

"Look around this table. We were all picked to appeal to a certain demographic. The producers get thousands of applicants, maybe more. Do you really think we were the twelve most talented? We're all here for a reason."

Shannon folded her arms against her chest, nurturing a newfound respect for Alice. She would have expected Alice to agree with Ned just because she apparently had a thing for him. Instead, she'd spoken her mind against him.

After they finished their meal, Shannon seized the opportunity to separate from the group and head back to the hotel. When she left them, they were headed into a blues bar in Printer's Alley.

❖

"The network is about to start airing the new season. In fact, tonight's the premiere. You won't see it." Hugh waited out the chorus of boos that followed. He paced around the cluster of tables where the chefs were seated. "Remember, your phone calls are still being monitored. And the ban on talking about the show's progress is still in effect. This may be even more difficult now, because naturally your friends and family will talk about things they've seen. But you can't. And you shouldn't ask them about the show. Until we break before the finale, none of you are to know what's airing."

He covered a few more points, then led them to the kitchen and handed them over to Eric as filming began.

"There will be no immunity in today's elimination. Regardless of the outcome of this challenge, this could be the last day in the *For the Love of Cake* kitchen for any one of you," Eric said dramatically.

They murmured appropriately as they'd been instructed by Hugh, even though he'd just given them the same information before shooting started.

"Cupcakes are all the rage these days, so much so that whole shops are popping up dedicated only to gourmet cupcakes. Today, you'll be baking your favorite flavor of cupcake to donate for an elementary-school bake sale. You will prepare forty-eight cupcakes to set up at a table at the school. The contestant who sells the most cupcakes the fastest wins a reward. Would you like to know what it is?" Since this was the one part they hadn't been warned about, Eric paused for the expected chorus of yeses, then continued. "The top two contestants get one-on-one time with the mentor of his or her choosing."

Shannon flipped through her mental catalog of cupcake recipes. Chocolate-chip cookie dough? Kids love chocolate-chip cookies. No, cookie cupcakes weren't creative enough. She glanced at Maya, who was deep in conversation with Jacques. He and Wayne were both incredibly talented. If she won, she could choose one of them and still be the envy of every chef she knew. If she won, choosing one of them would be less complicated than spending time with Maya.

She had successfully avoided being alone with Maya since the night in the fitness room. During one exercise, the mentors had gathered their teams to teach them a new technique. Shannon had stood behind Alice as they clustered around Maya's workstation, keeping Alice between them to combat the butterflies in her stomach at being so close. As Maya bent over her cake, expertly applying icing in a complex pattern, Shannon gave in to the urge to look freely at Maya. She'd traced her eyes over the top of Maya's bowed head, imagining burying her hands in her white-blond hair. She could practically feel the point when the silky strands would give way to the texture of shorter hair over her ears.

She imagined bending to tease the shell of Maya's ear with her lips before kissing the back of her neck, just over the tattoo of a cluster of vibrant lilies. She leaned closer. The tattoo was very well-done, each delicate petal arching away from the center so lifelike that Shannon imagined she could reach out and run her fingers along the fine edges. Shannon had never been with anyone with tattoos. Would the colorful skin feel different against her lips?

Maya raised her head and looked right at her. Caught off-guard, Shannon didn't get her eyes away in time, and once Maya's had locked on hers, she couldn't.

"Chef Hayes?" Maya lifted a brow, letting Shannon know she'd been caught.

"Uh—yes?" Did she miss something important?

"I asked if you're ready to try this for yourself."

"Absolutely, Chef." Her face flamed, but, though she was sure Alice and Lucia were looking at her, she remained fixed on Maya. *God, yes, she wanted to try it for herself, and she wasn't talking about the technique.*

Later that afternoon, while working on her own cake, she'd looked up to find Maya watching her with an expression of confusion. When their eyes met, Maya's brow drew in tighter, then smoothed as her eyes dipped to Shannon's mouth and back up. Shannon broke the contact first. Since she had no idea how long the exchange had actually taken, she glanced around to see if they'd been caught and she came face to—well, lens with one of the camera guys. He'd kept his handheld trained on her, a smug smile on his face. She'd pressed her lips together and spun away.

Since then, she'd tried to become more surreptitious in her study of Maya, which only made her more aware of just how many times she sought her out. Even though Maya wore jeans and a white chef coat on the set, when Shannon looked at her, she still saw those short-shorts and the smooth planes of her abdomen giving way to the swell of her breast. If she could see her only as a spoiled, albeit hot young celebrity, she'd be a lot better off. But she couldn't shake the memory of the soft, slightly vulnerable look in Maya's eyes that hinted at more depth.

Still debating her cupcake flavors, she snuck another glance while Maya was still distracted by Jacques. She wasn't close enough to hear what they said, but Maya gestured as if she were physically describing something, sketching the shape with her strong, angular hands as she spoke. She paused to rub her neck, and Shannon followed the line of her deep-red fingernails into the collar of her chef jacket. When her hand stopped, Shannon continued to visually trace the neckline of the black tank top visible between the flaps of her jacket. She tore her eyes away and shook her head but silently acknowledged that she was kidding herself if she thought she would choose anyone but Maya. She wouldn't miss the opportunity for private tutoring from a chef of her caliber. Yes, that was why she had to win. She had absolutely no personal reason for wanting to be alone with Maya. Kidding herself again.

Two counters down, Alice appeared relaxed and confident. Given that she owned a cupcake shop, this challenge should be easy for her. Based on her opinion of Maya, she wasn't likely to want time with her. But she shouldn't be counted out as competition for the win.

Focus. Think. She couldn't afford to lose precious time planning. Teachers, staff, and parents would attend the bake sale along with the elementary students. She needed a flavor that appealed to the kids, yet enticed the adults as well. Peanut butter and jelly. Being in a school might make the grown-ups feel nostalgic toward the classic combination.

As Eric gave the cue for them to begin working, she quickly gathered her ingredients and constructed the batter for a vanilla cupcake. She stripped the insides out of vanilla beans to add a richer flavor to the cake. After she'd filled several trays with batter and slid them into the oven, she turned her attention to the filling and icing, working on both simultaneously. She was dimly aware of the other chefs moving around, gathering ingredients, going back and forth to the ovens, and running mixers. The aromas of various cakes baking mingled together, and the sweet bite of sugar cut through them as most of the chefs had moved on to toppings and fillings.

When she'd finished whipping her buttercream and tasted it, she glanced at the clock. The heavy mixture didn't have the right consistency, and the peanut butter overpowered the flavor. She debated for only a second before setting that batch aside and starting again.

She jogged to the oven and pulled a tray out, judging from the appearance that the cakes would cool to a nice spongy texture. After she'd removed all of them, she squeezed strawberry filling into each cake while they were still a bit warm, though she'd have to let them cool further before icing them.

While her second frosting attempt whipped in the mixer, she rolled her shoulders and stretched her neck from side to side. Eric and Maya, followed by a cameraman with a handheld, had started talking to the chefs at the other end of the room from Shannon, while Jacques and Wayne hung back and continued watching the progress.

Shannon tested her new batch of icing, pleased that it tasted exactly like she'd hoped. The light texture practically melted on the tongue, leaving just the right tease of peanut butter in the wake of the perfect sweetness. With only ten minutes left on the clock, she filled a pastry bag and pulled the first tray of cupcakes in front of her. As she swirled icing on top of her cakes, she heard Maya talking to Lucia, whose station was next to Shannon's. The low timbre of Maya's voice seemed to vibrate through Shannon, and she had to pause and steady herself. After a quick breath, she sprinkled the tops of each cupcake with a dusting of crushed peanut-butter-sandwich cookies to add a bit of crunch. When Lucia said something that made Maya laugh, Shannon's hand shook and she spilled some of the coarse crumbs across the counter. She cursed under her breath but kept moving. Any cupcakes that weren't complete couldn't go to the school and she'd start the bake sale at a disadvantage.

She reached under her counter and pulled out two prefolded bakery boxes, then glanced up and caught Maya looking at her. Instead of looking away, she held her gaze, steeling herself for the moment when Maya stepped closer to her counter. But when Maya moved, Eric caught her arm and pulled her in the other direction. Disappointment flooded Maya's expression, and though Shannon knew their exchange would likely have been brief and mostly impersonal, she missed having that moment with her as well. Maya glanced at Eric, shook off his arm, and walked over to Shannon's station. Without a word, she pulled the bowl containing her failed attempt at icing closer. She dipped a finger in, and then, while Shannon tracked every movement, she lifted it to her mouth. Shannon's heart beat like crazy as Maya's tongue slid along the side of her finger.

"Thirty seconds," Eric called out, giving Maya a pointed look. She nodded, glanced at Shannon, then returned to where Jacques and Wayne waited.

Shannon shook off her distraction and hurriedly finished packing the cupcakes inside and had just closed the lid on her second box when he called time. She held her hands up and stepped back almost in unison with the other competitors.

Chapter Ten

I hope you've thought of more questions than you had for that first consultation," Maya joked, as much to calm her own racing heart as to put Shannon at ease.

When she'd heard that Shannon and Alice had taken first and second at the bake sale, she hoped Shannon would pick her. Since the tutoring session would take place in front of the cameras, she knew spending time semi-alone with Shannon was flirting with danger. She didn't feel like expending the energy it would take to keep her expression neutral. She didn't usually have so much trouble controlling her own reactions and had never wanted so badly to completely let down her guard with someone. That thought alone should have had her curling into a fetal position and shutting Shannon out.

"I wish I could say I felt more prepared. But you tend to put me off balance," Shannon said.

They sat across from each other at one of the tables in the lounge, leaning forward and resting their forearms on the table in a mirror image to each other. The other chefs had been sent back to the hotel. Alice and Jacques had been taken to the kitchen to film their one-on-one time, and Maya and Shannon were instructed to wait until summoned.

"Why is that?" Maya toyed with a Styrofoam cup still half full of lukewarm coffee. Though she didn't want to drink it, she was grateful to have something in her hands. Otherwise, seeing

Shannon's nervous expression, she might give in to her urge to reach across the table and cover Shannon's fidgeting hands.

"You won your season. And I can't even begin to list all of your accomplishments since then."

"None of that is new since we last spent time together," Maya said a little too sharply, disappointed that Shannon focused on her professional achievement.

"I know you've been judging my work for almost two weeks now, but without the others as a buffer, it feels more personal." Her voice shook a little as she said *personal.*

"It could be," Maya said without even thinking.

Shannon leaned back in her chair, and Maya could feel her withdrawal in proportion to the increased distance between them.

"What's wrong?"

Shannon shook her head slowly. "Sometimes it feels like you're so focused on *me* that it's almost too much. But then you say something like that and it doesn't seem genuine—like it's all a game and I could be any woman sitting across from you."

Maya leaned even farther forward, stretched her arm, and brushed Shannon's knuckles with her fingers before pulling back. "You're not any woman." She suspected the tingle in her fingers could be soothed by touching Shannon again and nearly did, but she wasn't sure the caress would be welcome. And since they could be interrupted at any moment, she didn't trust herself to stop at a touch. When Shannon didn't respond, she waited a beat longer to let the tension between them ease a bit, then changed the subject. "You took a big risk scrapping that first batch of icing."

Shannon shrugged. "It wasn't good enough."

"You're right. But your end product really was amazing."

"Thanks. I needed to sell the most, desperately."

"Why's that?"

"I wanted you." The openness of Shannon's statement contradicted the distance she'd purposely put between them moments ago.

"Desperately?" This time she dropped her voice, letting her own desire infuse the words so Shannon couldn't doubt her sincerity. *I wanted you.* Maybe Shannon hadn't intended it to sound like a come-on, but the visions her words brought forth could easily seduce Maya. She imagined Shannon whispering them to her in a darkened room as they moved against each other.

"I mean—I wanted to learn from you."

If not for the tremor in Shannon's voice that matched the one vibrating within Maya, she might have believed Shannon's hasty correction. Desire made her honest when she said, "I didn't think you'd pick me."

Shannon lifted one shoulder in a half shrug. "Maybe I want to win more than I want to avoid you."

"Wow, if you keep up the glowing compliments, I'm going to get a big head."

"Seriously, you're an amazing chef. I would have kicked myself later if I'd chosen anyone else." Shannon's expression grew serious and she said, softly, "It had to be you."

"Shannon—"

Though she wasn't certain what she wanted to say, she wouldn't get a chance as Hugh strolled into the room whistling to himself. "Okay, ladies, you're up."

As he walked them back toward the kitchen, Hugh told them to relax and interact naturally. Several cameras would film them and the editors would cut something together later, but the producers wanted it to look like a casual conversation rather than something rehearsed. He asked only that Maya demonstrate an advanced technique and Shannon ask a lot of questions.

Maya stood beside Shannon, their shoulders close enough to touch, though very carefully not making contact. She rolled her eyes at Shannon as Hugh described his desire to have her come off as a starry-eyed amateur to Maya's seasoned-professional status.

"So, how would you like to spend our time together?" Maya asked once they were in front of the cameras.

Shannon blinked, as if completely caught off guard by the question. Maya replayed her words in her head and wondered if Shannon's mind had gone someplace intimate. She enjoyed the idea that Shannon might have sexy images playing in her head at that moment.

Shannon recovered, clearing her throat, and said, "When I found out I'd—for lack of a better term—won you, I thought about your strengths versus my weaknesses."

"And what did you come up with?" Maya struggled to focus on the scene, for she certainly was playing a part. But the little twist in Shannon's voice when she said she'd *won her* made her think about submission in ways she never had before. She managed to stop from actually shaking her head in an attempt to clear the visions.

"I would love some pointers on sculpting. You're brilliant at it." Shannon actually batted her eyes, obviously enjoying playing the fresh-faced fan.

"Okay." Maya went to the area of the kitchen they referred to as the pantry and retrieved several pieces of modeling chocolate. "What should we sculpt?"

"You're the *artist,* surprise me." Shannon grinned.

Maya shot her a warning look, lest she think she could push this little game too far. She picked up a piece of the dough-like chocolate, then rolled it between her hands. "It's one thing to have a vision. The important thing is how you translate it to your medium. What does your customer or, in this case, the judges or the audience, see?" She worked the chocolate like clay, pressing and pulling quickly.

"Hopefully, they see what's in my head."

"It's not enough for them to see it. They have to buy into it."

"Is that really what it's about—business? What about the art?" Despite the bitterness in her tone, Shannon kept her eyes on Maya's hands.

"Once you start getting paid to do it, it's never purely art again. On any level from a small-town bakery to a five-star restaurant, it's about getting return business. Otherwise, who'll ever get to sample your art?" Maya paused to gesture in the air and their eyes met briefly. When she returned to sculpting, Shannon once again watched her work. Maya slowed her hands, in part so Shannon could study her technique and because the scrutiny made her nervous and she didn't want to get sloppy.

"That seems jaded. Isn't there a balance?"

"Of course there is. I'm not suggesting you compromise your quality or originality."

"So, how do you hold on to your creative energy?"

"Well, that definitely becomes more work. Decorating doesn't feel as pure as when I first started out. On the other hand, success isn't all bad. I've met and worked with so many talented, passionate chefs, that I often get inspired by what I see others doing."

"Yeah? Like what?"

"Wayne Neighbors, for example, is a master in sugar work. That's an area I haven't trained much in. I fully intend to pick his brain about technique before this show is over." Maya smiled. "Actually, if I'd been in your shoes, I probably would have bid on some time with him instead of me."

"With three very talented mentors, it was a difficult decision for sure."

"That's a diplomatic answer." Maya leaned closer and winked at Shannon. "But it's just you and me here, you can tell me—I'm your favorite, aren't I?"

Shannon turned her head, just the tiniest bit, before she stopped herself, but she'd obviously been about to look at the nearby camera. Maya laughed and Shannon jerked her eyes up to her. She smiled and tapped her shoulder to Shannon's. "Relax. Let's have a little fun. You won a challenge today. The competition is stressful enough. Enjoy this small victory before you throw yourself back into it."

"Okay." Shannon nodded, but she didn't seem convinced.

"Okay. I can see you're not going to take my advice on that. So, if you don't hear anything else—this show is a blessing for the competitors. You each have your talents, and you get the opportunity to explore areas you might never be brave enough to expand into in your daily lives."

"Because, as you said, it's all about business in the real world. And no one is going to buy my cakes if they look like I spent the morning practicing but not quite perfecting new techniques."

"Exactly." Maya set her finished figurine on the cutting board in front of her.

Shannon bent and examined the miniature woman, who wore a chef coat and had her hair pulled back in a tight bun. Though she had tiny features, the lift of her brows and the jut of her chin as she stared back bore a resemblance to Shannon.

"Wow, she's great," Shannon said.

"Your turn." Maya grasped her wrist and pressed a ball of modeling chocolate into her hand.

"I can't possibly do anything like that—"

"Haven't you been listening? You don't have to do it like I do. Take what I did and do it your own way." She released Shannon, then shoved her hand under the hem of her chef coat and into the pocket of her jeans, hoping to ignore the tingling Shannon's skin left behind.

❖

"So, you have a daughter."

Shannon nodded. "Regan. Actually, she's about to give me my first grandchild." She glanced down at the lump of chocolate in her hand that, so far, she'd been unable to manipulate into accurately reflecting her vision. She raised it in a helpless gesture. "I don't think I'm much of a sculptor."

"You think too much. Just keep working and talk to me about this incredible revelation that can't be true. You're going to be a grandma?"

"Yeah. I can just now say that without wincing."

"I wouldn't have guessed you were old enough." Maya grimaced. "Wow, did that sound as much like a cheesy line to you as it did to me?"

"A little maybe." But apparently she was a sucker for a cheesy line, which was completely out of character for her. Now, for some reason, Maya's self-deprecating grin and the sparkle in her eyes charmed Shannon. Whereas she'd chastised her earlier for being insincere, now she practically melted under Maya's attention.

"Sorry, that was beneath me. I'm usually so much better at this."

"At this?"

"Never mind." Maya diverted her eyes, and though she never looked directly at the camera, Shannon got the impression she'd just become aware again that they weren't really alone.

Apparently, Shannon needed the reminder as well. She didn't want to be known as that woman who flirted with the mentor presumably to get ahead on the show. She knew Maya's reputation, so why did she suddenly feel so ready to be another in the line of people, both men and women, who had fallen for her beautiful face, amazing body, and unattainable magnetism?

"Tell me about your daughter," Maya said.

Shannon took a breath to adjust to another quick subject change. "She's smart, beautiful, funny—"

"And you're not biased at all." Maya smiled. "So obviously she got all of those traits from you. What did she get from her father?"

Shannon narrowed her eyes. "Another line?"

"Only if it works."

"I've never met her father so I don't know what she inherited from him." Discussing Regan's biological parentage was only slightly less uncomfortable than examining the disappointment Shannon felt realizing Maya was probably just playing a familiar role.

"How does that work? It seems like you must have met him at least once."

"Regan is adopted—from foster care when she was eleven."

"Now that you mention it, I think that was in your application file."

"I, uh—I couldn't have children."

"Oh, I'm sorry. I didn't know."

"It was ages ago." She glossed over the shadow of loss that snuck in whenever she talked about the past. "Anyway, I guess that's why I'm so excited about my grandchild. I missed out on the cool baby stuff with my daughter—all the firsts. I'd come to terms with never experiencing them. Do you know what I mean? Ah, you're so young. You've got plenty of time to have your kids."

Maya nodded stiffly, her lips pressed in a tight line. Though she didn't move, Shannon could feel her withdrawing, and the stories about Maya's abortion last year flooded Shannon's mind. Anger rushed through her, making her own body go rigid—that someone could throw away a child as if it were nothing, that the Maya she'd been getting to know could do such a thing.

She set her piece of chocolate down next to Maya's. The little statue of a dog didn't come close to the quality of Maya's, but measured against any of her previous sculpting attempts, she saw some improvement.

"Well done." Maya sounded polite but detached.

"Thanks." She kept the same careful distance in her voice while wishing their time together hadn't been studded with reminders of who Maya really was.

❖

"Okay, ladies, we've got what we need. Maya, there's a car out front to take you back to the hotel. Shannon, your driver is having car trouble. I'll let you know when we get another one here."

"She can ride with me." Maya didn't really want to spend any more time in Shannon's company tonight. But she could hardly leave her waiting here for a backup car.

Hugh shook his head. "We've called for another transport."

"Come on, Hugh. She's got to be here early tomorrow. Who knows when that other vehicle will get here."

"Maya—"

"Fine. Let her take mine. I'll wait for the next one."

"I can wait. It's fine," Shannon said.

"Hugh." Maya lifted her chin, watching conflict scatter across his expression. He wouldn't make her wait, but he didn't want to let them ride together. "If you're worried about unfair advantage, I'll promise we won't talk strategy." If the tension that had fallen between them was any indication, they might not talk at all.

He sighed.

"It's a five-minute ride."

"Fine. I'll cancel the other car."

"Thanks." She barely glanced at Shannon before she took off toward the door. "Come on. Before he changes his mind."

In the parking lot, she held open the door to the SUV and waited until Shannon climbed in. Though she was irritated she didn't have to forget her manners. She circled and got in the other side.

"All set," she called to the driver as she clicked on her seat belt.

Shannon stared out the opposite window as the vehicle rolled out of the lot and onto the street. The tension in the car filled the space between them, pushing Maya toward her side of the seat until her shoulder pressed into the cool metal of the door. She wanted to ease the strain but didn't know how without explaining why she'd shut down. She'd seen the judgment in Shannon's expression and could guess what Shannon assumed she'd done. But as usual, when faced with an unfair assessment of herself, she fell into a defensive posture. Only, now, with Shannon, she wanted to explain—wanted to see if the truth would change Shannon's mind about her. But despite that desire, the words remained locked in her throat behind a dam of fear.

So when they passed the gay bar she'd gone to, she offered a safe topic of conversation. "I was not impressed with that place at all." She pointed at the sign.

"You went *there*?" Shannon looked at her, obviously surprised.

"Yep. Something wrong with it?"

Shannon bit her lip. "Not really. It's just not my scene. I'm a little too old for the place. But you wouldn't have that problem."

"Yeah, you mentioned how young I am." She didn't care that she sounded like a spoiled brat.

"Maya, I didn't mean—"

"It's fine." She waved a hand between them. "I don't want—" She sighed in frustration. She'd thought after the time they'd spent together, Shannon would see her differently than everyone else did. But perhaps she'd manufactured that connection between them. Was it just pride that kept her from being honest with Shannon? Maybe she wanted Shannon to inherently see through her usual act. Was that too much to ask?

After another stretch of tense silence, Shannon said, "So what didn't you like about it?"

Maya shrugged. "I guess it's not my thing either."

"Not big enough for you?"

"Why do you say that?"

"I imagine you're used to bigger places, more lights, louder music, and a better show."

"I've been in my share of those establishments." She had to admit the truth, but that didn't mean she was one-dimensional. "But actually, I'm more of a beer-and-pool-tables kind of girl these days."

"Hey, there's my bakery," Shannon said as they passed Drake's Desserts.

"I know."

"That was in my bio, huh?"

"Actually, yes." She glanced at the driver, but he didn't appear to be listening to them. She lowered her voice anyway. "I probably shouldn't tell you this, but I've been there."

"Drake's? Really?"

Maya nodded.

"When?"

"A few days ago. I passed by and couldn't help myself."

Shannon nodded. "It's next to impossible for me to pass a bakery and not go inside. Could you get in trouble for that?"

Maya shrugged. "It wasn't specifically addressed. But I'm sure it's not encouraged. I even met your boss."

"Jori?"

"Yes. I felt bad, but I couldn't tell her how you were doing."

"She knew you couldn't. I'm surprised she asked. She's a by-the-book kind of person."

"That must be why you two get along," Maya said. "It was more of an off-hand inquiry really."

"We are alike in a lot of ways, yes."

"She's gorgeous." Another way you're alike, Maya thought as Shannon's gaze clashed with hers across the small backseat.

"She is. She's also very much taken." Again, cautious assessment filled Shannon's expression, and Maya had the feeling once more that she wouldn't come out favorably.

"I noticed the ring."

"Her partner, Sawyer Drake, runs the restaurant next door with her family."

"Hence the name."

"Exactly. They're both pretty amazing."

"Out of curiosity, why the emphasis on telling me your boss is taken?" The strain in Maya's voice was like a garrote on her throat, strangling the question that she almost didn't want answered. She didn't want to hear that Shannon thought she was just a player with no integrity.

"I don't know. You made a point of saying how gorgeous she is."

"So it follows that I want to sleep with her. Because you read in some magazine that I'm such a slut."

"Whoa, I didn't say that."

"But you were thinking it. The tabloids say I'm a player so it must be true."

"Isn't it?" Shannon's words carried a hard edge that cut through her indignation.

Maya didn't really have a right to be angry about a reputation she'd earned. Sure, the press exaggerated their stories, but they were based, at least in part, in truth.

The car pulled to a stop in front of their hotel, not a moment too soon for Maya. She jumped out and, forgoing chivalry this time, left Shannon to get her own door. She strode through the hotel doors and across the lobby. But Shannon caught up with her at the elevators. Maya stared up at the display, watching the numbers until the car reached the lobby. When the doors slid open, she stepped inside and Shannon followed.

"Thank you for the tutoring session. I meant it when I said I wouldn't have chosen anyone else," Shannon said quietly from her side of the elevator. "I'm sorry things got—um, tense. That's not how I wanted it to go."

Maya sighed, feeling like an ass. She'd been enjoying their time together. Then she'd overreacted to Shannon's comment about having kids, and the evening had disintegrated from there.

"I'm sorry, too. I'm obviously sensitive about how much of my business is out there for the world to see. I just have to remind myself that it comes with the territory."

"I didn't intend to invade your privacy. But clearly I'm a fan, and maybe I read too many magazines. Even now, it's surreal to me that we're having this conversation."

"Why?"

"I've admired you—um, your work for a long time. But before this month, I never dreamed I'd get the opportunity to meet you, not to mention spend as much time personally with you as I have."

"But you have. I've been alone with you more than I have anyone other than my assistant in months." And more than she'd wanted to be with anyone in even longer. She stopped short of asking Shannon to look deeper than the magazine articles, because the idea of having to ask made her feel weak.

The elevator stopped and the doors slid open. Maya moved forward and stuck out her hand to hold the door just as Shannon stepped into the center of the small space. Maya grasped Shannon's waist with her free hand to steady them both. Since they were nearly the same height, their eyes met naturally, though Shannon flicked hers to Maya's lips and back twice. Maya swayed toward her, intent on erasing the remaining inches between them.

"This is me," Shannon whispered as she pressed her hand to the center of Maya's chest, halting any forward movement.

"I'm on fourteen. You could come up." Maya issued the invitation before she had time to consider its prudence. But her brain seemed to have given up control of the situation, taking with it all of the reasons she'd been irritated with Shannon a short time ago.

"That's not a good idea."

Maya glanced down at Shannon's hand, still flattened against the center of her chest. "You know, this is the second time you've said those words to me, while touching me in exactly that manner. And if it's meant to be a deterrent, it doesn't work."

"No?"

"No." She leaned closer, now only a breath from kissing Shannon. "It only makes me think of all of the other ways I want you to touch me."

"Oh, God."

The words escaped on a moan so low and hungry she was certain Shannon hadn't meant to say them aloud.

Maya released the door, letting it close, wrapped her arm around Shannon's waist, and pulled her in. When their lips met, Shannon's response was instant and as hot as the need that flared within Maya. Shannon traced her lower lip with her tongue and she met it with hers, dizzy with the taste and feel of her. Needing an anchor, she pushed Shannon against the wall of the elevator and braced her hands against the paneling on either side of her hips to absorb the impact. She pressed the full length of her body against Shannon's, trapping Shannon's hand between them, still flat against her chest. Shannon pushed against her, and disappointment flooded Maya as she thought Shannon would break the embrace. Instead, Shannon freed her hand, wrapped her fingers around the back of Maya's neck, and pulled her in for more. Maya moaned into her mouth as they stroked and gasped and held tight to each other.

The elevator dinged and the doors slid open on Maya's floor. Shannon jerked her mouth free.

"This is you." Shannon's panting breath teased Maya's sensitive lips.

"You could still come in." She wanted her to, so badly.

"This is you." Shannon repeated, walking her backward out of the elevator. She pulled free and stepped back inside, leaving Maya on the outside alone as the doors slid shut between them.

CHAPTER ELEVEN

Maya stretched out on the sofa in her dressing room and rubbed her head. That spot over her left eye had been throbbing all morning, so during the first break in filming she'd fled the set. The competitors had been sent on a field trip of sorts, to a local restaurant specializing in an upscale twist on Southern cuisine. After they returned, the afternoon's challenge featured putting their own stamp on a classic Southern dessert.

For now, Maya planned to soak in every moment of silence she could, in hopes that the medication she'd taken fifteen minutes ago would kick in soon. She would never visit the South in the spring again. She'd grown up in the Northeast and, until now, experienced minimal issues with allergies, but the Tennessee pollen count had her praying for relief from the pressure pounding in her head.

After their kiss the night before, Maya had gone to bed to the most pleasant and frustrating dreams. She'd awakened with a feeling of anticipation and lack of fulfillment that she rather enjoyed. For a few minutes in that elevator, logic had left them both and all the reasons she constructed that they couldn't be together fell away. But when Shannon had stepped back and left her there alone in the hallway, they rushed back. She'd let herself into her hotel room with self-doubt weighing heavily on her shoulders. Shannon was a commitment kind of woman, and Maya hadn't done committed in years. She didn't think she'd be very good at it. Besides, in a matter of weeks, the show would be over and they'd each return to their life.

It had been so long since Maya felt this tangled up over anyone. She'd been celibate for a year, and even before that, when she did get physical, she was going through the motions. Sure, she could do what needed to be done, but she didn't feel much beyond that. With Shannon, she'd coiled so tightly so quickly, and she kind of liked not knowing when she might get to release that tension. She'd stayed in bed this morning as long as she could without being late for her morning call. It wasn't until she got up and tried to move around that the congestion fogging her head had started to take hold.

She'd arrived on set, hoping to catch Shannon alone for a moment to gauge how she felt about last night. But she hadn't been granted more than a quick glance across the room of competitors and crew, and Shannon's expression had been unreadable. Hugh had sent them off before she could catch her in conversation.

So with the rest of the morning off, she'd retired to her dressing room. Before she could really get settled, a sharp knock sounded on her door. She didn't open her eyes even as the door swung open.

"I brought you some coffee. Just how you like it," Hugh said as he set a take-out coffee cup on the table next to her and dropped into the opposite chair.

"You still remember how I take it?"

"Sure. I got a lot of coffee while I was paying my dues seven years ago, and I remember every order."

"Or you bribed a production assistant to tell you." Maya sat up, swung her legs over the edge, and leaned back into the leather cushion behind her. She squeezed her eyelids shut, then forced them open again, but she didn't reach for the coffee yet. Some of the ache behind her eyes might have eased. It might hurt just a little less. She took a deep breath and, moving slowly, sat forward to pick up the cup. She took a careful sip and sighed.

"Ah, nice. Thank you." The hot liquid soothed her scratchy throat.

"You've got a couple of hours until they're back. Did you take anything?"

"Yes. I think it's starting to work, but my head's still pretty full."

"Great. Listen, I need to talk to you about something." Hugh had his business face on, familiarity giving way to professional detachment.

"Shoot."

"We've been watching the dailies." Now he seemed uncomfortable. "I—we need the old Maya back."

"The old Maya?"

"The hardcore, take-no-prisoners chef I met in season one."

Maya laughed. "Okay, maybe I've mellowed a little, but—"

"Yeah, well, I didn't sell mellow-Maya to the producers. I told them you'd kick these kids' asses." He stood and paced the tiny space between his chair and her sofa.

"Hugh—"

"We need the ratings, and airing a mediocre cake competition isn't going to do it. I need some tension, some drama. Just give me a little more of your rough edges, okay?" His voice rose and the cadence of his words sped up until he ended at a high-pitched squeal.

"Stop squawking before my head splits open." She clasped her hands on either side of her head. "I didn't agree to do the show to be a puppet."

"I put myself out there for you. With all your bad press this year, the producers didn't want to take you on. I talked them into it. I told them you'd make the difference on the show."

She stiffened when he mentioned her media coverage. They'd never talked specifically about what had happened, and she didn't feel she owed him an explanation. But he'd gotten her here and unknowingly given her a place to hide—from the spotlight and from herself. She threw her hands up. "I'll try to be tougher on them."

"Thank you. If this season doesn't do well—"

"I said I'll try." She sipped her coffee. Just because it was part of an apparent guilt trip, she didn't intend to let it go to waste.

"Good. Get some rest. I'll send someone when we're ready for you on set later."

She leaned back and closed her eyes once again, trying to relax as she heard the click of Hugh closing the door carefully behind him. If this headache didn't abate, being grouchy and critical would definitely come a little easier this afternoon.

❖

"Time's up," Eric called.

Shannon stepped back from her workstation, convinced she wouldn't win this challenge. Her red-velvet cheesecake tasted good, but it hadn't set as well as she wanted so her presentation looked sloppy.

The mentors started their critiques a few workstations away.

"Your flavors are bland and the texture isn't good, too grainy. I think you might be in trouble today." Maya's voice carried down the row of chefs. Shannon felt sorry for the chef cowering under her sharp gaze.

As Maya made her way from one dessert to the next, her comments didn't get any more favorable. She picked apart the plates, one by one, judging much harsher than both Wayne and Jacques. Shannon's apprehension grew with every step Maya took toward her counter. She was ripping each chef apart. And Shannon would be willing to bet that none of *them* had pushed her out of an elevator and left her standing in the hall after being kissed senseless. So she didn't expect to fare any better.

She had kicked herself the entire way back to her hotel room, or she would have if she hadn't been too busy replaying the kiss in her mind. In fact, even today, she couldn't stop reliving the incredibly sensual encounter in vivid detail. She'd always enjoyed kissing, and good lord, Maya was great at it. But one very hot kiss didn't erase all the reasons she should stay away from Maya Vaughn.

Even if she set aside the restrictions of being mentor/mentee on the show, she couldn't ignore her personal fears. The way Maya seemed to hold herself apart, never completely opening up, supported her well-documented reputation as a player who didn't get seriously involved. Shannon had no interest in becoming attached only to be heartbroken when the show ended and Maya went back to New York without a second glance. She'd come to the set this morning conflicted, yet, almost against her will, eager to see Maya. Her reasons nearly faded into the background the first time they made eye contact. But she'd managed to shut down the quick burst of attraction and school her expression into something more neutral.

"Red velvet?"

Shannon flinched at Maya's words and discovered her standing with the other judges directly in front of her. She met Maya's hardened gaze and thought she saw a softening in her badass expression. Maya raked her eyes down Shannon's body, then snapped them back up. The aggressive perusal sent a flash of heat through Shannon.

She exhaled a shaky breath and rounded her shoulders slightly, hoping to pull her chef coat away from her hardening nipples enough that they wouldn't show up on camera.

"I wanted something more—creative from you. This far into the competition, this," she waved her hand over Shannon's plate, "just isn't going to cut it."

"Yes, Chef," Shannon responded between tense jaws. A flash of hurt feelings warred with an even stronger shaft of arousal. Maya's "in control" persona definitely turned her on. Wayne and Jacques both complimented her flavors but didn't offer anything further. Given their bland delivery, she guessed they made the comments to counteract Maya's obvious criticism.

Had Maya ripped only *her* dish, she might have thought her harshness had something to do with last night. But she spread her rancor evenly among the contestants. Shannon studied her surreptitiously as she faced the others. She moved stiffly and rubbed her temple often between sentences.

She got the chance to ask Maya about it ten minutes later when she caught her in the hallway while they were on break. She'd just left the restroom when Maya rounded the corner. Maya had been walking with her eyes downcast and pulled her head up in surprise as Shannon stopped in front of her.

"Hey, are you okay?" Shannon controlled the urge to touch Maya's cheek. She looked fatigued, slight discoloration marring the skin under her eyes.

"Sure. Yeah, I'm fine." Maya glanced around as if looking for someone else before she settled on Shannon.

"Okay, good. I—you look tired and I didn't know if you—if last night—"

"No. It's just a touch of sinus congestion." Despite Maya's impersonal tone, she searched Shannon's face as if seeking a deeper connection.

"The climate's catching up with you." Shannon heard the hitch in her voice. She felt Maya's eyes as surely as a caress and couldn't keep from leaning closer.

"I guess so. Since you brought it up, about last night—"

"Actually, let's just pretend I didn't bring it up." She didn't think she could force herself to tell Maya it had been a mistake. But she couldn't say anything else. She couldn't tell her that she was afraid her crush might be developing into real feelings. She couldn't admit that she'd replayed that kiss so many times and right now, she wanted another one more than anything.

"Shannon—"

"I need to focus on what I'm doing." She forced a laugh. "After all, if I don't do better than I did today, my hard-ass mentor's going to run me off the show."

For a moment, Maya didn't look as if she would let it go, but then she nodded. "Okay." When Shannon began to step around her, Maya touched her arm. "But if you're taking any more late-night hotel hallway strolls, you should be aware that I'll be in the gym tonight. You know, so you can avoid that part of the hotel."

"Are you sure you're feeling up to working out?"

"You know what they say, starve a fever, sweat a cold, or is it the other way around?"

"I don't think it's either. There's something about eating in there. Maybe you should stay in your room and get some chicken soup."

"I didn't see that on the room-service menu. Do you know anyone who might want to bring me some later?"

"You're persistent, I'll give you that."

"So, I'll see you later then?"

Shannon laughed and, as she walked away, said over her shoulder, "Enjoy your workout."

❖

"Okay, ladies. Design time is almost up. What do you have?" Maya asked as she approached the three women gathered around a piece of paper on one of the workstations.

The contestants had been given the topic of the next challenge. Each group had four hours to construct a birthday cake with a Southern theme. No more specific direction was provided. During the last ten minutes of the designated planning period, the mentors could consult with their teams.

Alice launched into a description of their idea. "What's more Southern than a good old-fashioned picnic? The kind where the whole extended family gets together and everyone brings their specialty. The main cake is shaped like a picnic table, complete with checkered tablecloth. On top of it, we have fried chicken, biscuits, corn on the cob—all made of cake or sculpted in modeling chocolate."

"And a pitcher of sweet tea," Shannon added.

"We haven't decided on a miniature dessert for the table yet," Lucia said.

"Maybe not red-velvet cheesecake." Maya looked at Shannon with a raised brow.

"Funny."

Alice snapped her fingers. "What about a birthday cake? It's not specific to the South, but this cake is for a birthday. That could be the occasion for the picnic."

"Grandma June's eightieth?" Shannon quipped.

Maya looked over their sketch, penciling in a few suggestions of her own. Their idea could work, but at this point in the game, their execution had to be near perfect. When time was up, she took her place across the room beside Wayne and Jacques. Eric called for the start of work and the chefs sprang into action.

She watched her team work for a few minutes before she retired to her dressing room. She wouldn't be allowed to coach them along, and she couldn't sit silently and watch for four hours. Hugh would let her know when she was needed back on set. She settled on her couch with her phone and scrolled through her emails. She returned a few and flagged some for later.

Two hours later, she heard sounds outside her door. The chefs must be taking a break for hydration and using the restroom. Working under the hot lights could be draining. Though the show would be cut together as if they worked nonstop, with the exception of certain challenges where part of the goal was to physically and mentally exhaust them, typically they got short, frequent breaks.

Maya listened for Shannon's voice, but she could hear only the sound of feet and the murmur of voices. She resisted the urge to leave her dressing room. Hugh had been watching her more closely since his warning. She refused to be mean for the sake of ratings, but she could strive to be more aloof and constructively critical of their work.

The noises faded and she imagined them jumping back into their work. She tried to picture the cake her team had described and hoped they were bringing it to life. She was surprised by how difficult the elimination process was. She remembered how hard she'd worked on her season—the stress of wondering if she'd survive the next cut—and watching these chefs go through a similar experience made it harder to judge who should go next. She'd always thought the mentors on her season had the easy job. Now she could respect both sides of the process.

Two hours later, she was back in the middle of that process. She stood next to Wayne and Jacques while Eric guided them through critiquing the three teams' cakes. Jacques's group, led by Ned, had the cleanest cake. She could already tell their creation was the front-runner. They'd built an antebellum mansion surrounded by beautifully constructed magnolia trees. So the race for second place came down to Wayne's group or Maya's. She followed the other two mentors as they all walked completely around the display tables.

When they were done, she took her place in front of the chefs again. She barely listened to Wayne and Jacques give their evaluations because she already knew the outcome. Her team had been edged out, and one of the three would go home. She glanced at Shannon, who was staring at the floor in front of her as if she knew what was about to happen as well.

"Maya?" Eric looked at her expectantly.

"I don't think we need to deliberate, do we, guys?" Out of the corner of her eye, she saw Shannon jerk her head up. Maya looked at Wayne and Jacques. While they both appeared surprised that she wanted to bypass any general comments and jump to the elimination, they shook their heads. She nodded. Not bothering to consult with Eric about the slight change in plan, she turned to her team and made eye contact with each of them. "It wasn't a bad idea, ladies. But we're getting to that point in the competition where every little detail matters. The food pieces were good. Shannon, I could practically smell that fried chicken. Your sculpting has improved already. Who was responsible for the picnic table?"

Lucia raised her hand.

"The tablecloth looked great, but the wood grain on the benches lacked detail. It should have looked more realistic. Alice, the miniature birthday cake was very well done. But you spent too much time on that one aspect and not enough helping out with the rest of the project." She checked again with Wayne and Jacques and saw agreement and respect in their expressions. "We needed a little more teamwork and communication today."

Eric recovered quickly and sent the competitors out of the room so the mentors could determine which one to send home. Maya felt several pairs of eyes on her as they filed out, but she kept her expression neutral and avoided looking at them.

"Who are you thinking?" Hugh hurried over.

In her mind, the choice was between Lucia and Alice. She took a moment longer to ensure that she wasn't letting personal feelings rule out sending Shannon home. But she didn't have to worry. Shannon's work today as well as thus far on the show had really earned her another week in the competition.

"Based on performance today, Lucia was the weakest," Maya said.

"But Alice is weaker overall," Hugh insisted.

Maya narrowed her eyes at him, and before he looked away she thought she saw guilt flash across his face. She shook her head. "In the beginning maybe, but she's come a long way."

"I have to agree," Wayne added. "Alice and Shannon have both shown marked improvement, and Lucia, though slightly stronger in the beginning, hasn't had much of an arc."

"And Alice's dessert during the immunity challenge was better," Jacques said.

Maya pulled in a deep breath and slowly let it out, feeling relief pour in to take its place. Having Wayne and Jacques echo her decision took some of the stress out of the situation.

"Send Alice home." With Hugh's tense words, Maya's anxiety ratcheted back up.

"I thought this was my decision."

"The producers are taking this one for you." Hugh's voice was tight, as if he knew what he was saying was wrong.

"But Alice deserves to stay."

"Don't be naive, Maya. You know by now that it's not always about who deserves to stay."

"Why are the producers stepping in on this particular elimination?" She suspected she knew, but she wanted to hear him say it. He kept his mouth shut, though, so she tried another approach. "If my team hadn't lost, would you be telling either of the guys who to send home?"

"If it were Wayne, I'd advise him to keep Mason."

She stiffened her shoulders, feeling sick at the idea that no matter how hard the chefs had worked, their success depended on a trait so completely out of their control. "This isn't fair—"

"Just do as I say," Hugh snapped, then spun around and left.

Maya stared at the door he'd exited through. Not far away, the contestants awaited their fate. This far into the competition, every elimination got a little more nerve-wracking because the top three was now in sight. Both Alice and Lucia were strong chefs, and of course, she'd prefer not to send either of them home. But now was the time for tough decisions, and it irritated her to have that decision taken out of her hands. Especially when she'd already weighed the options and made her choice.

Now she had to walk back in there and send Alice home. But what would happen if she said Lucia's name instead? They weren't live so they could just make her reshoot the segment. But how would they explain to the contestants what was going on? They couldn't admit the truth, which Maya was pretty certain had to do with wanting to ensure ethnic diversity in the final three.

"Don't do it," Wayne said quietly from beside her.

"What?"

"I can see the wheels turning in there. Just do what they ask."

"It's not right."

"I know. But unless you want your affiliation with the show to end this season, don't push it."

Wayne and Jacques left the room, but she hung back. She didn't even know if she'd want to mentor for another season, but she wanted the invite. This decision wasn't a career killer, by any means, but it could potentially end her connection to the show that had launched her success.

Chapter Twelve

C an you believe Lucia got sent home today?" Alice set a plate in front of Shannon. Since they came home exhausted most nights, one of them prepared a simple dinner, and the other two took care of the dishes. But today, they'd lost the third member of their team. "I thought I'd go before Lucia, for sure."

Me too, Shannon thought.

"Both of us really."

"Thanks."

"No offense."

"Sure." Shannon took a bite of grilled chicken with mango salsa. Then, to change the subject, she said, "This is amazing. The salsa tastes so fresh."

"Cilantro and lime juice, right before it's served."

"Yeah. I can taste it."

"I just can't believe it."

And we're back on Lucia. Shannon kept chewing, knowing that if she stayed silent Alice would carry her share of the conversation as well.

"It just goes to show, this game is unpredictable. Anyone can have an off day, and that can cost you your whole future."

"You sound like one of those television promos for the show."

"Seriously. Here I am, in the top five now, and after that first day, I didn't even know if I'd make it through the first couple of eliminations. And Lucia—I mean, she was the strongest of the three of us—the woman has ice in her veins. She just doesn't get rattled. Like ever."

"I get it." Shannon stood, unable to stand the chatter any longer. She stacked her plate in the sink. "But she's not here. And we are." She headed for her bedroom. Without turning back, she said, "Just leave the dishes. I'll do them later."

She closed the door behind her and leaned back against it. She sighed and crossed to flop onto her bed, then rolled over and stared at the ceiling. She'd been short with Alice, but actually Alice wasn't the source of her irritation. She'd apologize later. For now she turned her frustration inward. She glanced at the clock on her nightstand and groaned. They'd left the set only two hours ago, and already Maya dominated her thoughts. Maya had been critical, distant, and downright grouchy all day. Still, Shannon wanted to see her, to find out what was bothering her, to offer her a shoulder. She wondered if she was in the gym yet. Knowing where to find her only made it harder to stay away.

Going downstairs tonight would be just another thing she shouldn't have done today. She shouldn't have followed Maya into the hallway on their break or asked about her well-being as if they were anything more than acquaintances. And she definitely shouldn't have responded to Maya's flirting—she hadn't been overt, but she hadn't shut her down when she should have either. Truthfully, a little part of her liked the attention, even though she knew how complicated and messy getting involved with Maya would be.

She picked up her book from the bedside table. After she'd read the same page three times, she flipped it shut in frustration.

She stood and paced the room, looking again at the clock. Barely ten minutes had passed since she last checked. She was in for a long night. Though her alarm would buzz very early, she had no hope of going to sleep this soon. Maybe if she went downstairs and fatigued herself with a good workout, she could get a little shut-eye later. Chuckling to herself, she stood and paced the room. She'd just talked herself into a good excuse to see Maya.

But it wasn't a ploy if she actually did work out, was it? Grabbing hold of the weak logic, she stripped off her T-shirt and swapped her bra for a sports bra, then pulled her T-shirt back on. She tugged on a pair of yoga pants and laced up her cross-trainers.

By the time she'd finished dressing and returned to the living room, Alice had already cleaned the kitchen and was putting away the final plates.

"I told you to leave that."

"It's no problem." She turned and looked Shannon up and down. "Where are you going?"

"Um, down to the gym."

"I can't believe you have the energy to work out."

"It helps with the stress."

"Really? Maybe I should try it. Hold on, I'll join you."

"Ah—I don't think—"

"Wait right there. I'll go change."

Alice disappeared into the bedroom that she now had to herself. Shannon sighed and sank onto the edge of the sofa to wait. She owed Alice for being short with her earlier. And maybe if Alice was breathless on a treadmill or something, she wouldn't be able to talk about how broken up she was over Lucia's departure. Besides, now Shannon would have a chaperone with Maya and wouldn't have to worry about giving in to any inappropriate urges.

Maya pulled her arm across her chest and grasped her forearm with her other hand, stretching through her arm and back. After working slowly through a series of stretches, she moved on to warm-up exercises. She rolled her shoulders, then did a few big arm circles, trying to get the tightness out of her neck and shoulders. She'd been tense since the elimination two hours ago.

She hadn't completely known what she was going to do until the moment Lucia's name came from her mouth. Out of the corner of her eyes, she saw Hugh spring up from his chair and pace toward her, but he stayed out of camera range. She remained focused on the chefs in front of her, waiting for someone to stop filming and call her aside. But the cameras kept rolling and Lucia left the room looking dejected. Alice and Shannon stood there with shocked expressions until Jacques cued them to leave and return to the hotel as well.

Shannon had locked eyes with her, her expression full of questions. But Maya kept her face as neutral as she could. After what she'd just done, she couldn't afford to give anyone a reason to doubt her objectivity. She didn't question her motives for sending Lucia home, but she didn't want anyone else to either.

After the show broke for the day, Maya went directly to her dressing room and waited for Hugh to find her there. He didn't disappoint. When he arrived, she settled on the sofa, tucked her hands under her thighs, and listened to his tirade. As much as she wanted to, she hadn't argued, mostly because she'd quickly gathered that her decision to send Lucia home wouldn't be reversed.

When he'd finished shouting at her, she couldn't resist one dig. "You said you wanted the old Maya back." She gave an indolent shrug for effect. He clenched his fists and strode out of the room. Time would tell how her relationship with the show fared, but for now she wasn't being fired immediately. By the time she left the set, she was tense and ready for the release of a workout.

She bent and touched her toes, enjoying the pull through her hamstrings and calves. She lowered her shoulders, getting just a little deeper into the stretch, then shifted to hover near one foot and then the other.

As the door clicked open behind her, she straightened slowly, drawing the stretch out just a bit more. She turned and caught Shannon jerking her eyes away from her ass.

"Hey, you came." She smiled and winked as a blush spread up Shannon's neck. An answering flush of pleasure washed over Maya. When Shannon stepped aside and Alice followed her inside, Maya shifted her expression into polite acceptance. "And you brought a friend."

"The gym is open to all hotel guests, right?" Shannon didn't quite meet her eyes.

"Right."

"Well, we're here to take advantage of the amenities."

"Great. Hello, Alice."

"Hi." Alice's pointed glances toward Shannon indicated that she hadn't known Maya would be here. Alice put in a set of earbuds and waved the hand holding her iPod toward the machines along the far wall. "I'm going to hit the elliptical."

"I think I'll do the treadmill," Shannon said. She braced her hand against the wall, bent one leg behind her, and grabbed her heel, stretching her quad. As she arched her back and her lower body angled forward, Maya took a step closer, fighting the urge to grasp her waist and pull her in.

Maya glanced at Alice, who bobbed her head along with the music as she took big awkward strides on the elliptical. Then she spoke quietly to Shannon. "So you're really down here to work out."

"Yep." She climbed onto the treadmill and punched the button to start the belt, beginning with a moderate walking speed.

Maya got on the treadmill next to hers and matched her pace. Recalling the heat in Shannon's eyes when she'd walked in on her stretching, she said, "And you needed a chaperone."

"No." Shannon raised a finger in protest.

"Oh, that wasn't a question." Maya grinned.

"No. Alice saw me leaving and offered to come down with me. I thought it might be nice to have a workout buddy."

Maya laughed. "A buddy? I told you I was going to be here. I would have been your buddy." She purposely made the last word sound more suggestive than it should have.

Shannon cut her eyes at her, then back to the treadmill display. She sped up her pace to a light jog.

"You know you can't actually run away from me on that thing, right?" Maya enjoyed the deepening flush of Shannon's cheeks, certain she would attribute it to the physical exertion.

She kicked the speed on her own treadmill up a bit and settled into a comfortable rhythm. Her headache had abated, but her lingering congestion had her taking things at a slower pace than usual.

"I—I'm not trying to run away from you. I'm here, aren't I?"

"Sure, but you want me to believe it's a coincidence that you are. With Alice. After I told you this afternoon that I'd be here."

"Okay. I wanted to see you," Shannon hissed. Alice jerked her head toward them, and Shannon smiled tightly until she turned back to her workout. Lowering her voice even further, she ground out, "Is that what you want to hear?"

"Actually, yes." Maya kept her eyes on Alice, but since Maya could hear the pop music bouncing through her iPod from across the room, she was certain she couldn't make out their conversation. She leaned a little closer, without looking at Shannon. "I want to hear that you've been thinking about me just as much as I have you."

Shannon's slightly labored breathing hitched even more, but she didn't respond. Maya shook her head, wishing she hadn't let that last sentence slip out. Maybe Shannon would just chalk it up to harmless flirting instead of the desperate insecurity Maya feared it really was.

They jogged next to each other in silence, the steady cadence of their feet on the belts nearly in sync. Despite Maya's effort to keep her eyes on the treadmill display in front of her, she kept stealing glances at Shannon in the mirror on the opposite wall. She watched her ponytail swing back and forth with each step, because it kept her from staring at the way her breasts moved inside the sports bra that wasn't quite restrictive enough.

Shannon's face shone with perspiration under the fluorescent lights, and her features were a study in concentration. Obviously not as accustomed to cardio as Maya, she struggled a little to keep up the pace as they passed the first mile. When she began to pant, Maya started imagining ways she could make her out of breath that didn't involve a treadmill. Or maybe a more creative use of one at the very least. Her foot skidded against the belt as she lost her stride. She pulled the emergency stop cord on her machine and jumped off.

Startled, Shannon turned to her. "What's wrong?"

"Nothing." She paced to the other end of the room and back, pretending she wanted to stretch her legs. Actually, she needed a bit of distance from Shannon, who seemed completely unaffected by the stifling air in the suddenly too-small room. She'd invited Shannon here because she wanted to flirt with her—wanted to do more than that really. Until recently, she rarely fought those types of impulses and thought it ironically cruel that she desired Shannon more than she had anyone before yet couldn't act on it. And she apparently liked the punishment, because all of that only made her want to tease Shannon—and herself—even more.

Alice huffed as she pulled out her earbuds and climbed off the machine. "I don't think this is helping my stress at all."

"Me either," Maya mumbled, earning her a quick look from Shannon.

"A hot bath and a glass of wine would have done better. I'm going back to the room."

Shannon shrugged and kept running. "I'll see you up there."

Alice glanced at Maya, then back at Shannon as if she didn't want to leave them alone. But Maya suspected her hesitance had more to do with fear that Shannon might find a way to get an edge in the game rather than genuine concern for Shannon's well-being.

"See you tomorrow, Chef Vaughn," Alice said stiffly as she opened the door to the hallway.

Maya nodded and waved. "Actually a hot bath and a glass of wine would be nice," she said after Alice had gone.

Shannon remained silent.

"Don't you think? Sinking into some steaming water beats cardio any day. Especially with the right company." When Shannon still didn't respond, Maya stood in front of her treadmill so she had no choice but to look at her. "Not speaking to me? Or are you just that intent on your workout?"

Shannon met her eyes and flicked her brows upward. "I'm not responding to your flirty little comments."

"Well, that's no fun. Why not?"

"Because I'm sure everyone else does and I want to be different."

"Not everyone." Maya shrugged, then grabbed a balance ball from the corner of the room and brought it out to the center. If she couldn't get a verbal response from Shannon, maybe she'd go for a physical one. The hours she spent in the gym staying in shape for the camera should be put to good use somehow.

She set the ball where she knew it would be in Shannon's line of sight, then tugged her T-shirt over her head, leaving her in just a sports bra and running shorts. She sat on the ball and leaned back, then up, performing crunches that she knew accentuated her abs and thighs. She watched Shannon in her peripheral vision and smothered a self-satisfied laugh when Shannon nearly fell off the treadmill. But she bit her lip and quietly continued her reps, making sure to tighten her stomach muscles even more than usual.

Shannon slammed her hand against the treadmill display, stopping it. She strode across the room, saying over her shoulder, "I'll see you tomorrow."

"Don't go," Maya said, jumping up from the ball. Shannon paused with her hand on the door. "Stay and talk to me for a bit."

"Put your shirt back on," Shannon said stiffly.

Maya grabbed her shirt and pulled it over her head. She'd pushed far enough. And honestly, she didn't even know why she was doing that, except that she enjoyed seeing Shannon as flustered as she felt.

Shannon sighed, then retrieved another exercise ball and rolled it over next to hers. They sank down onto them together, bouncing a little as they got settled.

"So, was something wrong today, other than your sinus issues?" Shannon asked.

"No." A little white lie.

"You seemed, ah, more brusque than usual."

"Maybe I was just more honest. I've been taking it easy on you guys."

"Yeah?"

"We're mentors and judges, Shannon. We're not here to be friendly. We're here to make you better chefs."

"Really? Because it seems like you're trying to be friendly now." Shannon rolled back and forth slightly on her ball, as if the rocking motion soothed her. But watching the muscles flex in her thighs under the tight yoga pants didn't calm Maya in the least.

"I'm not working right now."

"I figured with reality television, you pretty much had to always be working."

"Yeah. I don't like that part of it." Bitterness seeped into her voice as she thought about the other aspects of the business she'd discovered she didn't like today.

"So you ignore the rules?" Her tone indicated that she thought this was how Maya lived all areas of her life. "Or just the ones you don't like?"

She shrugged. "If the producers were that worried about what we did at night, they'd have cameramen prowling the hallways. Come to think of it, we should probably be on the lookout for that."

"If you hadn't already seemed in an ill mood, I might have thought it had to do with Lucia's elimination. You didn't seem happy about that."

"I wasn't happy to be sending anyone from my team home. But Lucia was my choice."

"Well, something felt off about it all. Now that I think about it, the only person more on edge in there was Hugh."

Maya cringed, then hurried to change the course of the conversation. "More than you three? Did you think you were safe?"

"Apparently, we can never think that." Shannon smiled. "I hoped it wasn't me."

She wanted to tell Shannon to have confidence in herself—that she deserved to still be there. And if they were in the kitchen, in front of the cameras, and she were speaking as her mentor, she might have. But somehow, here, privately, when everything between them felt so much more personal, she wasn't sure it was her place.

From across the room, an electronic melody sang out from Maya's phone. She recognized the ringtone and didn't bother retrieving it.

"They let you keep your cell?" Shannon asked.

"Yeah. I'm not on house arrest. Just you contestants."

"It's only been about two weeks, but it seems like forever since I made a call that wasn't monitored." Shannon gave an exaggerated sigh, then smiled. "Should you answer it?"

"No. It was my mother. I'll call her back later."

"What if it's important?"

"She probably just wants money." She winced at the hard edge to her words. "That sounded cold, huh?"

"A little."

"I've been dealing with these calls for seven years now. It gets old." She hadn't realized just how little compassion she had for her mother until she thought about explaining their complicated relationship to someone else. "When I won my season, my mother began instructing me in how I should capitalize on my *fifteen minutes of fame*. You see, she never actually believed I had real talent, so she thought I should grab every opportunity to make money before the rest of the world caught on to that fact. After my season, before the money started coming in, when all I had to offer was fame, she figured out that certain journalists would pay for details about my life, past and present."

Shannon's brows drew together, and then as she made sense of Maya's words, her expression smoothed and settled into something that looked like anger. She pressed her lips tighter but didn't say anything. So Maya continued, "So the only way to control my privacy was to make a better offer than the reporters. I give her money, with the understanding that she keeps her mouth shut. If that ever changes, she's cut off."

"Wow. I'm sorry." Shannon touched Maya's forearm.

"Why?" Shannon's hand was warm and firm, and Maya's emotions came closer to the surface than they had in so long.

"You're paying off your own mother," Shannon said incredulously.

"We've never been close." She forced indifference.

"What about your dad?"

"Don't have one. Not a *dad*. I'm sure I have a father out there somewhere, but she never told me who."

"I didn't know things were so messed up with your family."

"Why would you? That stuff barely made it in the tabloids before I caught on to her tricks. Now as far as anyone's concerned, she's a hard-working single mother and we couldn't have a better relationship." Maya stood and paced away, needing distance from both the compassion in Shannon's eyes and the urge to seek more comfort in her touch. For too many years, she'd been dispassionate about her family, so why, today, should any of this bother her? "What about you? What skeletons are likely to come out when this show airs?"

"I don't really have any."

"Everybody does. Some people don't even realize it until your name and face are out there. Old friends and enemies you didn't even know you had suddenly surface."

Shannon shook her head. "My parents were supportive. Maybe overly so. But I never gave them a reason not to be. I fell in line— the well-behaved daughter. I married the boy I was supposed to, became the perfect wife." Despite describing the idyllic life, she looked sad. "How much of this do you already know from my bio?"

"Some. Keep talking. Reading it on paper doesn't tell the story." Maya sat back down next to her.

"Yeah, and I'm just getting to the good part. You know, where my life fell apart."

"You don't have to—"

"It's okay." She took a deep breath, then let it out slowly. "I'll give you the short version. I couldn't get pregnant. He left me. Found himself a fertile, younger wife and they have three kids, last I heard." She raised her brows and gave a self-deprecating laugh. "Did I manage that without sounding bitter?"

"Almost."

"We haven't actually spoken in years. I don't think he cares enough to say anything about me even if the media dug him up."

"You'd be surprised what people will say." Maya smirked. "I'm not even trying not to sound bitter."

Shannon shrugged. "I'm not worried. It's not like our marriage was very exciting. There's nothing to say."

"And now you're about to be a grandmother."

"Rub salt in the wound, why don't you? Yes. I'm elderly."

Maya smiled. "You're still hot for an old lady, though."

"Thanks." Shannon's answering smile chased some of the sadness from her expression, and Maya took too much pleasure in being the one to do that for her.

"Then sometime in the intervening years, you found the joy of women."

Shannon laughed. "Now that's a long and dramatic story."

"Isn't it always with lesbians?" Maya leaned back on her exercise ball as if she could assume a relaxed posture on the thing. "I've got all night."

As Shannon told her the story of discovering she was attracted to and subsequently dating a woman, Maya caught herself watching her face as intently as she listened to the words. Shannon's eyes lit up with easy humor as she talked about her disastrous first date with a woman, then comfortable nostalgia as she described several attempts at long-term relationships that ultimately didn't work out. After she adopted Regan, her priorities shifted and her life centered around being a mother rather than putting effort into dating.

Shannon's experience of finding women after having been married, and of adopting a child—a pre-teen, really—on her own was so different from Maya's path that it made her realize she'd never actually had to take responsibility for anyone but herself.

CHAPTER THIRTEEN

M aya stepped out of the steaming shower stall and grabbed a towel from the rack. She scrubbed it over her head, then quickly dried her body and hung the towel neatly on the bar to dry. Naked, she left the bathroom, circled the bed, and grabbed a bottle of water from the mini fridge. Unlike the full suites the contestants lived it, her room was a large open space with a king-sized bed, a small sofa and chair near the window, and a wet bar with a single-serve coffeemaker.

She didn't miss the kitchen, preferring to exist on salads from the deli downstairs and local takeout. One night, she'd sweet-talked the guy at the famous barbeque joint on Broadway into delivering to her hotel room. But after stuffing herself on pulled pork, ribs, amazing potato salad, and the best cornbread she'd ever had, she decided she'd have to stay away from that place for a while—for the sake of her waistline. She'd actually been so full she had to save her homemade banana pudding for breakfast the next day. As good as it was, that banana pudding didn't compare to the lemon cake she got from Drake's.

Somehow, every line of thought brought her back to Shannon. She could envision walking into Drake's and seeing Shannon behind the counter. She would flash that welcoming smile, and Maya would purchase baked goods she hadn't even known she wanted. She hadn't seen the kitchen, but she'd been in enough small bakeries to build a mental picture of what the space might look like. Having met

Jori, she imagined an efficient use of space, simple yet functional, quality equipment but not overly extravagant.

She set her water bottle on the nightstand, flopped down on the bed, then scooted under the covers. Somewhere else in the hotel, Shannon was probably about to turn in as well. They had fallen into a routine of meeting in the gym after filming. And every night, after working out, they rode the elevator back up to their respective rooms. Maya somehow managed to contain her desire to invite Shannon to her room. She retired to her own room, to torment herself with images of them showering together. She stopped herself before she could fantasize about getting into bed with Shannon. Even if Shannon was on board, which, given her "come-close-no-go-away" attitude, she certainly wasn't, trying to sneak in a sleepover during the show would be much too risky.

Her cell phone vibrated on the nightstand and she answered it, seeking distraction from the rabbit hole she hovered on the edge of.

"Hey, Wendy."

"I emailed you a list of interviews and public appearances I want you to consider while you're down there."

"I don't want to do any interviews until the show's over."

"You can't bury yourself down there. Besides, the producers want the publicity."

"So let them tell me to do it."

"After that stunt you pulled with Lucia, you need to get back in their good graces."

"You heard about that already?"

"I think Hugh has me on speed-dial."

"I think Hugh has a crush on you and wants an excuse to call you. Wasn't it nice of me to give him one?"

"Maya—"

"Okay. I'll look it over." Wendy wouldn't let it go until she at least agreed to that much. She'd pick one interview and one public appearance, maybe a benefit for a good local cause.

"So what else is going on? New York's boring without you."

Maya laughed. "Yeah? The most exciting city in the country is *boring* because I'm absent?"

"Yes."

"You said you needed a break. Consider this your vacation. Hey, maybe you should take a trip while I'm out of town. Go to the beach." When Wendy didn't respond right away, Maya knew she was thinking about it. But as much as Wendy complained about wanting to get away, she was a workaholic. Maya couldn't even picture her taking a whole week just to herself. "At least take a long weekend. If you need a reason, you could go to Provincetown and check on the condo. No one's been there in months." The small beachfront condo had been one of Maya's first splurges. The little town on the tip of the cape was a close-enough drive yet still far removed from the city. She loved the ocean air and the acceptance she found there. Also, depending on what type of distraction she sought, she was easily as able to blend in with the summer tourist crowd or find solitude in one of the nearby coastal towns or remote beaches.

"Hmm. That's not a bad idea. I'll let you know." Maya was about to make an excuse to get off the phone, but Wendy wasn't done with her yet. "How's it going with Soccer Mom?"

"What?"

"Let's not waste our time doing that thing where you deny it, and I say I know you better. Skip to the part where you just tell me what's going on."

Maya laughed. "I don't know what you mean. I'm very busy, what with filming and trying to stay in shape. You know I struggle when I travel. I've been in the hotel gym every night this week."

"So other than on the show you haven't seen her?" Wendy's tone said she wasn't buying it.

"If I happen to go to the gym and other people are there working out, well, that's out of my control, isn't it?"

Wendy's husky chuckle vibrated through the phone. "Really? So every night this week? If that's how you're hoping to sell it to Hugh, you need a little more practice. Granted, I can't see you right now, but I happen to know your innocent-face isn't very good."

"There's nothing to sell."

"Hey, I get it. Sneaking around is a turn-on."

"Wendy." She did get excited to see Shannon. During filming, she'd catch her eye and Shannon would give her that small smile, the one that said they shared a secret and she liked it. For a moment, Maya could convince herself there was something special between them. But she always forced her eyes away, forging two reminders in her brain—first, that she was there to do a job and getting caught staring at a contestant wouldn't be good—and second, that whatever was going on between them would probably end sooner than she was ready for.

Then each night when she returned to the hotel, she dressed in workout clothes and headed to the fitness room. She always arrived first and got a pretty good workout in before Shannon arrived. After Shannon had dinner with Alice, she joined her. Maya had expanded her routine and continued exercising with Shannon. She might actually be in even better shape than she'd been in when the show started.

"Okay. Nothing to sell? So no flirting, and definitely no physical contact, then?"

She never could lie to Wendy—not even over the phone. And her second of hesitation was all Wendy needed for confirmation.

"I'll ask you again, how's it going with Soccer Mom?"

She didn't know how to answer. They'd shared a lot of conversation, both on casual and more serious topics. She'd snuck in some light flirting. But despite how hot their one and only kiss had been, Shannon hadn't let it go any further since.

"I'm trying to be supportive here, even though I don't think this is the smartest play. So talk to me as a friend. We'll both forget I'm your assistant and I have to worry about you tanking your career over a woman."

She shoved a hand through her hair. The sides had gotten longer than she liked, so she made a mental note to talk to the show's stylist about giving her a cut.

"She's doing great on the show. I just have her and Alice left on my team. And yes, okay, I've seen her the past three nights in the gym after filming. But nothing's happening. There was a kiss, but—"

"Maya—"

"But that was days ago. We both backed off and since then it's just been a lot of talking." *A lot* of talking. One night they'd stayed down there until two a.m. The next day, she'd dragged her ass into the makeup chair begging for concealer. She'd seen traces of fatigue around Shannon's eyes as well and vowed not to keep her up so late again. This show was hard enough without being exhausted. She felt noble until she realized that if she was really that honorable she'd cut off the nightly visits altogether.

"Yeah? You're just enjoying the conversation, huh?"

"I'm a little offended that you think I can't."

"I know there's more to you than everyone thinks. But you also have to admit it's been a while since you invested that much time."

"What else do I have to do while I'm here? I've already checked out the one decent gay bar."

"Be careful."

"I admit, I'm attracted to her. And I may even be in deeper than I thought."

"Deeper than you can handle?" Had anyone else asked her that, she would have blown up in response. But Wendy's softly posed question simply deflated her. She had no idea what she could handle anymore. She'd earned her reputation as a player, especially since the show exploded her popularity. She'd dated, had casual sex, and even got involved in a committed relationship or two along the way. But in the past year, she'd changed.

She growled in frustration and pushed her hand through her hair again.

"Hey, as your friend, I'm happy to hear that you're getting a little torn up over someone."

"Yeah? You love my misery, friend?"

"It means you're healing. After the baby—"

"I don't—"

"Hear me out. After last year, I thought you'd keep yourself shut off forever." Wendy's gentle tone took a bit of the sting out of her words. "I want you to be happy. But when the show's over, you and Soccer Mom will be going your separate ways. Are you considering a long-distance relationship?"

"You're getting so far ahead of what I've even thought about."

"Is she thinking about it?"

"I don't know."

"Maybe you should ask her."

"Maybe I should just keep my head down and finish this show and get my ass back to New York." She couldn't start thinking about the future. The last time she let herself plan for happiness, she got her heart broken. She couldn't take another loss right now.

"Yes. Because avoidance usually works. Except when it doesn't."

"Give me a break. I thought you didn't want us together. Yet when I agree, you get snarky. What do you want from me?"

"You didn't agree that you shouldn't be together. You agreed that you're afraid to be with her. Anyway, it doesn't matter what I want from you. *You* want *her*. But you also want to give in to your urge to flee because it's less complicated."

"What I want to give in to right now is this monster headache you're giving me. I have to go." She didn't wait for Wendy's response before she disconnected the call.

❖

"During today's challenge and going forward, you will each compete on your own. No more teams." Hugh's announcement came as a relief. As their team dwindled, Shannon had worried that another loss meant she had a 50/50 chance of going home. But now, her fate rested in her own hands.

She lined up behind her workstation alongside Alice and the other two remaining chefs, Ned and Mason. After yesterday's elimination, she'd made the top four and finally began to feel optimistic. One elimination stood between her and the live finale.

Perhaps for the first time since she'd arrived, Shannon had started to consider that she could win this thing. At first her goal had been to not go home first, then she wanted to make it halfway, and then she thought maybe top five would be respectable. But now that she was one spot away, she wanted top three more than anything. During these next competitions, her entire focus had to be on that end. After she achieved that, she would let herself think about actually winning.

The door on the opposite end of the kitchen opened and Eric entered, followed by the three mentors. They talked quietly among themselves, ignoring the bustle of activity around the kitchen that signified the many crewmembers getting ready for today's filming. Shannon had gotten better at tuning out the flurry as well. The distraction she'd faced with the cameras had faded, and, while on some level, she remained aware of their presence and locations within the room, she barely caught herself looking directly into a lens anymore.

Since Shannon had claimed one of the center counters, Maya, standing between Wayne and Jacques, was directly across from her. Their eyes met and the corner of Maya's mouth twitched as if she wanted to smile. Instead, she looked away. She'd been doing that a lot lately. During the competition she was distant, impersonal, and often constructively critical of all the chefs.

At night, when the two of them met in the hotel gym, Maya became a different person. She was warm and funny, and their conversation flowed easily. When Shannon tried to ask about her demeanor during filming, Maya deflected. The only other subject that seemed to shut Maya down as quickly included anything about the rumors surrounding her alleged abortion last year—not that Shannon brought that one up. But she could feel when a topic traveled too close to that time period and Maya backed away.

❖

"Chefs, please welcome our guest judge for this challenge, Greta Haus, chef-owner of Klett Haus, a local German restaurant."

Maya turned a laugh into a subtle cough as Eric mangled the pronunciation and it actually sounded like he called it "clit house." When he glared at her she averted her eyes, cleared her throat, and shot her gaze to the floor.

The shapely woman that entered turned nearly every head on set. Her flowing dark-blond hair framed cheekbones made even more prominent by artfully applied makeup. Her obviously tailored, light-pink chef coat funneled from her full breasts down to her narrow waist, although the two open buttons displaying impressive cleavage drew the eye back up. Clear eyes, dark blue or green— Maya couldn't tell for sure from where she stood—lighted on everyone in the room as she curved full lips into a warm smile. She was stunning. And Maya didn't think she imagined that Chef Haus's eyes lingered just a bit longer when they reached her.

"Almost five years ago, Chef Haus opened Klett Haus to celebrate her German roots. She has built her reputation by putting her own spin on her family's traditional recipes, creating lighter, healthier dishes that carry echoes of home." Eric welcomed Chef Haus with a hug. "Welcome to our kitchen."

"Thank you. It's so wonderful to be here." Judging from her minimal accent, Maya guessed if she wasn't born in the United States, she might have emigrated at a young age.

"Chef Haus and her staff are about to celebrate five years in business, and they're throwing a party. You'll each have three hours to complete a design, and the winning cake will be featured in the celebration."

"So, Chef Haus, why don't you tell our chefs a little about yourself and your restaurant?" Jacques said.

She thanked him politely and launched into an abbreviated version of her family history. Maya scanned the four faces across from her, recalling how excited she'd been on this day during her season. She'd been so cocky and certain that she'd make the finale. Actually, she'd been that way through her entire tenure. She faced every day feeling fearless and certain she was going all the way to the end. Aside from Ned, none of the other chefs seemed to possess that level of confidence. She'd always told herself it was necessary— that if she didn't fully believe it would happen, then somehow she didn't deserve it. But she couldn't look at the nervous expressions of any of the competitors before her and say they didn't deserve it.

Each of them had worked hard, and though she had a clear favorite, any one of them could easily compete in the finale.

Thoughts of the finale reminded Maya that in just a few days, the show would break for eight weeks while the episodes continued airing. Then the three finalists would return to participate in the final show, before one was declared the winner.

A sudden burst of movement from the competitors shook Maya from her thoughts. She'd completely missed the rest of Greta's intro and apparently Eric's call to begin.

"What do we do while they're working?" Greta touched Maya's arm. "Please, tell me we don't have to watch them for three hours."

"No. We'll come back when they're almost done."

"Hmm, so how could we pass the time?" Greta winked, an invitation shining clear in her eyes. "Do you have any interesting suggestions?"

Maya glanced down at Greta's hand, now encircling her bicep. The old Maya would ask her back to her dressing room and show her a number of interesting ways to pass three hours. Apparently taking Maya's moment of hesitation as consent, Greta stepped closer, her breast brushing Maya's arm. Maya could now tell that her eyes were green—clear and green like sea glass. And she smelled like strawberries. The dilation of Greta's pupils and the way her tongue peeked out to moisten her lips sent a shot of arousal through Maya that felt familiar and more comfortable than anything she'd experienced in months. She'd been trying to be someone else, but maybe this was just who she was—maybe the tabloids were right and she couldn't be anything more.

"Lunch?" she suggested, raising her brow in a way that had won over countless women. She knew the moves so well, they were second nature. Men and women required different tactics—the aggression that made women melt didn't work with men. Their egos required a more submissive approach. And she'd shifted between the two personas effortlessly when it suited her needs.

"We can start with that." Greta practically purred.

Maya nodded and led her from the kitchen. As she pushed open the door, leaned into the doorway, and waited for Greta to precede her, she caught Shannon watching them. As Greta passed, she squeezed Maya's ass so briefly she might have thought she imagined it if she didn't seen Shannon's eyes dip and then go cold.

"Chef Vaughn, are you coming?" Greta called over her shoulder.

"Oh, hell. No time soon, I suspect," Maya mumbled as she stepped across the threshold and released the door. Before it swung shut she saw Shannon go back to work.

"There's a great deli down the street if you don't mind walking a couple of blocks." Maya guided her through the backstage area.

"I had something a little more intimate in mind. Can't we send someone to get takeout—" Greta waved her hand at the crewmembers moving around them. "Then we go to your dressing room."

Shannon's disappointed expression lingered in Maya's mind and suddenly she didn't want to be alone with Greta, but she didn't want to admit it. So she flagged down a production assistant and gave him an order.

In her dressing room, Greta settled on the couch and patted the cushion. Instead, Maya leaned against the desk on the adjacent wall and folded her arms across her chest.

"Your producer hasn't announced this yet, but the fifth-anniversary party is tonight and you all are invited," Greta said.

"That's great. I'm sure the chefs will enjoy getting a break from the competition for a night."

"Yes. But getting you, Wayne, and Jacques in the restaurant is the real coup. When I was contacted by the show, I thought I might get to spend a few minutes with you at the party. But I never dreamed I'd get so much uninterrupted time alone with you."

"It's hardly uninterrupted. Our food will be arriving soon. And people are constantly coming and going around here." Bringing Greta in here was a mistake. If Maya wanted to hold onto the hope that there might be something between her and Shannon, she couldn't let anything happen with Greta.

Greta stalked across the room. Maya straightened, prepared to move. Greta slipped her hand inside Maya's jacket, skimmed her stomach, then touched her waist.

"I don't want to be rude, but what you're thinking—it's not going to happen." Maya tamped down the instinctive flutter of arousal stirred by the touch of a beautiful woman. She was human, after all.

"I'm not doing a whole lot of thinking right now." Greta ran her hands up Maya's chest and clasped them behind her neck, then leaned in and pressed her lips to Maya's. Before she could stop herself, Maya returned the kiss. When Greta eased back, she said, "I'm a big girl. I don't expect anything from you."

Maya grasped her upper arms and pushed her back farther. Greta's assumption that she knew all about Maya was like a bucket of cold water. "It's not happening."

"I didn't think 'hard to get' was part of your game." Greta's eyes glittered with confidence. She clearly thought she still controlled the outcome of this encounter.

"I'm not playing games." She stepped around Greta and strode to the door. She clamped her mouth closed against the urge to shout that Greta didn't know anything about her, then opened the door. "Our lunch should be here soon. We should wait in the lounge."

"Maya—"

"Chef Haus." She made sure her tone left no room for argument. Greta flashed her one more sultry look, but this time she had no trouble shutting it out. She waved her hand at the door, waiting for Greta to pass through it.

"What's going on with you and Vaughn, anyway?" Alice asked before taking a bite of her turkey sandwich.

"What do you mean?" Shannon kept her voice low, though the other chefs had taken a table on the opposite end of the room.

"All those nights in the gym. And the looks you guys exchange when you think no one's watching. I'm not an idiot."

Shannon stared at her, trying to ascertain Alice's angle. Could she be trusted? Or was she hoping for a reason to cry foul if she lost the competition? A part of Shannon wanted to talk to someone about Maya. Normally, Jori was her go-to for personal advice. But since their phone calls were monitored, she'd been keeping their conversations short, doing little more than checking in and asking how business was at Drake's.

"I'm not getting any special treatment." In the end, she just couldn't bring herself to fully trust her. At Alice's hurt expression, Shannon winced. Maybe she'd called that one wrong.

"I wasn't implying that you were."

"I just didn't want you to think—"

"I know. She's just as hard on you as she is on us. I can see that."

Shannon nodded.

"So come on, dish with me."

"There's really nothing to tell. We work out at the same time. Just because we're both gay doesn't mean we're automatically compatible." She couldn't take the risk. She'd grown to like Alice, but she wasn't the type of person who engaged in girl talk. "I'm a forty-something mother—about to be a grandmother. What would someone like Maya Vaughn want with me?"

"Well, I wasn't going to say she was out of your league, but since you said it." Alice chuckled and Shannon clenched her teeth. "It's just that she has a—um, certain reputation. And I wouldn't want you to get hurt by having, you know—unrealistic expectations."

Shannon pressed her lips together and shook her head slowly. Alice wasn't saying anything Shannon hadn't thought herself. And somehow it sounded even more credible when Alice said it aloud. Maya was young, hot, and in demand. The image of Greta Haus grabbing Maya's ass flashed through Shannon's head. Greta was the kind of woman someone like Maya would be with—confident, innately sexy, and much more sophisticated than Shannon would ever be.

She hadn't imagined the spark between her and Maya. They were both stuck in this fishbowl until the show finished filming. Maybe Maya was just looking for a diversion until something better came along. And, with a sick feeling, she realized that Maya might see Greta Haus as something better.

"I wish they'd just come and get us already," Alice whined.

They'd finished their cakes and been dismissed to grab lunch while the mentors and Chef Haus looked over their submissions. Their lunch break had passed its usual hurried twenty-minute time frame and had extended for nearly an hour already.

"You know they want to make us sweat," Shannon said.

"I could look at the cakes and tell them how it should go. Ned's going to win. We could argue about which of us comes in second, but it's not an elimination challenge, so second doesn't really matter, does it?"

As if answering Alice's query, Hugh rounded the corner. "Let's go, kids."

He led them back to the kitchen where Greta Haus and the mentors were already waiting for them. Shannon slipped behind her counter. Their cakes had been moved to a display table a few feet away. The mentors stood opposite the competitors along with Greta, who kept sneaking glances at Maya. Maya didn't appear to be returning her attention, and Shannon would know because she was watching Maya closely.

Eric had started talking, but Shannon missed a lot of what he said. Somewhere she registered it as his usual spiel for the camera. After the first few days, she'd learned to tune some of that out and listen only for key phrases that indicated he was about to reveal something important. As his voice changed timbre and cadence, she focused on him once again.

"The winning cake, and the one that will be featured at the anniversary party at Klett Haus this evening, belongs to Ned."

Ned gave an exaggerated fist pump. Alice nodded, and Shannon wondered if she was even more pleased that she'd called it right than she would have been had *she* won.

"Chef Haus, I believe you have another announcement."

"I do." She paused and looked at him. He gave the tiniest nod, and she began speaking again as if she'd been waiting for his cue. "I'd like to invite all of you to attend the celebration tonight as my personal guests."

The chefs exchanged glances and smiles. Anything except the inside of this warehouse or their hotel suites was a welcome change. And a party at a restaurant meant conversation with people who weren't connected at all to the show—again a novelty for them these days.

"Okay, chefs, head back to the hotel. The cars will return to pick you up for the party in an hour. We'll see you there."

After the cameras stopped rolling, Hugh gathered them together for some additional information. They weren't to discuss the show with anyone at the party. Their interactions should be kept casual yet professional. Several cameramen would be moving around the party with handhelds to capture the evening. They would go as a group, and when it was time to leave, the cars would return and they were to leave together as well.

Shannon took all of this in while mentally reviewing her closet and thinking that she hadn't brought anything to wear to a party. Sure, she'd included some more formal clothes, but likely nothing that would compare to how Greta would probably dress. Comparing herself to Greta irritated her. If her suspicions about what had gone on while Greta and Maya were absent were correct, Maya had pretty much proved that she was exactly who the press portrayed her to be, yet Shannon still couldn't stop competing for her attention.

CHAPTER FOURTEEN

Jori pressed the mute button on the television remote long enough to confirm that she'd heard the garage door going up. When Sawyer's car engine quieted and the door connecting the garage to the house didn't open right away, Jori imagined her sitting in the driver's seat staring straight ahead. Sometimes the drive home wasn't enough to completely decompress, and Sawyer needed just a couple of minutes more to separate herself from being a restaurant manager before she came inside.

Jori pulled a throw from the back of the sofa and curled up at one end of it, trying to appear as if she hadn't been eagerly waiting for Sawyer's return. At times like this, a bit of the old Jori—the one who had to prove she didn't need anyone—snuck out.

The door from the garage opened, then closed quickly.

"I'm sorry." Sawyer called out the apology as she entered the living room. "We were swamped and down a server. The shipment of the new flooring came in, and I had to pull a couple of the guys to help stack it in the back room. So I ended up working in the dining room."

Jori nodded wordlessly.

Sawyer sat beside her with a sigh. She glanced at the television, recognizing the set of *For the Love of Cake*. "You're watching the new episode without me?"

"I didn't know how long you'd be. It's on the DVR."

Sawyer nodded, and though she didn't say anything, Jori suspected she might be hurt that Jori hadn't waited for her. Regret made Jori want to reach for her. She didn't complain about Jori's early hours, so why should Jori make her feel guilty about her late return?

"It's still weird seeing her on television," Sawyer said.

"Yes. Very. She looks nervous. I've seen her do much better work than she has so far. Maya didn't seem too impressed, either." Jori slid closer and snuggled against Sawyer's side. Sawyer gathered her close, easily accepting the olive branch. They'd both been much more stubborn in the early days of their relationship, holding grudges and staying mad over minor irritations.

"I thought you said you picked up on something when she was in the bakery?" Sawyer rested her hand on Jori's thigh, inched her fingers under the edge of her pajama shorts, and traced small circles on her skin.

"I did."

"Are you sure you weren't trying to live vicariously through Shannon? I remember how you both drooled over that picture."

"Maybe a little. You should be sorry you missed her, babe. Maya's even hotter in person." When Sawyer pressed her lips together and nodded, Jori smirked. "No, really. Tonight on the show, she barely noticed Shannon. She was just another person on the team. But when she was in the shop, there was a look—when she talked about Shannon. I don't know what it was, but she definitely wasn't dispassionate."

"I don't know, hon. You know I think Shannon's great. But I can't imagine they have much in common."

"You're probably right." Jori handed her the remote and headed for the kitchen. "I'm going to make cocoa. Do you want some?"

"Sure, that sounds good. You know, people can change. If you'd told me five years ago I'd be happily committed and domesticated, I wouldn't have believed you."

"Are you complaining?"

"Of course not. That's my point," Sawyer said.

"Honey, I know you like to think you were a badass when I met you. Don't take this the wrong way—but are you comparing yourself to Maya Vaughn?"

"Maybe a little."

Jori laughed. "A very little, I hope. She's way wilder than you ever thought about being." Jori set two mugs on the coffee table in front of them. She sat on the couch, pulled Sawyer into her arms, and gave her a lingering kiss. "Not that I'm complaining. I fell in love with you then, and I still love you now."

"My point was, you and I were very different, and even wanting different things in our lives when we met—"

"But we work," Jori said. "I'm not saying they're hooking up. But I did get the feeling she had some degree of respect and affection for Shannon beyond just the professional."

❖

"I've been imagining you here. In my restaurant."

Maya grimaced and stepped back as she turned, in order to put a bit more distance between herself and Greta.

"It's a charming place," she said politely, ignoring the innuendo in Greta's voice. Once, such a line might have had her picturing them doing dirty things alone here after hours. But now, she remained focused only on the restaurant.

Greta hadn't overdone the German theme, yet the influence was definitely present in the dark woods, exposed beams, and the array of German beers lining the shelf behind the bar that spanned one entire wall of the restaurant.

"I'm lousy at decorating. I hired a pro." Greta nodded toward the bar. "We have a lot of loyal beer patrons, so dedicating a little extra space for the bar saved us from the groups that come in just to drink and tie up the tables."

Strings of clear bulbs decorated the dining room, and a table had been set up in a corner where Ned's cake was featured.

"Any chance you've reconsidered my offer from this afternoon? I have a private office in the back—"

"I haven't changed my mind." She lifted a glass of champagne from the tray of a passing waiter. She'd learned that she could carry a full glass around most of the evening, and if she already had one in her hand, she was less likely to get one foisted on her.

"You're not at all what I expected, Maya Vaughn." Greta tilted her head and regarded her with an amused expression.

"I'm going to take that as a compliment." She gave her most polite—most fake smile. "If you'll excuse me, I need to go check in with Hugh."

She didn't wait for a response before heading across the room. She wandered over to where Hugh stood with Jacques in case Greta was still watching. And when she turned to speak to Hugh, she caught Greta looking away.

She exchanged a few pleasantries, enough to make Greta think she'd had a substantial conversation. After all the guests arrived, Hugh planned to present the cake and introduce Ned, as well as the other three chefs. Other than that, Maya only had to mingle and be friendly tonight. She'd been here only fifteen minutes, and every time she turned around she found a camera in her face. She already couldn't wait until the night was over.

She'd just started chatting with one guest, who had pompously introduced himself as Nashville's next district attorney, pending the tiny detail of an election, of course, when she caught sight of the four competitors entering.

Despite the producers' concerns about diversity heading into the finale, they couldn't have ended up with a more different group of competitors, and tonight their appearance reflected their personalities. Mason's classic dark suit and tie represented him perfectly, understated and steady, whereas Ned's electric-blue jacket matched his hair. The collar of his black shirt lay open, and a thick chain with a large silver cross rested against his chest. Alice's flowered dress spoke of her small-town charm. Shannon's hair swept back from her face in a simple up-do, but not as severe as the buns she favored on the show. Now, loose tendrils fell against her cheek. The patterned gray scarf draped around her neck added an understated accent to her simple black dress.

The dress looked new, and given what she'd learned about Shannon, Maya guessed she'd purchased it to bring along to the competition. The producers would have told her to include several dressier outfits along with everyday clothes. Though Shannon wasn't given to extravagances, she'd admitted to Maya that she liked to shop when she had a worthy occasion. Maya, too, enjoyed browsing a clothing rack, whether it was at a high-end store or a thrift shop. She thrilled over the unusual finds and putting together cool accessories with the simplest jeans and T-shirts. In fact, she loved poring through local boutiques when she traveled. And for a moment, she imagined how much fun it would be to have Shannon with her, searching the racks for just the right edgy jacket to pair with Shannon's usual functional pieces.

"It was good to meet you, Ms. Vaughn," the future district attorney said, and Maya realized she'd missed most of his remarks for several minutes. He, however, didn't seem to notice. She smiled and nodded, a gesture she'd perfected over the years to encourage the other person to carry the conversation. He gave her an insincere grin of his own and continued. "We certainly have our share of celebrities in this town." He placed his hand alongside his mouth, palm out as if about to tell her a secret. "A few I've even aided during my days as a criminal-defense attorney."

He seemed to be implying that she might know what it was like to be on the wrong side of a courtroom, thus indicating he knew little to nothing about her. Despite her bad-girl image, she'd never been in trouble with the law. She didn't drink and drive, she'd never been arrested—hell, she'd never even assaulted a paparazzi, though she'd run into more than one who might have deserved it.

❖

Shannon paused just inside the door, hovering at the edge of the group of competitors. She scanned the room, telling herself she just wanted to see if she recognized anyone local. She located Greta near the bar, apparently giving instructions to a group of servers. She was inordinately pleased to find that Maya was nowhere in the vicinity. On some level, she'd been mentally preparing herself to see the two of them together again.

Resuming her visual voyage around the room, she found Maya talking to a rotund man near the center of the room. She seemed only half-interested in the conversation. In fact, it was difficult to tell from her distance and because she was angled slightly away from the door, but she actually felt Maya's attention directed at their side of the room.

Shannon gave her a quick once-over, surprised by the sedate black pantsuit. The well-tailored jacket traced the lines of her torso and ended a few inches below her waist, leaving Shannon the perfect view of Maya's amazing ass inside wonderfully fitted slacks. When Maya turned their way, the edges of her jacket gaped open to reveal a red, lacy bustier, and Shannon's mouth went dry. So much for a sedate pantsuit. If only she were close enough to see the swells of breasts lifted so perfectly by that garment.

Alice laughed and, startled, Shannon jerked her eyes away from Maya.

"What?"

"I wish you could see your face. You wouldn't be trying to convince me you're not lusting after her."

"Okay. She's gorgeous. I never denied that."

"We probably have a few minutes before they corral us so we can all pat Ned on the back. You should go talk to her."

"You don't even like her. *And* you already warned me about getting my hopes up. So why are you encouraging me to spend time with her now?"

Alice shrugged. "I may not like her, but that doesn't mean I don't see the way you light up when you look at her. If you're determined to get your heart broken, who am I to stop you?"

She wasn't sure if Alice was being a friend or not. She still seemed to believe Maya couldn't possibly return her interest or that Maya was capable of being more than the player everyone else saw her as. Maybe she hoped heartache would distract Shannon from success on the show.

Shannon looked at Maya again. She'd shoved her hands in the front pockets of her pants, pushing the lower edges of her jacket behind them. The contrast of the very feminine flash of red smoothing over her breasts and stomach and into the somewhat masculine low-rise waistband of her tuxedo-like pants did strange things to Shannon's heart rate. She stepped forward, with only a little regard for their surroundings. She glanced discreetly around for the cameras, but even if one of the guys with the handhelds was following her, she didn't think she could stop her feet from propelling her forward. She couldn't be in a room with Maya without talking to her—without wanting to be near her.

Maya turned away from the gentleman she'd been talking to just as Shannon walked up. And as she spun, she almost ran into Shannon.

"You got a haircut," Shannon blurted.

"Yeah. I asked one of the stylists to stay after filming today and do it before the party." Maya rubbed her hand over her hair, ruffling it in the most adorable way. "He went a little shorter on top than I'm used to."

"Turn around." Shannon circled one finger in the air.

Maya spun slowly. The sides and back were as short as always, but the top had been cut a couple of inches shorter than she usually wore it and had been styled into a faux hawk.

"I like it."

"Really?"

"Yes. Especially with that outfit." She couldn't seem to keep her eyes from dipping toward Maya's cleavage for an obscenely long moment of appreciation.

Maya raised her eyebrows. "If I didn't know better, I'd think you were tempted to flirt with me a little just now."

She smiled, the laid-back atmosphere of the party apparently keeping her more relaxed than usual. She didn't even care that she'd so obviously cruised Maya just now. "Maybe the champagne is going to my head."

Maya laughed. "I don't believe you've had any yet."

"Are you sure? Because I'm feeling a bit light-headed already." She shouldn't have said it, and she certainly shouldn't have allowed that teasing lilt into her voice. But a part of her wanted to prove that she hadn't imagined the attraction between them. Though Alice didn't believe Maya would be interested, and because Greta so obviously was, Shannon just might have a chance, even if she still contended that she didn't want one. By the time she'd finished thinking she'd confused even herself.

Maya tilted her head but didn't respond, almost as if she could see the circular logic running around in Shannon's head. She pressed the flute she'd been holding into Shannon's hand, letting her fingers trail along the backs of Shannon's knuckles as she let go. "Take mine."

Shannon drained it quickly, then looked around for someplace to set the empty glass. She grinned and gave a half shrug. "In the movies, right now I'd place this on the tray of the perfectly timed passing waiter and grab another glass."

"Sadly, things so rarely happen like they do in the movies."

"That's right."

Just then a waiter walked by with a full tray. Maya grabbed another glass and switched out the empty one in Shannon's hand. "Not quite as smooth as if it was directed, but close enough."

Shannon lifted her glass in a salute before taking another sip. She held back with this glass, because even though she wasn't opposed to a good buzz right now, she really was a bit of a lightweight when it came to champagne.

"Have you ever been here before?" Maya asked.

"Once. On a horrible first date."

"How can a date that begins at the Clit House go wrong?"

The champagne Shannon had just tried to delicately sip almost came out her nose. She managed to contain it to just a tiny cough and a tickle of bubbles that made her eyes water.

"That's horrible," she rasped.

"Tell me that's not what it sounded like when Eric said it."

"It really did." She laughed out loud, then covered her mouth with her hand when she accidently snorted. Her face burned with embarrassment, and she looked around quickly but no one else seemed to have heard it. After a flash of confusion across her features, Maya smiled so widely it didn't seem she could be holding anything back, and another rush of heat raced up Shannon's neck. "What?" Shannon waved a finger in Maya's face. "What's that expression?"

The smile dropped from Maya's lips, and she pulled the lower one between her teeth. For a moment, the anticipation of what she might say had Shannon's heart racing. But whatever had brought the serious look flew away just as quickly, and her eyes shifted to neutral. "Nothing."

Shannon was about to question her further when she caught a movement out of the corner of her eye. A cameraman skirted around a large group, apparently angling for a shot of the two of them. Shannon quickly assessed their positions, assuring herself that with the respectable distance between them, they could simply look like mentor and mentee.

While she was keeping an eye on the cameraman, Greta had approached and purred a greeting to Maya.

Shannon spun back around, and her head swam a little at the too-quick motion. How many glasses of champagne had she had?

"Good evening, Chef Hayes." Greta greeted her politely but with an air of detachment. But when she spoke again, to Maya, her voice dropped to a more personal tone, and she wrapped her hand around Maya's bicep. "Are you going to hide over here talking shop all night?"

Shannon bristled at the implication that they had nothing to talk about except the show. Maya didn't seem as adversely affected. Granted, her smile seemed forcibly polite, but she also covered Greta's hand and gave it an obvious squeeze.

"I think we're both here for work, at least a little bit, aren't we?"

"Well, of course, but that doesn't mean we can't enjoy a little pleasure as well, does it?"

Shannon rolled her eyes at the way Greta drew out the question. She obviously imagined herself as some type of siren, but truthfully, she wasn't even very good. She was beautiful, Shannon had to give her that. Maybe when you looked like that, it didn't matter so much what you said.

"Unfortunately, tonight is all business for me." Maya winked at Greta as if they shared some private secret, and Shannon began looking for a way to escape the awkward situation. These two probably wouldn't even notice she was gone. She'd just taken two steps away when Maya grabbed her arm. "Actually, Greta, I think Hugh is going to need Shannon and me soon for the cake presentation. So if you'll excuse us. Perhaps I'll catch up with you later."

Shannon tried to jerk her arm away, but Maya held on.

"I hope you'll find me when you're through."

Maya led Shannon toward the other end of the room where some of the chefs had gathered.

"You just can't help yourself, can you?" Shannon ground out when they'd cleared Greta's earshot.

"What?"

Now she did pull her arm away, irrationally angry that she missed the contact as soon as it was gone. "The touching, the flirting—it's part of who you are."

"I guess I don't always think about it." When Shannon gave her a look of disbelief, she said, "Okay. I never think about it. Stuff just comes out of my mouth."

"So you think you can flash that sexy smile and it's okay—it's just who you are?"

"You think my smile is sexy?" Maya raised her pierced brow and one side of her mouth in that way that made Shannon melt and, now, made her even more irritated with her inability to control her reactions.

"Oh, you know it is. That's why you do it." The champagne made her more honest than she'd intended.

Maya steered them off to the side of the room and slowed their progress toward the rest of the group. When they got close to a door leading to an unoccupied patio, she pushed Shannon through it. "Yes, it's an automatic reaction. What do you want me to say?" She continued forward so Shannon had no choice but to back up.

"Nothing. Never mind." She liked thinking that it didn't mean anything when Maya flirted with Greta, but she didn't want to hear that Maya wasn't engaged when she flirted with *her*—that it was reflex.

"Nothing happened." Maya met Shannon's eyes, but her expression was unreadable in the shadows of the darkened patio.

Shannon laughed harshly. "I don't believe that. I saw her grab your ass in the kitchen earlier today. Women don't typically do that without encouragement."

"They do when they think they'll get something out of it. Women don't always come on to me because they're interested in *me*." Maya tugged at the front of her hair in seeming frustration. "Okay, you want details? Yes, she kissed me. In my dressing room. I stopped it there."

Shannon smothered a gasp at the ache that stabbed her chest at the thought of Maya and Greta in her dressing room. "No. No, I don't think I want the details," she whispered.

"This is ridiculous. You're mad at me because someone flirted with me?" Maya backed off, lowering her voice, and leaned against the brick half wall that separated the empty patio from the parking lot.

"I didn't see you fighting her off." Shannon spoke softer as well. She glanced through the glass panes in the patio door to make sure their raised voices hadn't drawn any attention, then shook her head to clear away her inappropriate possessiveness. "I'm not *mad* at you. I don't have any right to—"

"I was being polite."

"Please don't insult me. I saw what I saw."

"What do you care who I flirt with?" Maya snapped.

"I—I don't—I just—"

"What?" Maya sounded frustrated.

"Because you—I don't know."

"Ah—God, just say it," she growled. "Just—say it. Why would it bother you if something did happen with her? That's obviously exactly what you and everyone else expect of me anyway."

"Because I want you to flirt with me," Shannon practically shouted, then winced as her words echoed across the parking lot around them. Her declaration was made even bigger by the silence that followed it.

Maya stared at her.

"I want you to flirt with me and mean it," Shannon whispered into the stillness.

"Well, why didn't you say so?" Maya smiled.

"Because it's not a good idea."

"You keep saying that to me. And I'm supposed to—what—just accept it?" She pushed away from the wall and took a several frustrated steps toward Shannon, still keeping an arm's length between them.

"Yes."

"Then tell me why."

"What?"

"Why isn't it a good idea? Why shouldn't we give in to the incredible urge to do something that feels so good—something I promise we would both enjoy very much?"

Shannon's response died as the force of Maya's words hit her, coupled with images of them together that only a masochistic mind could conjure up. "I—we—I can't think when I look at you."

"Tell me why we can't." When Shannon would have looked away, Maya grasped her chin and forced her to meet her eyes. "We were just opening this conversation up. Don't stop now."

"You already know," she said, resignation making her voice heavy.

"I don't."

"The show—"

"No. Not good enough." Maya shook her head. "The show is so temporary. It'll be over in a couple of months."

"But Hugh—"

"Forget about Hugh. He doesn't have to know. Next?"

"We're from two different worlds." She resorted to generalities, because, even half drunk, she knew better than to bring up certain things with Maya, especially here where neither of them could escape when the conversation got too hard.

"Honey, I hate to break it to you. But you're about to be from two different worlds yourself. Do you think you'll just step back into your old life once the show is over?"

"That just makes my point. You'll go back to New York and I'll—who knows what I'll do. I have a lot to figure out."

Maya gave a resigned sigh and nodded. But she looked like she wanted to say something more. Without another word, Maya turned and walked back inside.

Shannon squelched the bubble of hope that Maya had wanted to ask Shannon to make her a part of those decisions. She'd admit to some harmless fantasizing about Maya, probably since the first time she'd seen her on her own season of the show. But she shouldn't delude herself into believing they had some kind of future.

CHAPTER FIFTEEN

Maya stared out the front window of the black SUV as if she could see into the matching one just ahead of them. Yet even if she could see Shannon, she wouldn't be any closer to understanding their conversation at the party. Shannon was jealous of Greta, that much she got. In fact, she kind of liked it. She even agreed with many of the reasons they shouldn't pursue the attraction between them. What she couldn't get her head around was why it bothered her so much. While she wasn't exactly the "love 'em, and leave 'em" chick people believed she was, she also didn't do much sticking around.

But when it came to Shannon, she wanted nothing more than to be there. Shannon had said she wanted Maya to flirt with her and mean it. And Maya really did. She found it difficult to be in the same room without wanting to be closer to her. And once she was near, she wanted to touch her—sometimes the urge for the kind of casual, comforting touches that couples shared came on surprisingly strong.

The two cars stopped under the portico of their hotel. As soon as Maya closed the door, both vehicles pulled away, leaving the group of them standing there together. Wayne and Jacques nodded at her, then disappeared inside, followed closely by Ned and Mason. By the time Maya tried to follow the others, Alice had stopped in the middle of the sidewalk, blocking the entrance.

"I'm not ready for bed yet. That party was a bit of a dud." Alice grabbed Shannon's arm. "Let's go out."

"What? Where?"

"I don't know. This is your town."

"I don't think we're supposed to—"

"Please?"

Maya moved to step around them. "Have a good evening, ladies. Don't worry. I won't rat you out." Her arm brushed Shannon's shoulder, and, as she eased past, she instinctively touched the small of Shannon's back.

"You should come along," Alice said.

"I'm not sure the producers would like that."

"My mistake. I thought you were a rebel." Alice was challenging her.

Maya raised her brows and glanced at Shannon, who shrugged. Maya couldn't decide if that meant she wanted her to join them or if she simply felt as trapped as Maya did. Now that she thought about it, Shannon hadn't actually agreed to go yet. What if she agreed and Shannon bowed out, leaving her alone with Alice?

"I'm in." She held Shannon's eyes and tried to convey her hope that Shannon wouldn't abandon her.

Shannon nodded. "Okay. I'll show you where you should have gone when you went out on your own."

"Great." Alice looped her arm through Shannon's and pulled her down the street. "And we already have our party clothes on. Where are we going? Can we walk there from here?"

As Maya followed them along the sidewalk, she couldn't hear Shannon's answers as each one was drowned out by the next question. Shannon stopped suddenly next to a taxi parked by the curb. She pulled open the door and waited for Alice to get in.

"We could walk, but this is faster." She jumped in behind Alice and slid to the center of the seat.

Maya got in last and pulled the door closed. With the three of them in there, Maya was pressed tightly against Shannon, and her other side hugged the door. She slipped her shoulder behind Shannon's and tried not to notice the way Shannon's arm rested on top of hers or how little effort it would take to hold her hand.

Shannon leaned up and gave the driver their destination. As she sat back, she looked at Maya. In the mix of darkness and streetlamp glow, the planes of Shannon's face appeared more dramatic, and, though they weren't alone, the moment felt almost more intimate than Maya could handle.

"Are you really okay with this?" Shannon asked quietly while Alice continued chattering about the architecture of the bridge they crossed.

"Which part?" She turned her hand over and caressed her fingers against the underside of Shannon's wrist, confident that their legs hid the move from Alice's sight.

"How much trouble are we in if we get caught?"

Maya let her eyes drop to Shannon's lips, purposely misunderstanding just what she thought they might get caught doing.

"Stop." Shannon's firm voice didn't erase the images in her head.

"You can't make me," she said stubbornly, then sighed. "Hugh will be pissed. But mostly because he didn't catch us in time to get someone to tail us. His biggest concern is the show. And he loves to ramp up the drama. Haven't you ever noticed that the questions in those *interviews* they pull us into every so often are geared toward pitting you guys against each other?"

"I never thought about it."

"They don't put you in teams so you can work together. They do it because if you have to work closely in very small groups, you're more likely to blow up at each other."

Shannon was quiet for the rest of the ride. Maya took the opportunity to watch the neighborhoods change outside the window. The tall buildings of downtown gave way to a four-lane street lined with old gas stations, discount beer and tobacco markets, and storefronts with iron bars on the windows. Two blocks later, she began to see signs of rehabbing—fresh paint and new fences.

The cab stopped and Maya handed the fare through the divider before she climbed out. Three bars lined the sidewalk. Across the street a bicycle shop had already gone dark for the night.

"This way." Shannon led them into the bar in the middle.

Inside, Maya immediately inhaled a mix of yeasty beer, fried foods, and cigarette smoke. A group of college-age kids clustered around the bar. And the two tables in the back held a crowd of hipsters obviously too cool for personal hygiene.

"When did beards come back in, anyway?" Maya asked as they settled around one of several empty tables.

"I don't like them," Alice said.

"Right. Too itchy." Maya rubbed her cheek.

"There are darts and pool tables in the back room, if you're into that," Shannon said.

"I love darts." Alice glanced around. "But first I want a beer."

"Me too."

"Great. You two have so much in common," Shannon murmured, clearly referring to more than the darts, but Maya didn't think Alice heard her.

Maya narrowed her eyes at Shannon but decided not to call her on the snarky comment. "You were right. This place is much better than that club I went to."

Their waitress came by a couple minutes later and introduced herself. She took their order, and Maya slipped her credit card to her in order to start a tab. She signaled to put all of the drinks for the table on it.

Maya wanted to settle back in her chair and watch Shannon, but she ended up fielding questions from Alice about everything ranging from New York City to how she got her hair to stand up the way she did.

When she bent her head and rubbed her hand over her head, still getting used to the shorter length, she caught Shannon's intent gaze. Maya could practically feel Shannon's fingers sifting through her hair and caressing her scalp. Goosebumps rose on her arms, and from the way Shannon stared, she wasn't the only one entertaining fantasies.

"Who wants another?" Alice asked.

"One is my limit," Maya said.

"One?" Shannon's chuckle turned to a cough as she must have realized Maya was serious. "Really?"

Maya nodded.

"Okay," Alice said. "Let me know if you change your mind." She headed for the bar, leaving Maya and Shannon sitting in awkward silence.

"Not what you expected?" Maya asked.

"Not at all."

"I don't like being drunk. It slows me down too much." She would have bet that Shannon was recalling the many grainy tabloid photos in which Maya seemed to be partying hard. But the pictures never told the whole story.

"Are you really that much of a control freak?"

Maya clenched her teeth and tightened her jaw, wishing she'd just taken the drink and nursed it like she always did. What was it about Shannon that made her want to open up?

Shannon covered Maya's hand and squeezed. "I'm sorry. I just meant—you seem to be fearless and fly by the seat of your pants in the kitchen. I assumed you were as—"

"What? Reckless?"

"Well, yes. But more like carefree, really. I didn't mean it in a bad way."

"It's okay. I think I know what you meant." Maya withdrew her hand.

"Maya."

"It's fine." Her first reaction was anger. She'd spent the past seven years being judged by people who didn't know her, and she wanted Shannon to be different. Sometimes she was, and then she said something to remind Maya of her complete lack of privacy. "I don't drink much. It's not a big deal. I don't have some hidden addiction or anything. You watched my season. You know I partied a lot during that time."

Shannon nodded.

"I saw people around me doing a lot of stupid things back then and using alcohol as an excuse. I witnessed how much someone can fuck up their life without a conscious thought, and I don't want to be one of those people. Despite those party days, I don't have a high tolerance for alcohol, so it doesn't take much for me to feel out of control. So, yes, I guess I *am* a control freak."

"I'm sorry." Under the table, Shannon laid her hand on Maya's thigh. "I understand. And that's actually admirable."

God, Maya couldn't resist when her voice went all soft like that. But something about Shannon viewing her as honorable in some way didn't sit right either. So many times she'd acted selfishly, and yes, she had been reckless, with her choices and with others by extension. She stood and wandered toward the back room. She could feel Shannon following her, but she didn't acknowledge her. The area around the pool tables was more crowded than the front had been. She waited while a guy took his shot then edged around to the far wall. She leaned against a bar stool next to the wall, not really sitting but just resting the edge of her butt on the seat. Shannon caught her and grabbed her wrist.

"Hey. Really. I'm sorry."

Maya stared at her for longer than was polite, then finally nodded before averting her eyes. No one was playing darts, and, in fact, no one could since the area in front of the boards had been turned into an impromptu dance floor. Couples of all races and genders swayed to the slow jazz coming from large speakers around the room. Maya watched them, jealous of their freedom to embrace each other. She pushed off from the stool, latching on to the excuse to hold Shannon in her arms.

"Dance with me."

"I can't."

"You can't dance?"

"I can't dance with *you*."

"Why not?"

"I can't be that close—"

"How close?" She took a step forward, leaving only inches between them. "This close?" She'd intended to tease Shannon a bit, but too late, she realized she'd tortured herself as well.

Shannon's eyes flashed with heat, but even though she had plenty of space behind her, she didn't move away. "I can't touch you without completely giving myself away." Shannon's words hit

Maya like a wave, crashing white-hot lust over her until she thought she might drown in it.

"It's just one dance." She forged the lie in an effort to recover from the naked desire in Shannon's expression and the answering pull within her.

"No. It's not."

"Do you know how bad I want to kiss you right now?" Desperate now, she threw the most honest words she could think of into the tense space between them.

"I have some idea."

Knowing that Shannon was just as affected by their exchange didn't make it any easier to restrain herself. She couldn't breathe without pulling in the fresh, lightly floral scent of Shannon's perfume. When Shannon looked away, she got a reprieve from the intensity of her gaze, but the smooth length of neck exposed by the turn of her head didn't ease the ache. She leaned closer and spoke near Shannon's ear, tormenting herself with a close-up view of the skin she wanted her mouth against. "I can't think of a good-enough reason not to."

Just then a blinding camera flash cut through the darkened room. She jerked back and looked around, but she was still seeing stars from the bright light and couldn't make out who had taken a photo and of what. Shannon stared at her with an expression of panic.

"That would be one reason." Shannon's voice sounded surprisingly calm, but Maya guessed it was numbness that dulled her tone.

"Shannon—"

"I have to get out of here." Shannon sounded like she might be starting to panic.

Before either of them could move, Alice hurried up to them. "What was that? Who was taking pictures?"

"I don't know." Maya glanced around, but apparently whoever it was had slipped away. Several bystanders stared at them, but none looked guilty enough to be the culprit.

"On my way over, I saw a guy watching you two, right before it happened."

"Let's get out of here." Maya herded them both toward the door, making a quick stop on the way to close out their bar tab.

By the time she got outside, Shannon and Alice had already flagged down a cab and waited inside. She climbed in and gave the hotel address. She considered trying to drag a more detailed description out of Alice, but most likely even a good physical description wouldn't tell her who he was or if he intended to profit from the picture.

"What do we do?" Shannon bounced her leg nervously.

"Nothing." She tried to sound calm. And honestly, she usually didn't worry about this kind of thing. But the idea that a picture could surface that might hurt Shannon had her more wound up than usual.

"Nothing?"

Maya put her hand on Shannon's knee to stop the bouncing. She didn't want to move her hand, but Alice was watching them both closely, so she pulled it back quickly.

"We don't know who the guy was or if he even realized who we were." She looked at Alice. "You're sure he was watching us?"

She nodded, uncharacteristically mute.

"But we don't know for sure the photo was of us. We weren't exactly looking around. We may have just caught the flash from someone taking a selfie."

"And if we didn't? If some photo of us looking as if—" Shannon stopped, flicking her eyes toward Alice. She rubbed her forehead. "Hugh will have a heart attack. He'll keel over and die right in front of us. The ambulance will come and carry him off and I'll feel guilty for—"

"Hey, stop talking. You're beginning to sound like—" Maya bit her lip and avoided looking at Alice. "Whatever happens, we'll deal with it. But we can't do anything but worry until the photo shows up."

Shannon nodded. They rode the rest of the way to the hotel in silence. When they got out of the cab, Maya wished she could go back to earlier in the evening when they stood in front of the hotel, only this time she would refuse the offer to join them. Chances were Shannon and Alice wouldn't have been recognized on their own.

When the elevator doors opened on their floor, Shannon and Alice barely looked back as they exited.

"Try not to worry. You need your sleep," Maya called.

"Yeah, right." Though Shannon didn't turn around, she raised her hand and waved behind her.

❖

Shannon turned over and punched the pillow next to her head. She flipped off the covers and stared at the ceiling. She'd been pretending she could sleep for the past two hours. She knew it had been two hours because she'd watched the numbers change on her alarm clock for the better part of that time.

She'd managed a few restless hours broken up by strange dreams involving paparazzi chasing Maya and her through the streets of downtown. Maya stumbled and yelled for her to go on, but she went back for her and they were both swallowed up by the mob. As the faces closed in around them she woke up. She didn't need help interpreting that dream. But then again, her dreams were never very mysterious. Stress always definitively affected her sleep.

Giving up, she got out of bed and headed for the kitchenette. She filled the coffeemaker and sat down to wait for the strongest brew she could handle. She had a feeling she'd need more than one cup to make it through this day.

Maybe she didn't need to worry. The flash didn't necessarily mean there was a picture of them out there floating around. People took drunken bar photos all the time. If she got through today and nothing happened, maybe then she could relax.

Alice's door opened and she stumbled out. "Coffee?"

"Working on it." Shannon poured two cups and handed her one. "Did I wake you?"

Alice shook her head. "Do you think we'll get busted for going out?"

"You didn't seem too worried about that when you talked us into it." She added just a splash of creamer to make her coffee palatable.

"You don't think they'll send us home for that, do you?"

"No. Besides, there's probably no proof you were even there. And I won't tell."

"What will you do if the photo comes out?"

Shannon shrugged. "I guess denial would be out."

Alice shook her head slowly. "I just don't know what will happen. I mean, they could send you home. The others might say you only made it this far because of her. It seems like the show would have to make an example of both of you. I'm so glad I'm not a lesbian. I just don't know what I would do if I got kicked off the show—"

Shannon interrupted with a sharp laugh. "I'm sorry. Did you just say you're glad you're not a lesbian?"

"Yes."

"You know this could as easily have happened between one of you and a male mentor, right?"

"Jacques is married and—well, old, but Wayne is pretty good-looking." She seemed to be giving the idea further consideration but then shook her head. "He's not like Maya though."

"What does that mean?"

"You always see stories about her and all these men and women. From the pictures, she seems pretty friendly. And then there's the way she was with Greta yesterday. Everyone saw them leave the kitchen together. They were gone the whole time we worked on our cakes. That's plenty of time to—you know."

"You know? Are you twelve?" Shannon snapped, then took a calming breath. "Nothing happened between them."

"She told you that?"

"Yes."

"And you believe her?"

"Why would she lie?" Shannon resisted the doubts Alice's words planted in her head.

"To hook up with you. I heard she was sleeping with one of the guys on her season. And that every time she comes back to consult or guest judge, she picks one of the chefs to try to seduce. And she usually succeeds."

"Where did you hear that?"

"One of the lighting guys told me. And he's been here since the first season."

Maya had a reputation as a player, she knew that. So this new information shouldn't be a surprise. But somehow it didn't fit with the woman she'd come to know. So was it just gossip? Or was Maya playing her as well? She could certainly point to moments when Maya's flirtation with her seemed less than sincere—like it was habitual behavior. But there had also been times, when they were alone in the fitness room, when she'd felt as if they truly connected—like they could be just two women getting to know each other. Could she be fooling herself to think someone like Maya could find her interesting? Maybe she was just this season's conquest, and next season the crew would be gossiping about her?

CHAPTER SIXTEEN

I'll be late getting home." Sawyer pulled the full carafe from the coffeemaker and filled two travel mugs.

"How late?" Jori spread a light layer of butter on her wheat toast.

"I don't know. Don't wait up."

"Are you going in now?"

Sawyer nodded.

Jori gritted her teeth to keep from complaining. She'd been surprised when Sawyer jumped in the shower right after she vacated it. Sawyer never got up this early. Yet, she already knew she would be home so late that Jori shouldn't wait up.

"Jori—"

Jori raised a hand, palm out, before Sawyer could continue. "It's fine."

"You're obviously not happy—"

"It's fine. I'm not going to say anything. Because then I'm the asshole who demands too much of your time. And I've never been that person, Sawyer. I haven't. And I'm not."

"Things are busy right now. But soon the bakery will make enough to hire someone else, and in a few months, our restaurant tourist traffic will slow down—"

"Nothing's going to change. Stop promising me things will be different." Frustrated, she rubbed the back of her neck.

She'd been working so hard to stay ahead—in her business and in her life. She kept telling herself they would have time, later, to talk about the future—about kids. Maybe they would even want a wedding someday. But how long would they need before they felt ready? And would it be too late? She'd never heard her biological clock ticking—and she still didn't—but deep down she knew she would someday.

Years ago, she'd prepared herself for the disappointment of never finding that future. But since Sawyer, she'd let herself believe she could have everything she wanted. So when her dream of owning her bakery was within reach, she never questioned trying. She'd never thought about how it might affect her relationship or their future because she'd had faith that together they could do anything. And though she knew it wasn't right, on some level, she blamed Sawyer for making her believe she deserved her dreams.

"Jori?" Sawyer touched her shoulder gently and Jori felt guilty for her doubts.

She shook her head. She wanted to reassure Sawyer they would be okay—that she was just stressed. But the words wouldn't come. Despite all of her hope that they were doing what was right for both of them, she had serious concerns.

Sawyer's heavy sigh conveyed her frustration as well. "What do you want me to do? This isn't all on me. The bakery takes as much of your time as Drake's does mine. It isn't my fault you had to open a business that requires the exact opposite schedule as mine."

"So it's all my fault."

"I didn't mean—"

"What did you mean? Because it sounds like you're saying that your business is more important than mine."

"No. But I had mine first," Sawyer blurted out, then quickly sucked in a breath as if she wanted to pull the words back in.

"What?"

"You knew what you were getting into. I've worked the same schedule practically since we met. The same schedule you worked when you were at Drake's and would have continued working if you'd stayed there."

"Well, now I realize how you really feel. That would have been nice to know when I was actively soliciting your advice while making *life-changing decisions.*"

"I can't do this right now. I have to get to the restaurant." Sawyer crossed to her quickly and kissed her cheek, then was out the door before Jori could say anything more. On her way out, Jori heard her say, "I love you."

Jori dropped into a chair at the kitchen table. Now she had to drop by the restaurant later today and apologize. Yes, she'd picked a fight. But it had been easy to do, given Sawyer's distraction and short temper of late. Ultimately, Sawyer wasn't wrong. Since she'd opened the bakery, they'd had precious little time together. Early on in their relationship, Jori would have been angry that Sawyer left without resolving things. But now she understood, Sawyer needed space and work to distract her. Later, they'd make up.

She gathered up her breakfast dishes and had just put them in the sink when her cell phone rang.

"Hello." Aggravation still colored her tone.

"Bad time?" Shannon asked hesitantly.

"No." She took a breath, trying to get the edge out of her voice.

"Okay." Shannon drew out the word, letting Jori know she didn't believe her.

"Maybe. I don't know. Sawyer's acting strange."

"Strange how?"

"I don't know exactly. But something is going on, and she just tells me it's nothing. She hasn't been this closed off since we first started dating. I'm frustrated and getting short with her over the littlest things."

"Maybe it's just Drake's."

Jori laughed. "Yeah. When I met her, she didn't care one bit about Drake's. But the restaurant and the success of her family have come to mean so much to her I really think this is just a continuation of that. But maybe she's more worried than I think."

"Sure, she is. Come on, what else could it be? You two are the most deliriously happy couple I know."

"You know as well as I do that no one who's been together more than a year is delirious. But yes, we're very happy. And you're right. We'll get through this and probably be stronger."

"Right."

"So what's going on in your world?"

Shannon sighed. "Nothing I can talk about. I can't wait until I can go home and watch the episodes."

"I wasn't sure if you'd want to see them. We're recording them so you can catch up on what you're missing right now."

"I have so much to tell you."

"Can you give me any hints?"

"Ah, no. I definitely can't be breaking any rules right now." Shannon chuckled.

"Did something happen?"

Shannon was quiet for several seconds. "How's everything at the bakery? Is New Girl working out?"

Jori smiled. "It's cute how you keep calling her New Girl so you don't have to admit that you aren't coming back."

"Okay. Is *Mackenzie* working out?"

"She isn't as talented a decorator as you, but she's doing well. And she's a fast learner." Jori glanced at the clock display on the microwave. "I hate to cut this short, but I need to get to the bakery."

"Of course. Sorry. I didn't realize what time it was. I should be getting ready to go in as well." She paused for a moment, then said, "Jori…"

"Yeah?" Jori said when she didn't continue.

"I miss you."

"I miss you, too." Jori smiled, warmed by the sentiment though she knew Shannon wanted to say something more. Whatever it was must have to do with the show. If it was as important as it sounded, she'd find out as soon as Shannon was free to talk.

❖

Shit. Shit. Shit. Maya chanted the word in her head as she left her dressing room and headed toward Hugh's office. He'd just summoned her via a production assistant, and she didn't have a good feeling about it. They'd made it through a full day of filming with no mention of a photo showing up. She'd been starting to think they were safe. If anyone had it, and knew what they had, surely they would have done something with it quickly. She got a little worried when Hugh was absent for most of the afternoon. He rarely handed over his duties to another producer, especially this late in the season. But she'd stuffed her concern down and followed the scene instructions of his proxy.

That morning the contestants had gone to the performing-arts center to meet the cast and crew of a popular musical. They watched a matinee performance of the show, then returned to the set to plan a cake commemorating the show's tenth anniversary on tour. Tomorrow they'd begin to construct their cakes.

After they finished for the day, Maya had escaped to her dressing room. She just needed to make it to the SUV and back to the hotel and she'd be home free, for the day at least. She'd planned to head down to the fitness room and see if Shannon showed up. After a good workout, she could go to her room for a hot shower with thoughts of Shannon still in her head. And she'd been just minutes away when the production assistant knocked on her door.

As she approached Hugh's door, a familiar sick feeling started in her stomach—the same one she always got when a new tabloid story first broke. Shannon was already there pacing—well, if you could call three steps and a turn pacing. The photo was out. And she didn't know how the hell she was going to do it, but she had to fix this.

"Did he call you, too?" Maya stopped in front of Hugh's door, effectively putting an end to Shannon's pacing in the cramped space.

"Yes. How much do you think he knows?"

"I'm not sure. But don't cop to anything until he spells it out for us."

Before either of them could say anything more, the door opened and Hugh waved them inside.

"Have a seat, ladies."

"What's going on?" Shannon asked as she took the chair next to Maya, across the desk from Hugh.

"See for yourself." He turned his computer screen around to reveal a photo of two women standing very close. Even in the low light, Maya's distinctive hairstyle was easily recognizable. Shannon wouldn't be so easy to identify, but anyone who watched the show could figure it out. Despite knowing she was likely in some trouble, as Maya relived the moments in the shadows of the bar, her body reacted to the image of the two of them. Her heart pounded, and she curled her hands into fists to resist leaning in for a closer look.

"Where did you get that?" Maya asked.

"Urgent email from a reporter. It goes public tomorrow." He leaned back and crossed his arms over his chest, obviously angry. "And please don't insult me by telling me that's not you."

"Okay. But it's not what it looks like." Out of the corner of her eye, she saw Shannon whip her head around, but Maya didn't look at her. Okay, maybe it was exactly what it looked like, but Hugh didn't need to know that.

"Damn it, Maya, I know you have a reputation, but I expected you to know better than this. Couldn't you have found someone anonymous to—"

"There are two people in the photo, Hugh," Shannon said.

"Hugh, it's not a big deal," Maya said, as if Shannon hadn't spoken. She needed to keep Hugh's focus on her until she could figure out a way to make this okay.

"You're looking very cozy with one of our contestants—whose success or failure in this show depends at least in part on you. How is that not a big deal?"

"You know how the press can make things look. A picture from the right angle. Okay, yes, we snuck out and went to a bar together but—"

"Hugh, let me—" When Shannon started to talk, Maya put her hand on her arm to silence her.

"Nothing more than that happened. It doesn't affect the competition." Uncertain how much he knew, she didn't let on that they weren't the only ones there.

"It only has to *look* like it could affect the show." He looked pointedly at her hand still resting on Shannon's forearm, and she pulled it back.

"Well, you did ask me for more drama," Maya said.

"Not funny." Hugh's face turned red and, for a second, she worried about his blood pressure. "Even I can't sell this one. The producers are already talking about how it would look to replace you this far into the season."

"You took it to them without talking to me first?"

"Of course I did. We only have until tomorrow to figure out how to do damage control on this."

"Get me a number for the reporter. I'll take care of it. I'm used to doing *damage control.*"

"I used every threat I know. He's not going to kill a story this juicy just because you ask him nicely."

"He will if I promise him an even juicier one."

"Maya—" Shannon jerked forward in her seat, her spine stiffened, and her eyes went dark with an emotion Maya hadn't seen in them before.

"It's okay." Maya held her gaze, asking for trust, then looked back at Hugh. "I'll give him an exclusive about what I went through last year. But he has to agree to never use that photo. And I won't do it until after the show is over and has aired."

Without waiting to be dismissed, she stood and headed for the door.

"What if he—"

"Make the call, Hugh. He'll take the deal."

Shannon caught up with her just as she entered her dressing room. She slammed her palm against the door before Maya could swing it shut.

"Maya, please don't do this." Shannon stepped inside the room and closed the door behind her.

Maya turned quickly, causing Shannon to stumble backward. "Why not? They already think the worst of me. The truth can only make me look better."

"What do you mean?"

This was the moment—Maya should sit Shannon down and tell her the whole story. She knew Shannon had heard the abortion rumors. She should tell her about the miscarriage. If nothing else, Shannon's reaction would be a good gauge for how the rest of the public would receive the truth. Some, she suspected, wouldn't believe it, would call it a publicity stunt. Others would pity her. And then there was the small faction of fine, upstanding Christians who would be so happy to point out that the miscarriage was God's way of punishing her for being bisexual. Those would probably be her favorite.

What had she done? She'd promised to subject herself to all of that to keep Shannon's reputation clean. And not only that, but by waiting until the show wrapped, she now had over eight weeks to anticipate the fallout.

"Why does everyone keep acting like this is your decision alone? I'm in that picture, Maya. I have a say in this." Shannon closed the scant distance between them until they stood toe-to-toe, their breasts nearly brushing.

"I'm trying to protect you."

"I'm a grown woman. I decided to sneak out and go to that bar with you—"

"I remember the moment in that photo quite vividly. I leaned in to you." Maya raised her voice to speak over Shannon.

"You don't have to do this. You don't have to take this all on yourself. I'm here."

Those last two words, spoken so tenderly, nearly undid Maya. She wanted to believe them. She wanted to shelter herself in Shannon's embrace and pretend that nothing else existed. She wanted it so badly that, just then, she'd do anything to spend more time alone with Shannon.

But just then the production assistant knocked on her door and announced that her car was ready to take her back to the hotel. They didn't know Shannon was in there and were most likely looking for her as well.

"Have dinner with me."

"What?"

"Have dinner with me. Tonight."

"Were you not in there just now? Us being in public together is what started this mess in the first place." Shannon's voice was high and tight with disbelief.

"Then come to my hotel room." Before Shannon could protest, Maya held up a hand. "Just dinner. With no chance for photographers. I'll behave."

"Stop changing the subject. I want to talk to you about giving this interview, or rather *not* giving it. You shouldn't have to—"

"We can discuss that over dinner." She made sure her tone left no doubt that she wasn't discussing it further right now.

"You're impossible."

"Is that a yes?"

Shannon sighed. She looked like she was about to give in when the dressing-room door flew open and Hugh entered. Though they had several feet between them, Shannon guiltily jumped back a step.

"What's going on in here?"

"Nothing." Shannon's defensive tone came off as deceptive, and Hugh narrowed his eyes.

"She's trying to talk me out of doing that interview." Maya hoped an explanation would lower his suspicions.

"It's already arranged. I just made the call. You were right. He practically salivated through the phone."

She shrugged. "If there's one thing I know, it's how to handle reporters."

Hugh turned to Shannon. "We just got a call. Your daughter's gone into labor. She's on her way to the hospital. I have a driver ready to take you there."

"Oh, my God. Okay. Thank you."

Shannon looked at Maya. She clearly wanted to say more, but Hugh wasn't about to leave them alone again. So she hurried through the door he held open. He glared at Maya once more before following Shannon through it.

CHAPTER SEVENTEEN

No baby, yet?" Alice asked as soon as she answered the phone.

"Not yet. She's being stubborn." Shannon wedged the hospital-room phone between her cheek and her shoulder and handed Regan a cup of ice chips. When the night turned to early morning, then to late morning, she'd called Hugh to check in. He told her to stay as long as she needed to, but she sensed he did so out of obligation. Certainly any break in filming would cost the network money.

Her next call had been to her hotel room, where she caught Alice and filled her in on the progress, or lack thereof.

"Hugh gave us today off since they can't shoot the next challenge without you. Well, we have to go in to do some interviews that they can cut in to the earlier stuff during editing. But after that, we're free."

"I'm glad I could get you guys a day off. I know I'm enjoying mine."

Alice laughed. "Actually, at this point, we're so close, I'm just ready to get it over with."

"Me too. Both there and here."

They finished the call and Shannon turned her attention back to her daughter. After ten hours of very slowly progressing labor, Regan's frustration grew exponentially. Not having any experience to draw on, Shannon had to trust the doctors when they told them both to be patient.

Despite Regan pleading that she needed to be distracted, Shannon refused to tell her anything about the show. She didn't realize how little else she had to talk about until she had to sit in a chair next to her bedridden daughter for hours on end. A couple of times she had to cut herself off just when she was about to mention Maya. She typically didn't discuss her love life with Regan, but she desperately wanted to talk to someone about what was happening with Maya and the threat of the photo getting out. She'd purposely avoided calling Jori so she wouldn't slip up and say something. Instead, she borrowed Regan's cell phone and texted Jori that Regan had gone into labor. Jori replied that they would come up to visit once the baby was born, and Shannon resolved to be gone before they arrived.

Regan's husband, a contractor, had been back and forth between the hospital and his job site, which was luckily only ten minutes away. He'd been busy making all the preparations so he could be there as soon as the delivery was imminent. Every time he left, Regan soothed his guilt by assuring him that since Shannon was there, she wasn't alone, and that she wouldn't have the baby without him. However, the nurses didn't think much of her plan to try to hold the baby in so he could make it back in time if need be.

He arrived by late afternoon, when she finally delivered. He had tears in his eyes when the doctor handed the baby to Regan. Shannon stepped back and watched her daughter's first moments with her family. She swallowed hard and took a deep breath, determined not to lose control of her emotions. Regan had a tough childhood before Shannon took her in, and seeing her today, Shannon swelled with pride. That her once-distrustful child had opened her heart and found a wonderful man to share her life with made Shannon believe in the redeeming power of love. Not only that, but Regan was a smart, accomplished young woman and would now be a great mother and example to this baby girl.

Similar emotions still swamped her later, when mother and baby had been cleaned up and had rested. She sat once more in the uncomfortable chair at Regan's bedside.

"Mom, do you want to hold her?"

Shannon nodded and took the little bundle. Her eyes burned with happy tears as she stared at her granddaughter. The birthmark in the center of her forehead looked nearly purple against the rest of her blotchy skin. A shock of hair, as black as her father's, had been smoothed down against her head, and Shannon wondered how much of it she would lose in the coming weeks.

"Hello there, little Annabelle, I'm your grandma," Shannon whispered as she bent to kiss her head. As she touched one tiny fist with her finger, Annabelle grabbed on and held for a second.

"Mom, don't cry. If you do, I will, and I'm so exhausted, once I start blubbering I may not be able to stop."

"She's so beautiful."

"I know. I did pretty good," Regan said, and when her husband cleared his throat from across the room, she said, "*we* did good."

"I'm so glad you waited until I was almost done with the show to have her. I only have to be away from this sweet face for a couple of days."

"Yeah, but you still have to be secretive for several weeks yet."

"Until the show catches up with the live finale."

"Any idea what role you might be playing in said finale?" Regan asked coyly.

"Not yet."

"Ha. So that means you're still in the running, at least. And this late there can only be one more elimination."

"Damn it." She'd tried to stay evasive in her answers.

She turned the conversation back to the baby in her arms, not relinquishing her until her other grandparents arrived to visit. She stayed for another hour, then called Hugh to check in and let him know she'd be returning to the hotel. He refused her offer to take a cab and insisted that he'd send a car to pick her up. He also said they were done filming for the day and told her what time to be ready in the morning.

She made one more call before she left Regan's room. When the phone picked up she said, "Do you still want that dinner?" When the answer was affirmative, she added, "I'll be there in twenty minutes."

❖

Maya paced near the door of her hotel room, straining to listen for a knock from the other side. She'd decided that Shannon had happily taken Regan's labor as an out to avoid dinner and maybe even would see it as a sign that they shouldn't try to sneak in this visit. So she'd been pleasantly surprised to get a call thirty minutes ago asking if she wanted to see Shannon. She hadn't hesitated to answer, giving no thought to what was prudent, only what she selfishly wanted.

Now, she told herself that, even though Shannon's twenty minutes had come and gone, she hadn't changed her mind but simply underestimated her time of arrival. When, a couple minutes later, the knock came, she reached for the doorknob, then pulled back. She smoothed a hand over her shirt and tucked it more neatly into her jeans. She didn't want to seem like she'd been waiting on the other side of the door, even though she had.

She shouldn't even be so excited to see her. Shannon probably only wanted to try to talk her out of the interview. And Maya definitely didn't want to discuss that. She took another deep breath, then opened the door.

"Is it too late?" Shannon asked right away.

"Of course not, come in." Maya stepped back and waited for Shannon to enter. She leaned out and checked the hallway before closing the door.

"I wasn't followed." Shannon's voice carried a note of humor.

"Good." Maya laughed.

Shannon glanced at the array of covered dishes Maya had arranged on the coffee table in the sitting area.

"I took the liberty," Maya said. "I didn't want the room-service guy to see you here and sell his story."

"Good thinking. A little paranoid maybe."

"When you've been doing this as long as I have, there's no such thing as paranoia."

"Doing this? You mean inviting women back to your hotel room?"

"You invited yourself."

Shannon shook her finger at her. "No. You extended the original invitation yesterday. I'm just a day late showing up."

"Anyway, I meant living in the public eye. But, yes, that too."

"Well, you're honest."

"I haven't pretended to be anything I'm not. Not with you, anyway." She purposely injected a self-deprecating tone. Shannon stepped closer, grasped Maya's chin, and lifted her head. Her eyes raced over Maya's face, then narrowed as if seeing something she didn't approve of. But as quickly as her expression changed, it was gone again.

"And you don't have to." Her response was so sincere that Maya allowed herself to believe things could really be that simple. Here was a person she could truly be herself with. But believing something like that might only get her in trouble.

"Let's eat before it gets cold." Maya took Shannon's hand, pulling it away from her face. But she didn't let go of it as she led her to the sofa. "Have you had any sleep at all in the past two days?"

"Yes. I had a nap in an extremely uncomfortable hospital chair."

"That sounds lovely. Maybe we should skip dinner. You have a big day tomorrow. You need to be alert and at the top of your game in just eight hours."

"I'm too wired to sleep right now."

"I'll bet. How's your daughter?" Maya uncovered several dishes and began piling food onto two plates.

"She's good."

"And the baby? Everyone happy and healthy?"

"Yes. The baby's beautiful." Shannon's eyes welled up. Maya moved toward her, intent on deepening the conversation, but Shannon took one of the plates and said, "I want to talk about the interview."

"There's nothing to talk about. I'm giving the interview and that's final."

"You said if I had dinner with you, we could discuss it."

"Okay." Maya settled onto the sofa beside her, laid a napkin in her lap, and picked up a fork. She looked at Shannon expectantly. "Go ahead."

"What?"

"Tell me why you don't want me to do it."

"Why do I get the feeling you're only indulging me and you'll do what you want to do anyway?"

"I won't let that photo go public. Can you think of another way?"

"Are you that worried about your relationship with the show?"

"My relationship with the show?" Maya set aside her plate, flew off the sofa, and threw her hands up. "That's already toast. I wouldn't come back next season if they asked me. I've been getting pressure from the producers, through Hugh, to be the same person they brought onto the show as a competitor. It's been seven years. I'm not that stupid kid anymore. But I'm not allowed to grow up?"

"Then what's this about? Why stop the photo? Let it go public."

"I won't let them do that to you."

"What are you talking about?"

"Your advancement in this competition is in no way due to my feelings for you. I won't let it appear as if it were. I know how easily the press can tarnish a reputation and how difficult it is to earn it back."

Shannon froze with her fork halfway to her mouth and stared at Maya. Uncertain, Maya played back her words in her head, and realization brought an ache to her chest. Had she just admitted she had feelings for Shannon? And, more importantly, had Shannon picked up on the fact that she'd admitted it?

Shannon patted the sofa cushion beside her and said, "Sit down and eat. We'll finish this later."

"It's decided," Maya said stubbornly.

Shannon picked up her own fork and began pushing her food around, neither agreeing nor disagreeing. They didn't talk any more about the interview. In fact, the only sound in the room was the clinking of their forks against the plates.

When they finished Maya gathered their plates, including Shannon's half-full one, and stacked them on a table by the door. "Did you not like the food?"

"No, it was good. I guess I wasn't as hungry as I thought. After a couple of bites, I just lost my appetite."

"Were you sneaking all of your daughter's hospital food?"

Shannon smiled halfheartedly. "No. But I should have. She wasn't eating it anyway."

"What's wrong?" Maya sat back down beside her. Shannon had been subdued since she arrived. She looked exhausted, but Maya sensed there was more to it.

"Nothing."

"Then why do you look sad?"

"I'm not. Not really."

Maya waited patiently, not content with the answer but sensing that pushing wouldn't get her anywhere.

Shannon sighed. "I'm so happy for Regan and the amazing journey she's beginning. Adopting was the best decision I ever made. But a part of me will always wonder what it would feel like to be pregnant, you know?"

If it was physically possible for all of a person's breath to leave their lungs in one sudden, painful moment, Maya's did. The agony that pierced her chest hit her surprisingly hard, even after a year.

Shannon kept talking, apparently unaware of Maya's pain. "I—I've been a parent for the past thirteen years. But I don't—I've never felt a life growing inside me." She rested her hand against her own stomach, still not meeting Maya's eyes. Maya wondered how much of the guilt that kept her looking away was for Maya—for what Shannon believed she'd done.

She wanted to tell her, but she didn't know how to force the words out. In all of these months, she'd never talked about it to anyone except Wendy, and even those conversations had been stilted. Maya had kept herself as emotionally distant as she could, and Wendy clearly didn't know what to say. Now, Maya was no more eager to revive the pain. But, today especially, she couldn't stand for Shannon to think she'd had so little regard for another life—for the life that had grown inside her.

"This all probably sounds silly to someone who doesn't even want kids," Shannon said.

"I never said I didn't want kids." Maya's body went cold. She stood and walked to the window, every step made more difficult by her urge to flee the room. Every second that went by brought her one step closer to the truth.

"I—well, I guess I just assumed, considering—"

"I know what you assumed." Her voice was as hard as she could make it, like a brick wall she wanted to keep between them. Her anger surged—anger at the press and at Shannon for believing their speculation and lies. But though she tried to cling to the safety of the wall, she could feel it crumbling and somehow knew that if she looked at Shannon, she'd find her holding the bricks as she took them down one by one. She took a breath. "I didn't have an abortion."

Shannon's reflection glowed in the surface of the darkened window in front of her. Though she didn't turn, she could see Shannon staring at her.

"I got pregnant. I wasn't exactly with the father so, yes, it was unplanned and unexpected, but I was so—" Maya's voice broke and tears fell down her cheeks. She swiped the backs of her fingers against her face, not stopping them, only diverting their path. "When I found out, I was happy. I didn't abort my child. I had a miscarriage." When she reached the words she'd been dreading, they spilled out surprisingly easy. Shannon stood and approached, but Maya kept her back to her. "And to answer your question about being pregnant, it was amazing. And heartbreaking."

"Oh, sweetie." Shannon touched her arm, gently turned her, and pulled her closer.

When Shannon tried to guide her back to the sofa, Maya jerked away. She stumbled back two steps until her back hit the wall.

"Maya." Shannon reached for her again.

"No." With a sob, she slid down until she sat on the floor and pulled her knees into her chest. "I—damn it, I'm—this is not me. I'm not a crier."

Shannon knelt in front of her and grasped both of her hands. "It's okay." She sat beside her and pulled her into her arms.

Maya resisted at first, but Shannon's arms around her felt like the haven she'd needed for so long. While she didn't break down completely, she stopped trying so hard to stifle her tears. She relaxed against Shannon's chest and wrapped her arm around Shannon's waist. Shannon cupped the back of her neck, and something about the touch soothed her. Feeling Shannon's fingers firm against her neck grounded her when it seemed everything was out of her control.

As she began to quiet, Shannon eased back a little. "This is what you intend to reveal in that interview?"

Maya nodded, not trusting that she could speak without sobbing.

"No." Shannon's voice was harder than Maya had ever heard it.

Maya sniffed and pulled in a deep breath. "It's not up for debate—"

Shannon stroked Maya's jaw, then lifted her chin until she met her eyes. "You're right, it's not. You're not doing it."

"I have to." Maya pulled out of Shannon's arms and scrambled to her feet. The concern in Shannon's eyes made her feel more vulnerable than she was ready for. But escaping to the other side of the room didn't lessen the pressure in her chest.

"You don't. Honey, you don't have to do anything you don't want to do. You don't owe anyone anything." Shannon stood, too, but remained a couple of feet away. "Least of all, me."

"If I don't, they'll run the photo." She couldn't shield Shannon from the reality of media scrutiny forever. But if she could keep this photo under wraps, maybe she'd buy Shannon a bit more time before it really became a factor in her life. "Maybe it'll be a relief to get the truth out."

"What you went through—it's so personal. I won't be the reason you can't keep it private." Shannon's eyes shone with unshed tears.

"Let me worry about that."

"Why do you dismiss my part in this? You did it in Hugh's office and you're doing it now. I'm not some innocent you corrupted. I was in that bar with you."

"And if you'll recall, I was the one putting the moves on you." Maya closed the distance between them much the same way as she had that night, with several quick strides. She leaned in, demonstrating how she'd gotten in Shannon's personal space.

"And I wanted you to," Shannon whispered quickly. She turned her head as she spoke, and her breath feathered across Maya's cheek.

"You can't say things like that and still expect me not to kiss you." Maya turned her head, too, bringing her mouth within inches of Shannon's.

"I want you to. I haven't stopped thinking about it since you kissed me in the elevator." Shannon wrapped her arms around Maya's waist.

"Well, I'm not going to." She used every bit of willpower to keep herself still in Shannon's arms.

"No?" Shannon leaned in a bit more, her nose brushing Maya's, but their lips didn't touch.

"This time you'll have to kiss me."

"No problem." Shannon's lips moved against Maya's as she answered.

Maya held still for as long as she could while Shannon's lips caressed hers. In reality, she lasted only a handful of seconds before she buried her hands in Shannon's hair and pulled her even closer. Where their first kiss was urgent and passionate, this one was tender—a slow exploration of the burn between them. Maya deepened the kiss, pouring her need and the lingering emotions of the evening into every stroke against Shannon's lips.

Reluctantly, Maya eased back far enough to rest her forehead against Shannon's, but not because she was done kissing her—she didn't think she could get enough. She needed a moment to regain control. Shannon pressed her body closer so Maya wrapped her arms around her and held her, using the pressure against her to center herself. Over Shannon's shoulder she glimpsed the time on the alarm clock by the bed.

She took Shannon's hand. "Come lie down. You need to try to sleep. You'll be exhausted tomorrow."

"I should go."

"Please, don't. Stay with me."

Shannon resisted, pulling back on Maya's hand when she began to guide her across the room. "It's been an emotional night for both of us."

"I'm not trying to get in your pants, Shannon. Not tonight anyway. Despite what everyone thinks of me, using that situation to get laid is beneath even me."

"I don't—" Shannon said, then sighed.

"I—I just don't want to be alone right now."

Shannon nodded and let Maya lead her toward the bed. Maya released her hand and went to the dresser. She grabbed two T-shirts and two pairs of boxer shorts. After tossing a set to Shannon, she turned her back, pulled off her jeans, and put on the boxers. She replaced her shirt as well. When she faced the bed again, Shannon hadn't moved. She stood staring at her, with the clothes clutched tightly to her chest.

"What's wrong?"

"You can't tell me you're *not* trying to get in my pants and then strip down to your underwear in front of me."

Drawing courage from the stark, hot lust burning behind the exhaustion in Shannon's eyes, Maya crossed to stand very close to her. "I can and I did. But I'm trying to control myself because, as you said, it's been an emotional night and you're nearly dead on your feet. So if you don't get your sexy behind in that bathroom and change so we can go to bed, I'll have to help you do it."

Shannon made a breathy sound, like a cross between a sigh and a moan, but she didn't move toward the bathroom. Emboldened, Maya took the clothes from her arms and set them on the bed. Then she grasped the hem of Shannon's sweater and lifted it slowly, giving her ample time to stop her. Once she'd freed the sweater, she folded it carefully and placed it aside. Shannon looked down at herself and folded her arms around her stomach. Maya gently moved them aside.

"I want to see you." Maya risked speaking, hoping she wouldn't break whatever spell allowed her to behold this vision. Shannon's bra was a simple beige number with a front clasp that Maya's fingers already itched to undo.

"Maya," Shannon said, but she didn't seem to know what she wanted to say after that. She just stared at Maya, her eyes soft yet a bit wary.

"Please." Maya trailed her fingers up the pale skin of Shannon's stomach. She flicked the bra clasp between them, deftly releasing it.

"I suppose you've done that a few times before." Shannon's voice vibrated with nervous laughter.

Maya said the first thing that came to her mind. "Never once that mattered more than now."

"Another line?" Disappointment colored Shannon's tone.

"Not at all." As she eased Shannon's bra off, she couldn't tear her eyes from the ivory swells of her breasts or their dusky tips. She cupped one breast and brushed a thumb over her nipple, feeling the texture change as it tightened immediately.

Shannon's sharp intake of breath lifted her breasts. Maya wanted nothing more than to lay her down and have her way with her. And from the way Shannon trembled under her touch, she was certain she could. Instead of the expected surge of power at that knowledge, she felt humbled. She'd just emotionally opened herself more than she had with anyone. Ever. And in this moment, if Maya indicated it was what she needed, Shannon would set aside all the reasons they shouldn't be here together and give herself to Maya. Something in her eyes told Maya it wouldn't be just a physical surrender.

Maya dropped to her knees and rested her forehead against Shannon's stomach, pouring the trust she felt into the submissive bend of her head. Shannon cupped one hand around the back of Maya's head, threaded the fingers of her other hand into the longer hair on top, and held her close. Maya wrapped her arms around Shannon, resting her own hands against her bare lower back. She pressed her cheek to Shannon's stomach.

They stayed that way for several long seconds while Maya warred with conflicting desires. Talking about the baby had flayed open old wounds, and she desperately wanted to alleviate that pain. But being with Shannon wasn't a carefree hookup. Maybe it could have been in the beginning, when she was just flirting with the cute competitor, but they'd long passed that point.

When she'd sufficiently bolstered her control, Maya opened the fly of Shannon's jeans and eased them over her hips. Shannon braced her hands on Maya's shoulders as she stepped out of them.

She grasped Shannon's hips, hooked one finger in the waistband of her panties, and raised an eyebrow.

"Panties on or off?"

Shannon covered her hands. "If you're thinking sleep, *on* is probably the safer choice."

"And if I'm not?" Maya squeezed her hips and pulled her closer. She pressed her lips to Shannon's stomach. She tilted her head back and met Shannon's eyes. She could tell they were in the same place—both wanting each other but still feeling like they should fight it.

"Then I don't need to put this on." Shannon held up the T-shirt. She pulled it over her head and paused with it pooled around her neck. "Hugh would—"

"Oh, God, okay. Please don't talk about Hugh right now." She stood, still holding Shannon's hips. "We've already crossed several lines, here. What's a few more?" She searched Shannon's face for signs of weakness, and, though it was there, she decided against exploiting it. She sighed. "All right, put the damn shirt on."

Shannon shoved her arms into it and let it fall to her waist. She turned to pull back the bed linens, and Maya caught a peek of her panties under her shirt hem.

Maya groaned. "How is it possible you're even sexier in a T-shirt and panties?"

Shannon laughed. "I'm sexier with my breasts covered? Wow, you really know how to make a girl melt."

"Yeah, well, you know, I've got lots of practice at that," Maya said as she climbed in bed beside Shannon. She settled against the pillow and folded her hands behind her head.

"So I hear." Shannon's voice sounded strange. Much of the intimacy from a moment ago had drained away, making her words sound empty and slightly cynical.

"You can't believe everything you hear." She turned on her side and rose on one elbow.

"How do I decide what stuff to believe, then?"

Maya tilted her head, trying to decide how serious Shannon was. "Well, you should believe everything I say and nothing you hear from reporters." Maya grinned.

Shannon didn't smile. "What about others?"

"Who?"

"It doesn't matter."

When Shannon didn't meet her eyes, Maya touched her chin and lifted her head. "Someone's been running their mouth. And you've been trying to decide if anything I've told you is true." At Shannon's look of surprise, Maya nodded. "This isn't my first time on this ride, Shannon. You don't think you can trust me because someone else is whispering in your ear."

"Can I? Trust you?"

"Of course." Maya sighed. "I just told you the most personal thing I could tell anyone."

"Which, if you have your way, is going to come out in several weeks—"

She shook her head. "I can't make you believe any of what I'm about to say. I've never denied that I deserve some of my reputation. I've dated plenty of men and women. I've gotten caught up in my own hype at times. But I never lied to any of them about what we had. I never pretended they meant more than they did. And in the past year, since the miscarriage, I haven't gotten close to anyone— despite what the tabloids like to report."

"Maya, you don't have to—"

"I want to." She stroked a lock of hair off Shannon's forehead. "I don't know what this is between us. But I meant what I said earlier. Every moment I spend with you somehow means more than with anyone before. And no matter how many times I tell myself I should, I can't seem to ignore that fact."

CHAPTER EIGHTEEN

Shannon woke to a warm body pressed against her back, an arm around her, and the gentle caress of fingers tracing over her stomach. Her bare stomach. Her T-shirt had worked its way up around her ribs. She lay still for a moment, prolonging the surreal and amazing sensation of being in bed with Maya.

"Good morning," Maya said, kissing her shoulder.

She rolled to her back. Maya's hair was flat on one side and stood up at odd angles on the other. Without makeup, she looked even younger.

"Hey." She touched Maya's cheek. *God, she's beautiful.* Maya bent and gave her a lingering kiss. When she began to pull back, Shannon grasped a handful of her T-shirt and pulled her in for one more. Then she lifted the covers and made a show of looking under them. "It hardly seems fair that you have so many clothes on."

Maya raised the sheet and looked for herself. "If I was going to keep the promise I made to myself, I needed more than just your panties as a barrier between us."

Shannon smiled and gave an exaggerated sigh. "You see, that's the problem. You're always trying to put barriers between us."

Maya laughed. "You're right. It's all my fault." She moved over Shannon, settled her lower body against her.

Shannon sucked in a breath at the feel of Maya's strong thighs against hers. She grabbed Maya's hips, getting hold of the waistband of her boxers as well. Maya pressed into her. Shannon groaned.

"Keep that up, and even these won't be enough of a barrier." She tugged at the waistband.

"I don't know if I can stop." Maya closed her eyes briefly, but when she opened them, Shannon didn't see any more control. "You've been telling me no. And I've been fighting this." The corner of her mouth lifted in a half smile. "That was hard enough while you were telling me no, even when your eyes said yes."

Shannon laughed. "My eyes were saying no such thing."

"Oh, yes, they were. But I don't know if I can keep fighting my natural urges if you're just going to climb into bed with me."

"Your natural urges?" Shannon raised her eyebrows. Perhaps she should show Maya what some of her urges were. She wrapped her legs around Maya's hips, then raised her head and bit Maya's lower lip.

"Shannon," Maya moaned.

"What?" She'd been toying with Maya just as she believed Maya was with her. But now—was she willing to let this go further? Her body said yes, and it was quickly overtaking any other part of her.

"Have some mercy."

"Are you begging?"

"Yes," Maya said without hesitation. The sexy little growl in Maya's voice and the openness in her eyes made Shannon's decision for her. Whatever else she might believe was or wasn't between them, in this moment, Maya didn't hold anything back, and Shannon was determined to do the same.

"Wow. I can't believe I'm in bed with *the* Maya Vaughn and she's begging." She tightened her legs around Maya in case she took her teasing the wrong way.

Maya's eyes narrowed, but the rest of her face was relaxed and showed no sign of anger. "Will I be reading about this in the tabloids tomorrow?"

"Possibly. So if you want the story to be flattering, you'd better do something to impress me."

"No pressure, though, huh?"

"None," Shannon said, meeting Maya's eyes and making sure she knew she was serious now.

Maya sat back on her heels between Shannon's legs and pulled her T-shirt over her head. Shannon immediately reached for her, running her fingertips over her stomach and tracing the dips between her defined muscles.

"You are beautiful," Shannon whispered.

When Maya bent to kiss her, Shannon swept her hands up and palmed her breasts. She rubbed her thumb over one nipple, pleased when Maya moaned into her mouth. She caught her other nipple between her thumb and forefinger and applied a bit more pressure. Maya deepened their kiss, stroking her tongue against Shannon's.

Maya undressed her deliberately, paying attention to each inch of newly bared skin and driving her crazy with her mouth and hands. Shannon fought to get her hands on Maya as well, but Maya maintained control.

All of the reasons she'd been fighting this seemed to melt away under Maya's sure caresses. Maybe the reasons were still there, maybe they weren't, but they could certainly be dealt with another time. Right now, the only thing she seemed able to concentrate on was the swirl of pleasure rising within her.

Maya moved over her, supporting her weight on her magnificently carved arms, and met her eyes. She didn't say anything but, in a moment of silence, asked permission. Shannon granted it—all of it—for everything. She stroked her hands over Maya's shoulders and around to her back, then pulled Maya down on top of her.

"I want to feel all of you."

"You have all of me," Maya whispered in her ear, the warm feather of her breath against Shannon's skin adding a delicacy to the words.

"Oh, you are *really* good at this," Shannon moaned when Maya slid two fingers inside her. Pleasure weakened her legs, sending a tingle all the way to the tips of her toes.

Again, Maya sought her gaze. Shannon thought she read an insistence on the integrity of her words, but Maya didn't say anything. She moved slowly, as if mapping out Shannon's responses against each movement. And as Shannon's need grew and she began to frantically grasp at Maya's back, Maya responded with increasing speed and pressure.

Shannon closed her eyes and threw her head back against the pillow, submitting completely to Maya. Her body surged toward a peak, tightening against Maya's fingers, and she ground against her, seeking a little more pressure—just enough. With her one remaining fleeting thought, she wished she could hold onto this moment—this feeling. But, proving it was stronger, her body let go, sending waves of bliss through her. She arched into it, her heart beating out of control and her own cries rasping in her ears.

She pulled Maya to her, holding her tight, enjoying the pressure against her still-sensitized skin. Maya pressed her lips to Shannon's cheek, then her neck, and found her lips for a slow, thorough kiss. By the time she eased back, Shannon's recovering body had started to clamor for a different kind of satisfaction.

She rolled Maya to her back and began her own exploration. She covered her body with her own, slipping her thigh between Maya's. Right away, even through Maya's boxers, she felt heat and wetness against her thigh and rubbed her leg higher.

"Ah, slow down," Maya said as she moaned.

"What's wrong?"

"I know you were probably expecting more self-control from me. But it's been a very long—ah, God, Shannon." Her last words were a warning as Shannon slipped her hand between her thigh and Maya's center. "It's been—I haven't been with anyone in a long time."

"Do I want to know what a long time without sex is for you?"

Maya closed her eyes and exhaled slowly. "Since I found out I was pregnant. Over a year."

"Oh, wow. I—I'm sorry."

"No, please don't make this moment about apologies. Just slow down a little and let me really enjoy it."

Shannon nodded. She lifted herself away carefully, breaking contact with her. But before Maya could protest, she began trailing kisses along her torso, against skin that twitched in response. She covered one nipple with her mouth, teasing it but never applying enough pressure to bring Maya back to the edge. She paid close attention to Maya's reactions, giving a little, then easing up when Maya tensed or arched against her.

She held back, letting Maya set the pace. And it was only when Maya grabbed her wrist and guided her hand that she finally slipped her fingers between her soft folds. Her own moan melded with Maya's. She hadn't even imagined touching Maya could feel this good. Maya was as responsive and in control from the bottom as she'd been from the top, and Shannon enjoyed letting her set the pace as she pumped against her hand, quickly driving herself to orgasm.

"So much for slow." Maya's soft chuckle sounded breathy.

❖

"Mmm, well, that was definitely impressive." With their naked bodies still entwined, Shannon couldn't keep the satisfaction out of her voice. "Maybe I won't sell my story after all. I think I'll keep you to myself for a little while longer."

"You probably should. At least until after the show is over."

With that reminder, Shannon glanced at the clock, then sat up quickly. "Shit. Our car's going to be here in thirty minutes." She jumped out of bed and began putting on her clothes.

Maya leaned up on her elbow and watched her. After Shannon had her shirt on, she smiled and pointed. "Your shirt's inside out."

"Damn it." Shannon yanked it off and fixed it.

"I wish we could blow off the show and stay in bed all day." Maya flipped back the covers, got up, and crossed the room naked. While Shannon still rushed around getting dressed, Maya leisurely pulled the carafe from the coffeemaker as if she actually did intend to abandon her responsibilities for the day.

"You're not helping."

"Oh, was I supposed to be?" She put on a robe but let it hang open in the front. "I finally got with the woman I've been thinking about for weeks. Forgive me if I want to enjoy it a bit longer."

"Weeks, huh?"

"Let's just say I've had some interesting showers lately." Maya stepped close, grabbed her waist, and kissed her.

"Yeah? Try having them with another girl in the suite," Shannon said. When Maya's expression changed, Shannon laughed and pushed her away. "Pervert."

"You know, if you need a little more privacy, there's a very roomy shower stall right in there." Maya tilted her head toward the adjoining bathroom.

"I don't have time for that right now. Where's my purse?" She searched the room and found it where she'd dropped it by the sofa.

"Do you have your room key?"

Shannon dug into her purse, then held it up triumphantly. Maya handed her a travel mug of coffee and led her to the door. She closed her robe and tied the belt.

"Go down to your room. Shower and change, quickly. You don't have much time."

"Alice is going to ask where I've been."

"Tell her you were at the hospital. It's mostly true, anyway."

"Maya, I—"

Maya pressed her lips to Shannon's, stopping whatever she'd been about to say.

"We didn't have time for the kiss and for talking, and I really wanted to do that." She opened the door, stuck her head out to check that the hallway was clear, then pushed Shannon outside. "I'll see you on set."

She closed the door and left Shannon alone in the hallway before she could say anything more. Shannon got in the elevator and pushed the button for her floor. During the brief ride, she used the mirrored finish of the doors to frantically try to tame her hair. She wished she looked more like she'd spent the night in the hospital and less like she'd been rolling around in bed. Alice might buy it, if she kept her distracted with talk of the baby.

❖

"The winner of this challenge and the first chef to win a spot on the finale is—" Eric paused, scanning the four of them. Shannon counted to five in her head, having a feel for his dramatic rhythm by now. "Alice."

Alice covered her mouth and jumped up and down. She looked like she wanted to say something; in fact, she appeared to be bursting with the urge, but by now she'd learned that Eric would want to continue quickly.

"Ned, you are also safe and on to the finale."

He didn't waste any time with the next reveal, leaving Shannon stunned. Ned gave a fist pump on his way out of camera range. Shannon glanced at Mason, and he looked as nervous as she felt. She hadn't been confident going into this elimination.

Despite being exhausted and distracted by Maya, her work had been solid, but not as creative as Alice's. She'd thought she could edge out Ned for the second spot, but that clearly wasn't the case. So now it was down to her and Mason, and in just a few minutes it would all be over for one of them. The idea that she could come this far and be sent home shook her.

As usual the mentors stood opposite them, next to Eric. When she met Maya's eyes, she thought she detected a tiny smile, but she couldn't be sure. Maybe she'd imagined what she wanted to see, because when she looked again, Maya's expression was almost neutral. After the night—and morning, they'd just spent together, if she were going home, wouldn't she see some trace of that in Maya's face? Unless it really didn't matter to Maya. She had Alice in the finals, so her team would be represented either way. They hadn't taken the time to define their relationship. Just because sleeping with someone was a big deal for Shannon didn't mean Maya viewed things the same way. If even half the tabloid reports were true, she had plenty of casual sex.

"Mason." Eric's voice interrupted what might rapidly turn into a panic attack for Shannon. She braced herself to react gracefully either way and, if it went badly, not to let them see how destroyed she was. "Mason, you will not be competing in the finale this year."

"Oh my God," Shannon whispered. She turned to Mason and hugged him. Then she exited to where Hugh motioned for her, giving Mason his time to say good-bye to the mentors.

Hugh took her arm and led her farther away. "This was a close elimination, and some of the producers thought it might be safer to give it to Mason. That photo almost cost you this finale," he said so quietly only she could hear.

"What changed their mind?" She wasn't sure how she'd feel if Maya had been the one to save her. She wanted to believe she'd earned this spot on her own merit.

"It was Wayne's endorsement that saved you."

"But Mason was on his team?"

"Yes. He was." Hugh walked away without another word.

She turned and watched the rest of the proceedings on the kitchen set. Wayne had chosen her over his own team member. Just when she'd accepted that she had no control over the outcome of the show, she apparently had done something to convince Wayne she deserved to be in the finale.

Mason was escorted away, and Shannon knew he would be taken back to the hotel to pack. By the time the three remaining contestants returned, he would be gone. As she tracked him across the set, she caught sight of Maya, who was watching her as well. When their eyes met, Maya winked and Shannon smiled in response.

This morning, when Shannon had hurried into her hotel room after leaving Maya's, Alice came out of her bedroom. She immediately began asking about the baby, apparently assuming she'd just rushed in from the hospital. Letting her continue to think so was easier than she'd thought it would be. She went to her own room, mumbling about needing to grab a quick shower before they left. She raced through her morning ritual, not bothering to dry her hair before twisting it into an updo.

Once they'd arrived on set and finished in makeup, Hugh hustled them into the kitchen to begin the day's challenge, citing lost time yesterday as the reason for the rush. Shannon hadn't had even a second alone with Maya since she left her hotel room. She'd caught Maya looking at her several times, and each time, Maya seemed to be angling away from the nearest camera as if she didn't want to get caught. Though their eye contact remained brief, Shannon thought she saw the heat of their shared secret in Maya's gaze.

She hadn't had much time to evaluate her own feelings, and she had no more luck figuring Maya's out from a mere glance. If their situation were simpler, if their worlds weren't so drastically different, if they didn't have to worry about how their actions impacted the show and their careers, she might feel freer to just enjoy what could be between them. Their time together was about more than just the amazing sex they'd had this morning. If nothing more happened between them, yes, she'd have the memory of their physical interaction. But the closeness she'd felt the night before as they talked about Shannon's family and Maya revealed the truth of her miscarriage, those were the moments she cherished.

When she looked at Maya now, the attraction still flared, along with a renewed arousal at knowing firsthand what it felt like to be with Maya, but, even more amazing, underneath flowed an unexpected layer of intimacy that went beyond the physical. She desperately wanted to know how Maya was feeling. Maya had told her this was different than others she'd been with. She didn't know where they were going, or if they had a future, but she'd feel like a fool if this all ended along with the show.

CHAPTER NINETEEN

S ettle down, chefs. I know you're all excited about making the finale, but we have some business to attend to first." Hugh interrupted the round of hugs and exclamations among the three finalists. "We're going to be filming another segment, which will give you an idea of what your final challenge is. After we finish here today, you'll have a celebratory dinner with the mentors tonight. Tomorrow, you'll each head home until the finale. During that time, we'll be sending camera crews out to interview your families and friends, get some shots around your towns, and, in some cases, your former jobs. You'll also use this time to plan and practice your final cake. When you return, you'll be expected to create your cake from scratch. Someone will contact you regarding a list of supplies you'll need us to have on hand for the finale. Any questions?"

No one spoke up, though Shannon's head swam with questions, and she'd bet the others' did as well. Instead, she focused all her energy on listening to what Hugh said and trying not to get overwhelmed by the events of the last two days. She'd become a grandmother, slept with a woman who was closer to her daughter's age than her own, and made the finale in a nationally televised reality show. But listing those events in her head didn't help, and suddenly she felt like she couldn't breathe. Hugh gave them a few more instructions, then told them to take a quick break before meeting in the kitchen to begin the next segment.

As soon as he dismissed them, Shannon wound her way toward the door leading outside. Alice called out to her, but she kept going. She moved among the crew with ease, remembering how that first day there seemed to be so many of them. Now she barely noticed the commotion around her.

When she reached the door, she burst through it and immediately sucked in a lungful of fresh air. She leaned against the side of the building, bent at the waist, and grabbed her thighs. She closed her eyes and forced herself to breathe slowly. The door opened beside her, but she didn't look up.

"Hey." How could one softly spoken word from Maya send an ache through her chest?

"We shouldn't let Hugh find us out here alone. Apparently, my tenure on the show barely survived the last time." She forced a neutral tone into her voice. She had to regain control, and being around Maya wasn't likely to help.

"Yeah. Okay." Maya paced a few steps away from the door, then spun back toward her. "I—uh, I came out here to see how you were doing with what happened between us. And I guess now I know."

Shannon straightened and looked at her. But she immediately realized that might have been a mistake. The wounded look in Maya's eyes hurt her. "Maya—"

"No, it's okay. Really." Maya held a hand up to halt Shannon's words. "I didn't think you were the celebrity-notch-on-your-bedpost type. But hey, at least you'll have a good story to tell at cocktail parties about how you fucked Maya Vaughn and got her to fall for you." When Maya reached for the door handle, Shannon grabbed her arm and she froze.

"I don't go to cocktail parties." Shannon grasped Maya's shoulders, turned her, and pushed her against the door. She kissed her aggressively, pouring out the swirling emotions of the past two days. Maya clung to her, and Shannon could feel her granting access to every part of her. Shannon lifted her mouth only far enough to rest their foreheads together. "Say that part again about how you fell for me."

Maya took her face in her hands. "I really have."

Shannon sighed. "I hope you know that I'm not interested in you because you're famous. It's just—so much has happened in the last two days and I've had so little sleep. I feel a little like I'm going crazy."

"I know how that is." Maya pulled her in for a quick hug before releasing her. "We're begging to get caught out here."

Shannon nodded.

"You just have to get through one more day. Then you'll have some time off to recover and prepare before the big show. And since I haven't said it before, speaking both as your mentor and your friend, whatever happens, I'm proud of how far you've come."

"Since we brought Maya back from season one, we thought we'd bring back her final challenge as well. Maya, do you recall what it was?" Eric turned to her with his stiff posture and trademark toothy grin.

"Of course. We designed a wedding and groom's cake for a very special couple." She didn't add that the particular celebrity marriage hadn't survived the seven years since.

"Nashville is known for all kinds of music, but especially country music. For your final challenge, you'll be making two cakes. Chefs, please welcome country music's power couple, Viola Embers and David Nash."

The three competitors clearly recognized the duo as they entered. Maya did, too. She enjoyed their music separately and their collaborations as well.

David's reputation as a hard-partying but big-hearted country boy had endeared him to country fans for years. They loved that he looked like them, a thick guy who frequently wore blue jeans, T-shirts, and a ball cap onstage. He wasn't one of those guys who wore a western shirt and hid behind a guitar. His appeal had only increased when he teamed up with Viola Embers, America's young sweetheart from Oklahoma. He'd reportedly wooed her while they were on tour together. Since their engagement announcement, they'd done all the talk shows, and Maya had heard rumors of a reality show. She couldn't imagine ever giving the press that much access to her life, but they apparently didn't mind the lack of privacy.

"Viola, I understand David proposed to you onstage. Is that right?" Eric prompted her.

"Yes, he did." Her high-pitched speaking voice matched her bubbly personality. But when she sang, her tone deepened and took on a richer tenor that seemed too mature for her age.

"Is it fair to say this was love at first sight?"

"Oh, Lord, no. When we got put on the tour together, I couldn't stand him. Every night after the show, he and his band played poker until all hours. And soon he had my band joining in."

"She's just mad because my guys were winning all the money she paid hers. And her band *still* liked me better."

"Damn right." She grinned at him, the love between them evident in the light in her eyes. "But I taught him a lesson."

"I don't think they care about that," he broke in. "Aren't we here to talk about cakes?"

"I started sitting in on his little games. A couple of nights of getting his pockets emptied by a girl and the poker games suddenly stopped."

"Luckily, by then, I'd convinced her to sneak away and have dinner with me." David puffed his chest out.

"Ha. Dinner was just a means to an end for you." Viola swatted his arm.

"Hey, a boy's gotta eat, too."

Maya searched out Shannon's eyes, and when she found them, a wave of arousal swept over her. She'd used dinner as a ploy to get Shannon alone as well. It had worked for these two, and now they were planning their lives together. Maya hadn't made plans for the future in almost a year. But now, thinking about what she might have with Shannon after the circus of this show was over filled her with an overwhelming sense of hope and anticipation—and fear.

❖

Shannon watched from across the room as Alice interviewed David and Viola. They'd been brought to a downtown restaurant where the show had rented out a private room. The interviews were taking place first, in an area apart from the rest of the chefs. After they were through, the celebratory dinner would begin. She'd already sat through Ned's interview and now Alice's, her nervousness growing with each passing minute. Would it be inappropriate for her to down a shot—or two—from the bar while she waited?

She recalled her badly botched first consultation with Maya, and anxiety tightened her stomach. She'd definitely come full circle. Her ability to satisfy this couple, as well as her entire future, could hinge on this moment. She pushed her shoulders back and straightened her spine. She could do this. She wasn't the same starstruck woman she'd been when she started this show. She'd learned new techniques and grown as a chef, and this couple deserved to see that. She would do this.

"You're up," Hugh said, gesturing for her to join the couple.

She nodded and strode forward, projecting more confidence than she felt. David and Viola both rose to greet her.

"It's so great to meet you both. I'm a fan of your music." She shook David's hand. When she turned to Viola and extended her hand, she found herself pulled into a hug. Viola was surprisingly strong for such a tiny woman.

"Congratulations on making it this far," David said.

"Thank you." They exchanged pleasantries for a few moments longer, then settled in around the small table. While David tried to fold his large frame back into the small chair, he caught Shannon trying not to laugh at him.

"There aren't too many chairs around for a guy my size."

"At least your feet always touch the floor," Viola joked, lifting her feet and swinging them.

"David, could you describe Viola for me?" Shannon dove right in with her questions.

"Describe her?" He looked at Viola then back at her.

"Not physically. But who is she?"

He looked at her and smiled, showing off the dimples that no doubt made countless young fans swoon. "She's the strongest woman I know, but still feminine and dainty. She loves her expensive shoes, but when she wears them, she complains that her feet hurt. And actually, I think she's sexiest when she's onstage and she kicks them off and sings barefoot."

"No one is looking at my shoes when you get up there with me anyway. All of those young girls are just screaming for him."

"And what is it about him that appeals to you?"

"What makes *me* scream for him?"

Shannon laughed. "I suppose you could put it that way."

"He's gorgeous. Just looking at him makes me weak. I can be having the worst day, but then I see him and—well, maybe it's still a crappy day, but it's a little better."

Shannon nodded politely. He was a good-looking guy but not exactly her type. Across the room, she caught sight of Maya and decided maybe she understood. Just being close to Maya lifted her spirits.

"I can tell from that look on your face that you know what I mean," Viola said.

Shannon jerked her eyes away from Maya. She searched Viola's expression but didn't see any hint that she knew *who* had captured her attention.

"He's my best friend. Like the kid you grew up next door to and can share any moment with. But then there's this side of him—of us, and when we're together, I can't get enough of him, you know?"

"I do." She skimmed her eyes over Maya once more but brought them back to the couple in front of her.

For the next ten minutes, she talked to them about what they each envisioned for their wedding cake as well as for David's groom's cake. Their lives revolved so much around music, but neither of them mentioned it as a theme in their wedding. Viola talked about David's love of the outdoors and of being with his friends and family. His fondness for hosting poker games was mentioned once again as one of his favorite ways of bonding with his buddies, most of whom he'd brought into his band or road crew over time.

Shannon discovered that Viola harbored a fondness for photographing wildflowers. As they traveled, she would make the driver pull the bus over and would run out into a field on the side of the road to get a shot. She also cherished the memories of growing up in a small town—of cornfields and hanging out with her friends down by the river at the dam. No matter how famous she got, how many cities she visited, and how many homes they bought around the world, at heart, Viola remained the country girl she was raised to be.

When Shannon's time was up, she felt good about the interview, but she wished she had more time to visit with them.

Once more, Viola hugged her. "Best of luck, sweetie," she whispered.

"Thank you." She gave David a quick hug and rejoined the rest of the group on the other side of the room.

Hugh raised his hand and gave a loud whistle to get everyone's attention. "Okay, chefs. The interviews are finished. Dinner will be served soon. Tomorrow, you all head home to begin preparations for the finale. But for tonight, have a drink or two, relax, and enjoy the evening. David and Viola have agreed to join in the celebration." He held up a finger in warning. "But no talk about the finale or your designs. No work tonight, just play."

The atmosphere in the room relaxed as the contestants, mentors, and crew dissolved into a mingle of people, some of whom moved to the bar, and others clustered in groups for easy conversation.

Shannon saw an opportunity to catch Wayne alone and hurried to his side.

"I don't know if I'm supposed to know this or not, but I understand that I owe you some thanks," she said quietly.

Wayne smiled. "You don't owe me anything. I lobbied for the three most deserving chefs."

"Well, thank you, just the same. Your opinion means a lot to me."

"Best of luck in the finale." He raised his glass in salute. "Excuse me. I need to speak with Hugh before he disappears."

As he stepped away, she stood apart from the others for a moment longer, letting herself take in the surreal moment. She'd just made top three on *For the Love of Cake*. If she'd been told even a year ago that she'd be on the show, she wouldn't have believed it.

"Can I buy you a drink?" Maya's voice close to her ear made her shiver.

Shannon turned to find Maya holding two glasses of champagne. "I hope you don't think you're going to impress me with cheap champagne."

Maya narrowed her eyes. "Should I be concerned that you seem to constantly want me to impress you? If you're going to be this high-maintenance through our whole relationship, it could get trying."

"I am not high-maintenance." Shannon swatted Maya's arm, ignoring the reference to a relationship.

"We'll see." She touched the rim of her glass to Shannon's. "Congratulations, Chef Hayes."

"Why thank you, Chef Vaughn." She took a small sip. "What's next? Are you heading back to New York?"

"Tomorrow morning. I have an early flight. Unfortunately, before the show started, I gave Wendy free rein over my schedule during the break. She took advantage and filled my itinerary."

"I'll miss you," she said softly, because she couldn't contain her words.

Maya smiled. "Me too."

"It sounds like you'll be too busy."

"So will you."

Shannon sighed. "Don't remind me. I don't want to freak out about my lack of ideas for these cakes."

"What? You just did the interview. Give that time to marinate, and something will come to you. Besides, you heard the man—" she nodded in Hugh's direction—"for tonight, no work, just play."

"Ah, so you're just trying to comply with your contractual obligation."

"Exactly." She set her glass down and grabbed Shannon's wrist. "So let's go join the rest of the group and enjoy this night before you start stressing about the next step."

Shannon allowed herself to be pulled along, though she'd already started dreading saying good-bye to Maya tonight. She'd see her again at the finale, but they hadn't talked about whether they'd stay in touch over the break. She'd been telling herself Maya would flee Nashville at the first chance, despite her hope that she might stick around, and she'd just confirmed her suspicion.

CHAPTER TWENTY

Hey, welcome back." Jori hugged her, then pulled back and held her at arm's length. "It's so good to see you. How are you?"

"I'm good." She couldn't keep the smile off her face. "I'm great, actually."

"Great? Like final-three great?"

"I'm not supposed to say." Almost against her will, her head bobbed in an enthusiastic nod.

"Oh my God." Jori threw her arms around her again.

"Hey, I said I can't say. I'm neither confirming nor denying."

"Sure. Sure. I won't tell anyone." Jori winked. "Except Sawyer, and she can keep a secret."

"Seriously. This goes in the vault."

"Okay. I know."

"I actually came to see if you meant it when you said I could come back anytime."

"Of course I did. But I'm confused. Why would you need to come back?"

"I need to work, Jori. Otherwise, I'll go crazy sitting around and doing nothing and just waiting for the finale."

"Shouldn't you be preparing for said finale?"

She waved a hand dismissively. "I have time for both. Or I can make time for both. It's probably just as detrimental if I spend too much time thinking about it, too."

"Okay, but you'll probably want to stay in the kitchen. Let Mackenzie handle the front. We're already getting people in asking about you. And they all want to know if you're a finalist."

She grimaced. Hiding the fact that she'd made the final three for the next eight weeks would be harder than she'd anticipated. "I have another favor to ask."

"Shoot."

"Once I have concrete plans for the final project, I need to practice. Where better than a commercial kitchen—"

"Absolutely. You can do it here."

"It needs to be after hours. I'll need the peace, and I don't want anyone seeing it."

"You're going to work here all day, then spend evenings here as well? You'll be sick of this place."

"Maybe. But other than getting to know my granddaughter, I don't have any other plans during the break."

"No plans to see a certain chef we both know? Okay, I don't really know her, but I've met her."

"What? Why would I—"

"Don't even think about playing coy with me." Jori held up a finger. "I've been watching the shows. I see the sexual tension between you two. In the beginning, not so much, but lately—"

"Seriously?" Heat rushed to Shannon's cheeks. "It's that obvious?"

"Eh, maybe not to everyone. But I know you."

Shannon grinned. After again swearing her to secrecy, she filled Jori in on the progress of their relationship thus far. She skipped over most of the sex, but Jori did manage to pry a few illicit details out of her.

"She's amazing. She's gorgeous, obviously, but more than that, she's sweet and sensitive."

"And sexy," Jori added.

"Yeah, that too. I just feel good when I'm around her, you know?"

"It seems like she feels the same way about you. So what's the problem?"

"You know her reputation. Her lifestyle is way too fast for me."

"That doesn't sound like the woman you just described. So it seems like you need to figure out who you trust more, the media's image of her or your own interpretation after having spent time with her."

"I don't know if it's that easy."

"You're afraid."

"Of what?"

"That you won't be enough for her. Believe me, if anyone understands this, I do. Maya's a lot like Sawyer, both outgoing and charismatic. In the beginning, I didn't think I'd be enough to hold her interest. You think Maya is worldly and could have anyone, so, why you?"

Shannon shrugged. "Maybe."

"*If* those stories are true and she's dated all of those people, there must be a reason why none of them stuck. They weren't what she was looking for."

"And you think I am?"

"You have as good a chance as anyone. Don't sell yourself short. You have a lot to offer." Jori squeezed her arm. "So where did you leave it?"

"She went to New York this morning—prior commitments. She didn't say when she'd be back. I gave her my cell number. We'll see if she uses it."

❖

"We need to start thinking about what's next." Wendy picked the maraschino cherry out of her drink and dropped it in her mouth.

"Next? I'm not even done with the last project. And you've got me pretty booked for the two months I'm free." Maya pushed her salad around on her plate, wishing she could have ordered a burger. But the Southern food and sweets from her time in Nashville had caught up with her, and now it was time to tighten the belt—before she had to loosen hers.

"You've got several offers on the table. Your publisher wants to do another cookbook. Or I have a couple of quick consulting offers. And of course, there are a slew of interviews available."

"No interviews. Not right now." She shook her head. She still had the promised exclusive hanging over her head. And her contract with *For the Love of Cake* included multiple press obligations as well. "What if I wanted to slow down for a while?"

"Ha. And do what? Bake cookies?" Wendy laughed, and then when she saw that Maya was serious, she gave her a disbelieving look. "Please, don't tell me how sick you are of all of the fancy parties, amazing food, and free booze. Because I might have to punch you in the throat."

"No. It's not that. But I've been going nonstop for over a year now. And I know I set that pace. But maybe I need to slow down and think before rushing into the next big project."

Wendy narrowed her eyes. "Where's this coming from? Not that I think it's a bad idea, but what brought it on?"

Maya shrugged. "It's not like I need the money. Maybe I'll do some traveling—finally take that vacation."

"Are you thinking about traveling with anyone in particular?"

"Maybe."

"So it's serious with Soccer Mom, then?"

"I think I'm going to require you to call her by her name at least six times before I let you meet her. Then maybe you won't call her Soccer Mom to her face." She suspected Shannon might not think the nickname was so cute. She might even be offended. Maya worried that Shannon still thought, at least in part, that she was just another conquest.

"Oh, am I going to meet her?"

"Sure. Eventually."

"This is serious."

"Stop acting so astonished. I can be in a relationship."

Wendy nodded, but doubt painted her expression. Maya turned her attention back to the wilting lettuce on her plate. She wouldn't dwell on the fact that her closest friend didn't think she was capable of being happy.

❖

"Do you want to go again?" Maya asked, her eyes still hazy from her lingering orgasm.

"Again? I can't believe you talked me into doing that the first time." Shannon lay sprawled out on her sofa, weak from her own climax as well.

"It was fun, wasn't it?" Maya sat up and leaned forward, bringing her closer to the camera on her iPad.

"It sure was." Shannon didn't have the energy to move, though she did manage to remove her hand from the front of her pants. She turned her head in the general direction of her own tablet, which was propped up on the coffee table beside her. "But I didn't know this was what you had in mind when you suggested video chatting while we're apart."

"Why just talk on the phone when we can see each other?"

"Please don't remind me that I fell for that."

"Aren't you glad you did?"

She really was. She didn't know how she would have survived these past four weeks if it hadn't been for their almost nightly chats. Tonight was the first time they'd added this new physical aspect. Until now, they'd just been talking, flirting, and making promises about when they were together again.

Though she'd been extremely busy at the bakery and working on her designs for the finale, Maya still managed to invade her thoughts. When she tried a new recipe, she wondered if Maya would like it. As she practiced her cakes, she imagined being back on set and having her work judged by Maya.

"I have that benefit tonight. But I really want to stay here with you," Maya said.

"You're going to get me in trouble with Wendy if you don't show up."

"Maybe. But wouldn't it be worth it?"

"I suppose you have to get up and put on clothes, huh?"

"Things do tend to be less complicated when I put clothes on before I go out."

"Okay, fine. Go."

Maya reached toward the screen as if about to end the call.

"Wait," Shannon demanded. "Call me back before you go. I want to see this dress you've been raving about all week."

An hour later, she stared at Maya's image on her screen. The black sleeveless dress hugged her body all the way to her knees before it flared out to drape to the floor. When she turned, Shannon drew in a sharp breath. The keyhole slit down the center of her chest gaped open just enough to reveal the curves of her breasts. The tight torso accentuated her toned arms and narrow waist.

"That is an amazing dress." Shannon wanted so badly to be there with her, to touch her waist and know the texture of that fabric beneath her fingertips.

"You think so?"

"Oh, yes." She would kiss her neck, then that sensitive spot behind her jaw. She would slip her hand inside the slit in that dress and caress her breast. "It's damn near perfect."

She wanted to rake her fingernails into the short hair at the back of Maya's head and watch her shiver in response. "Have I mentioned how much I love your new haircut?" The edgy style contrasted nicely with her expertly applied makeup and the gorgeously feminine dress.

"I think you've mentioned it a time or two." Maya frowned. "I really do have to go."

Shannon nodded, taking a bit of solace in Maya's reluctance to let her go as well. She didn't want to be the only one pining.

❖

"Maya, a minute of your time?"

She turned toward the familiar voice as she reached the end of the red carpet. "Charlie? You clean up well." She guessed his classic-cut tuxedo had a designer label. Only his press credentials distinguished him from the rest of the VIPs milling about.

"Why, thank you. So?" He pulled a small recorder from the inside pocket of his jacket and held it up.

"You came prepared." Maya shrugged. "Sure, why not." After their last interview, she didn't feel she owed him anything. But maybe she was feeling generous today. She stepped out of the way of the others still coming down the carpet to enter the building. Cameras flashed nonstop with each new celebrity to emerge from a limo.

"You look happy. This new gig obviously agrees with you."

Maya nodded. "I am enjoying myself. The show's great. And we have some very talented chefs on this season."

"Have you finished filming yet?"

"Almost. We're actually on a break while the rest of the episodes air, but the live finale is coming up soon."

"Any hints about who's in it?"

"You know I can't do that."

"Worth a shot." He grinned. "What's next for you after this?"

She tilted her head to the side. "I'm not exactly sure."

They chatted for a few more minutes about the benefit and the charity it would serve. He asked predictable questions and she gave the expected answers.

"Thanks, a lot." He clicked his recorder off. He'd acted graciously, though she suspected he knew as well as she did that his interview hadn't yielded anything print-worthy. "I didn't expect you to agree after our last interview."

"It's all business, Charlie."

"It doesn't have to be just business." He wound his arm around her waist and pulled her close so quickly that Maya put her hand against his chest to brace from falling completely against him.

She stepped smoothly out of his embrace. "I think it does."

"Are you seeing someone new?"

"My reasons haven't changed since the first time we met." While she admitted he was a good-looking guy, she had no chemistry with him. During their very first conversation, she'd been turned off by his conceit and apparent belief that she should fall at his feet.

"I've never seen you so relaxed and happy."

"What do you mean? I'm always happy."

"So, are you seeing someone? Or since I haven't seen you on the society pages lately, before tonight that is, should I assume it's work that puts that smile on your face?" He studied Maya closely, as if she might give away the answer in her expression. But she had plenty of practice at keeping her face neutral.

"I've been in Nashville, working. Not much time for the society pages down there." She stepped around him and entered the building. She doubted he'd actually picked up on any indication she was seeing someone; he'd simply been fishing for a story. But his questions made her think about how much more she would enjoy this benefit if Shannon were here. She'd love to escort her down the carpet and wondered if she'd ever get the chance.

Though they rarely went a day without talking, they both seemed to be avoiding defining their relationship. And maybe it was best that they didn't until after the show wrapped. But the next four weeks couldn't pass quickly enough for her. Maybe she could get Wendy to rearrange her schedule so she could go back a little early.

❖

Maya woke to the sound of her iPad signaling a video call. She turned over and blindly reached for the nightstand, knocking her iPad and the television remote to the floor.

"Damn it," she muttered, half-crawling out of bed to retrieve it. The benefit had gone late and Wendy had talked her into a party afterward, although she suspected Wendy only pushed so hard because she wanted to go and Maya was her ticket in. A cab had dropped her at her place around five a.m.

She glanced at the clock as she flipped open her tablet cover. She didn't feel like she'd gotten nearly seven hours of sleep. She'd also let Wendy talk her into a couple more drinks than she normally would have, and, combined with the secondhand smoke from the party, she had quite the headache. Had everyone at the party been smoking?

She accepted the call and lay back down in bed, propping her tablet up on her stomach.

"Good morning," she said, barely containing a yawn until she was done speaking.

Shannon's face appeared on the screen but she didn't say anything. Her expression seemed distant, almost angry.

"What's wrong?"

Shannon raised a magazine, if you could even call a tabloid rag a magazine. But that didn't matter because there on the cover was a picture of Maya and Charlie looking way too close. The caption read MAYA VAUGHN GETTING COZY WITH NEW GUY? She flinched. Had she done something last night that she didn't remember? She sat up and leaned forward, trying to get a closer look. Squinting, she finally realized when the picture was taken.

"That was not what it looked like." She sure felt like she'd been saying that a lot lately.

Shannon's doubtful expression indicated she didn't believe her.

"Yeah, I've earned my reputation in the past, but not this time. He's a reporter. I'd just finished an interview. He put his arm around me and someone snapped a picture." She jabbed at the picture. "It happens all the time." Maya shook her head. "Only a couple of weeks ago, that photo made you and I appear a lot closer than that."

"You think that makes your case? We've slept together. You just said you've earned your reputation."

"I also said that's not what it looked like."

"And I'm supposed to take your word for it?"

"Yes. When are you going to see me for who I am, instead of what *they've* made me out to be?" Panic had her raising her voice.

"When are you going to *be* more than who they've made you?" Shannon shot back, then sighed heavily. "Look, I know that's not you—not completely. But do you? I mean, flirting and playing that playgirl role comes so automatically to you, and sometimes you don't even realize you're doing it. I don't believe you're even into it half the time. But it's what people expect of you, so you just give it to them."

"That's not what this was. I didn't even flirt with him. I'd just finished giving him an interview and he grabbed me. What you don't see in that picture is that I pulled away less than a second later."

Shannon didn't seem to be listening to her explanation, as if once she'd started talking she couldn't stop. "You start to open up with me. I know you do. But then, you—I don't know, do you get scared? Because it's like you realize what you're doing and you shut down."

"I don't need to be psychoanalyzed," Maya snapped. Shannon's words skated too close to the truth.

She leaned forward and narrowed her eyes. "Or, worse, you give me a wink and a line that makes me feel like I'm no different than the rest of them."

"Listen to yourself. The rest of them? Do you even really know how many others there have been? Or are you just taking the tabloids at their word?" Anger propelled Maya out of bed, and she fumbled to keep her iPad pointed in the right direction. She had opened up to Shannon. And this was what it got her? Accusations and distrust.

"Men, women, it doesn't matter to you, does it? But I should have already known that."

"Oh, so that's what this is about? Because he's a man? And you still have an issue with me being bisexual?"

"What? No."

Maya didn't believe her. "If you're going to be so quick to believe everything that's printed about me, maybe you *are* just like the rest of them."

"If that's the way you feel, maybe we don't have anything more to talk about. Because I certainly don't want to be just another one of many who only get your public persona."

❖

"Oh, sweetie." Jori pulled Shannon into a sympathetic hug.

She'd called Jori after her conversation with Maya. Jori told her to come over to their house and she'd make them both lunch while they talked. She'd just finished recounting the exchange with Maya, which had ended on a tense note without the usual promises to call the next day.

"It's just so frustrating, with her being there and me here. I know I'll see her again in a month. But then what? We haven't talked about our plans after the show. I have a home and family here. And she's—well, can you see her leaving New York for Nashville?" Shannon settled on one end of the couch, and Jori sat next to her.

"You're getting way ahead of yourself."

"Am I?"

"Yes. You've just had your first fight, and now you're stressing about who's moving where? I know long distance is hard. Sawyer and I struggle to make time for each other and we're in the same city. But it sounds like you guys have a lot to talk about before you even get to that point." Jori put a hand on Shannon's arm as if she needed to soften the impact of her words. "Honey, she's not a face in a magazine anymore."

"I know that."

"Do you?"

"What do you mean?"

"It has to be pretty surreal. She's someone you looked up to professionally, and let's admit it—lusted after personally. She's famous and unattainable. Then all of a sudden, she isn't so unattainable anymore and you're spending time with her. I can see where that would be an adjustment. If I'd told you two months ago that you would get close to Maya Vaughn and even sleep with her, what would you have said?"

"That you're crazy."

"Exactly."

Sure, parts of the last two months felt surreal, but she'd thought she stayed pretty self-aware as well. She had to admit, though, that this was the Greta Haus situation all over again. She couldn't expect to maintain a relationship with Maya if she was constantly waiting for her to leave her—to find someone else she'd rather be with.

"I overreacted."

"I think you may have. It sounds like she was trying to be straight with you, and instead of believing her, you took the word of a tabloid reporter. How do you think that made her feel? Certainly not trusted."

CHAPTER TWENTY-ONE

A bell attached to the door tinkled as Maya opened it, thwarting her attempt to sneak in unannounced. But she entered anyway, drawing in the intoxicating aromas as she went.

When Jori came through the door from the kitchen and saw her, she gave her a wary smile.

"Hi. I thought you were a customer."

Maya bent to look in the display case. "How do you know I'm not?"

Jori reached in and lifted a brownie from a stack inside and wrapped it in tissue paper. The tag in front of them read CHERRY CORDIAL BROWNIES. Maya's stomach growled loudly.

She grimaced. "I skipped lunch. But in my defense, I was on a plane."

"Not that I'm condoning sweets as meal replacement." Jori handed her the brownie. "I know it's not what you're really here for anyway, but I think you'll like it."

"I'm sure I will." She inched open the paper, lifted it to her nose, and drew in the scent of chocolate.

Jori laughed. "God, you really are just like Sawyer."

"Maybe one day I'll meet your partner. Sounds like we'd get along great." Maya gave in and took a bite, moaning as the tang of cherries and sweetened cream cheese cut the richness of the chocolate.

Jori raised a brow. "Maybe. Are you planning to be around here often?"

She didn't know how to answer that question, so she asked one of her own. "Is she here?"

Jori tilted her head toward the kitchen. Taking that as an invitation, Maya started to move around the counter, but Jori stopped her with a hand on her arm.

"I don't need to do the whole overprotective-friend thing and tell you how special she is, do I?"

"Um—"

"Because, with the show, she's under a lot of stress right now, and no matter how amazing a chef I think you are, I'm not afraid—"

"Okay." Maya held up her hands in surrender. "I'm not sure I want to know how you might end that threat. I'm not going to lie. I'm a little afraid of you right now." She met Jori's eyes and gave her as honest an answer as she could right then. "I don't want to make things harder for her. I just—I had to see her."

She didn't say that she hadn't stopped thinking about her and their last conversation. Or that she'd tried for two days to deny her urge to get on a plane and fix things face-to-face, and finally had given in and made Wendy clear her schedule. She didn't say that she knew how their almost certainly divergent paths complicated the situation and right now she didn't care. And she absolutely didn't say unless she could figure out how to restrain herself, she would probably grab Shannon and kiss her right there in Jori's kitchen. And she might have trouble stopping at a kiss.

"Okay. Go on."

Maya took another bite of her brownie and raised it in tribute to the woman who created such a heavenly confection. "Amazing. Seriously."

"Just go." Jori waved her away. "I know how easy you chocolate whores are to please."

Maya feigned an injured look that she knew Jori wouldn't buy. After she passed through the door to the kitchen, it made a soft thud as it swung closed behind her.

"I'm almost done with this one. Then there's just the one birthday cake left," Shannon said, not looking up from the cake she worked on. She obviously thought Jori had returned.

Instead of announcing herself, Maya watched her decorate. With her left hand she spun the pedestal, rotating the round two-layer cake while she applied an even line of lime-green piping with the pastry bag in her right hand. The number of different colors staining her fingers indicated this wasn't her first project of the day.

"Are you keeping up your skills?"

Shannon looked up from the cake, and the tip of her pastry bag smeared green icing into the pristine white edge of the cake. "What are you doing here?"

"Obviously distracting you." Maya rushed forward and picked up a spatula. "I'm sorry. Let me help you fix that."

"I've got it." Shannon took the spatula and began carefully lifting away the marred section of icing.

Maya waited while she expertly fixed the cake. Now that she was here, she didn't know exactly what to say. Maybe she should have been rehearsing that during the two-and-a-half-hour nonstop flight from LaGuardia.

"Is that the remaining birthday cake?" She indicated a stack of un-iced cakes on the rack behind Shannon.

"Yep. That one's going to take the rest of the day, so I knocked out the others first."

"What's the theme?"

"Pirate ship." Shannon nodded toward a pile of small wooden dowels and a spool of thin filament.

"Can I help?"

Shannon finished the last line of piping on the green cake with a flourish. She pulled a flattened box from under the counter, then expertly folded and tucked the flaps in place. "Is that really how you want to spend your time?"

Maya took a step closer. She'd held herself back for long enough, and now she just needed to touch her. She rubbed at a smear of pink icing along Shannon's jaw, flaking away the dried sugar. When she sought Shannon's gaze she found it locked on her own lips. Maya sucked her bottom lip between her teeth and Shannon jerked her eyes up, desire reflecting in them.

"I can't think of anything I'd rather do."

Shannon smiled. "You're getting better at this. That one actually sounded sincere."

"It was." When Maya kept her expression serious, Shannon's smile faded. "I'm sorry. I was a jerk."

"No. I was. I should have believed your explanation."

Maya nodded. "I got frustrated when you didn't, and I lashed out. But if you can't trust me, we can't have a future. I know that's true for any couple, but for us—for the life I'm living and the one you're about to be living, it's even more important and more difficult. Reporters will make something out of nothing. Jealous people will say things to break us up. And we'll have to spend time apart, more than we want to. You have to trust me." She took Shannon's hands and bent her head to meet her eyes. "When I tell you that I love you, you have to believe that is more important to me than anything else."

"You—did you just say that you love me?"

"I did."

"And you meant it?"

"Yeah." She circled her arms around Shannon's waist and pulled her close. "I love you."

"*The* Maya Vaughn just said that—"

Maya pushed her back against the counter and silenced her with a kiss. Had the counter not been full of decorating supplies, she might have lifted her onto the counter and shown her just how real she was. Actually, if it wasn't for Jori and the certainty that they would get caught, she might do it anyway and put the various colored icings to good use.

As they eased apart, Shannon stroked Maya's cheek tenderly. "Are you going to just hop on a plane to apologize every time we argue?"

"I hope not."

"No?"

"I hope we'll figure out how to be in the same state from time to time."

Shannon nodded. "We've got time."

❖

"Hey, I didn't think we'd see you here today." Sawyer strolled through the alley from the direction of the restaurant just as Shannon arrived.

"Is that why you're sneaking into the bakery? For a quickie?"

"I wish. I can't wait for those preg—"

"What?"

"Nothing." Sawyer sighed. "I was going to say, I can't wait for those pregnancy hormones I've heard so much about to kick in."

"Jori's pregnant?"

Sawyer nodded. "But keep it to yourself. She doesn't want anyone to know until after her first trimester. But she's busting to tell someone, so if she finds out I already let you in—"

"I'll act surprised when she tells me. Oh my God, that's so awesome. I didn't know you guys were trying."

"We only decided recently. Can you believe it took on the first attempt? I didn't think it would be so quick when I agreed to try." Sawyer pulled open the bakery door and waited for Shannon to go in before she followed.

In the kitchen, Mackenzie had just pulled a tray of sugar cookies from the oven. Sawyer gravitated toward her side.

"Nope. Step back," Mackenzie said. "These are for a customer order."

"You don't have even one extra?"

"Go out front and get one out of the case." Mackenzie put her body between Sawyer and the tray of cookies and sent Shannon a silent plea for help.

"But those are still warm."

"Leave the cookies alone," Jori called as she walked into the kitchen. She glared at Sawyer, then turned disapproving eyes on Mackenzie and Shannon. "Can't you two handle her? You outnumber her."

"But she outranks us," Shannon said.

"*I* pay both of you. Part of your job is to protect my inventory." Jori waved in Shannon's direction. "Shannon, can I speak to you privately?"

"Sure."

"I'll be up front." Mackenzie grabbed Sawyer's arm. "You come with me. I don't trust you with those cookies."

As the door closed behind them, Jori said, "Have you seen any tabloids today?"

"No. I haven't been to the grocery store in over a week."

Jori pulled a folded copy of one of the trashier editions from the inside of her bag and set it on the counter between them. Her nervous expression had dread building in Shannon. She didn't pick it up, but she didn't have to in order to see Maya's face across the entire cover. She sucked in a breath at the words in bold print scrawled across the front of the image. MISCARRIAGE SHOCKER! ABORTION RUMORS FALSE.

"Shit."

"Okay. You're mad, but you're not shocked. You knew about this."

She nodded slowly, a cold feeling squeezing her heart. "I wanted to tell you. But she asked me not to."

"According to this article, Maya revealed this voluntarily in an interview."

"It's a long story. She promised this interview to keep a photo of us from going public."

"What photo?"

"Don't let your imagination go crazy. It wasn't that risqué. But it could have tarnished my career before it really got a chance to take off, so Maya tried to protect me."

"Wow."

"Yeah. I was trying to talk her out of it. But apparently now I'm too late. Damn it." She wanted to talk to Maya—to see her. "She's at my apartment—"

"Really? I told Sawyer she wouldn't be getting a hotel room. I'm surprised you made it in so early this morning."

Despite the flush burning up her neck, Shannon didn't address her implication. "She's staying in town for a few days."

"Sure. She did fly all the way down here."

"Then in just three weeks she'll be back for the finale. And I have a ton of preparation to do before then anyway." Shannon's eyes fell on the tabloid again. She clenched her jaw against a resurgence of anger. "Do you mind if I go home early?"

"No problem. Whatever you need."

❖

"Maya."

"In here," Maya called from the kitchen. She'd hoped to have dinner ready when Shannon got home from work, but then she hadn't expected her so soon.

"Something smells good," Shannon said.

"Roasted turkey breast, with my secret ingredient."

Shannon glanced at the packaging on the counter. "Butterball?"

"I'm a pastry chef, not a line cook." Maya kissed Shannon's cheek, then returned to cutting up red potatoes for roasting. "You're home early."

"Are you okay?"

Maya stopped and laid down her knife. "You saw the story."

"Actually, Jori brought it to my attention. A little warning would have been nice."

Maya nodded. "I'm sorry. I know I should have told you, but—"

"What happened? I thought you were going to wait until the show was over."

Maya shrugged. "The story had to go a little early."

"Why?"

"It doesn't matter." She didn't want to tell her that Hugh had demanded she give the interview early. She'd tried to stick to her deal, but he said the reporter was getting antsy and threatening again to run the photo. She suspected the producers wanted the ratings associated with a sensational story heading into the finale. And of course, her personal tragedy made for better press than a controversy that could call into question the integrity of the show. She almost laughed aloud at the direction of her thoughts. After her mentoring experience, she no longer had any illusions about the show having integrity.

"When did you give this interview?"

"The day after we argued."

"So you knew it was coming out today."

Maya nodded.

"Is that why you came here?"

"Not entirely. Look, I wanted to apologize. I wanted to see you. Even though I chose this, I knew when the story ran, it would be hard for me, and I wanted to be with you. And yes, maybe hide out from where the press knows to find me."

"Maya, you didn't have to do this." Shannon sounded exhausted.

Maya led her into the living room and guided her to sit on the couch. She settled beside her. "I know you don't agree with this. But it's already done, so there's no point arguing. Please know that I had your best interest at heart."

"I know how you feel about your privacy, and I didn't need you to sacrifice it for me." She looped her arm through Maya's and stroked her forearm.

"I chose to. It was important to me."

"Well, as you said, it's done now. But promise me that going forward, you'll include me in these types of decisions. We're in this together."

"Fine." Maya sighed. "But I have to go back to New York in a couple of days, and I'll probably spend the next three weeks trying not to answer questions about the miscarriage." She leaned into Shannon. "So for the next two days, maybe we can focus on other things."

"Three weeks. That sounds so long."

"We've still got our video chats."

"Mmm, that's something to look forward to." Shannon caressed Maya's jaw, turned her face toward her, and gave a lingering kiss.

When she started to ease back, Maya cupped the back of her neck and brought her back for more. She traced her tongue across Shannon's lip, and when Shannon's tongue met hers, she sighed against her mouth.

"Was there something particular you wanted to focus on?" Shannon asked when Maya slid her mouth over her jaw to her neck.

Maya nodded. "You." She rose, intent on taking Shannon once on the sofa before moving to her bedroom.

"Hmm, judging by current conditions, that shouldn't take long. Then what?"

"More. More of you."

"That sounds wonderful." Shannon placed her hand in the center of Maya's chest and put some distance between them. "But first," she sat up, then moved to straddle Maya's lap, "there's something I want to take care of."

"Hey, I was in the middle of—"

"Please, let me."

Maya's own desire reflected in Shannon's eyes, but beneath it, she also saw fierce protectiveness. She'd kept the interview from Shannon until the last possible moment, because telling herself she needed to shield Shannon distracted her from feeling the tearing pain of reliving that horrible time in her life with a virtual stranger. But now, here with Shannon, she longed to give in to Shannon's obvious wish to take care of her.

"Okay," she whispered, letting Shannon pull her shirt over her head.

She grabbed the fly of her own jeans and practically tore it open, then lifted up to push them down. Shannon guided her back until she was lying against the arm of the sofa. Shannon trailed her hand down the center of her chest. When she smoothed it over her abdomen and rested it there, the tenderness in Shannon's eyes nearly brought tears to her own. Shannon bent and kissed her stomach.

She closed her eyes and immersed herself in Shannon's touch, finding escape from all the expectations, the stress, and, most important, her grief. Shannon kissed and stroked lower, and with each pass of her fingers and lips, Maya felt the dark, tight places within unfurl, and at the same time her arousal rose and filled in the emptiness—no, Shannon filled the emptiness. *Shannon.*

Maya opened her eyes and whispered her name as she let go. She surged and pulsed and called out, and all the while Shannon stayed with her, her head bowed over her, her hair spilling across her thighs. Only when Maya sagged back against the sofa arm did Shannon lift her head and meet her eyes again.

Maya let out a heavy breath, her body limp with satisfaction and drained of emotion. No one had ever looked at her like that before. Men and women alike had gazed at her with lust in their eyes. Some had shown her ambition or greed. But no one had ever given her a glimpse of such complete and unselfish love and generosity.

CHAPTER TWENTY-TWO

Okay, chefs, I know you've all been working hard on your designs. But we have a little twist for you. Only two of you will actually be constructing your cakes." Eric paused to let the contestants gasp in shock, and they didn't disappoint. For once, Hugh hadn't prepped them. Though the live portion of the finale didn't begin until tomorrow, as that time drew nearer, the element of surprise seemed to become more important. "You'll each be presenting your ideas to David and Viola, and they will decide which two they want to see built. Once you've done so, they will choose a winner from those two cakes."

Eric launched right into the presentations of their plans, giving them no more time to prepare. He asked Ned and Alice to head off set while Shannon explained her design. Shannon was grateful for the chance to go first. She didn't need any more time to build up her nerves.

Once everyone was in place to film her segment, she took her place in front of David, Viola, and the mentors. She took a moment to reflect on how far she'd come in just three months. She met Maya's eyes briefly, smiled, and prepared to give this presentation everything she had.

Once filming started, she looked first at David and then at Viola. "I enjoyed meeting you both and am honored to have a chance to create the cakes for your special day. Weddings are one of my favorite events to decorate for. It's always a treat to meet a couple on the verge of embarking on a new life together. David and Viola, you've been touring together for over a year." She glanced at Maya but didn't let her gaze linger there. "I'm of the opinion that spending time in such close proximity accelerates the formation of the bond of love. Wouldn't you agree?"

"That year did feel a lot longer to me," David joked, earning him a swat on the shoulder from Viola.

"David, your love for Viola is evident, simply in the way you look at her. You accept her for the country girl she is in private and the city girl she wants to be when she's onstage. And since we all know that the wedding cake really is all about the bride, Viola, this cake is for you."

Shannon propped her sketch for the wedding cake on the easel beside her. "The majority of the fondant work is done in classic white, smooth and simple. The base of each of the four tiers is ringed with woven strands of wild grasses. This side of the cake," she pointed, "features a cascade of wildflowers, all made of gum paste and modeling chocolate. This sketch is by no means concrete. What I would love to do is have you share with me some of the photos you've taken on your travels so I can try to duplicate some of the specific flowers and color palettes that you captured."

Viola looked impressed, bolstering Shannon's confidence. She picked up the sketch of the groom's cake, not yet revealing it to her audience.

"For the theme of your cake, David, I chose a subject that not only represents you but also the story you both told about your times on tour together."

Rather than describe the cake, she flipped the sketch and let the image speak for itself. She planned to build the cake in the shape of a poker table, complete with the padded rail and cup holders. She had sculpted figures of both David and Viola. David, clad in a tuxedo, had a paltry stack of chips pushed out in front of him. His cards lay in front of him, flipped up to reveal only a pair of twos. Viola sat across from him, in a wedding dress, looking around her towering stack of chips at him. Her cards, a royal flush of hearts, were poised to take the rest of his money.

❖

"Which two designs would you like to see come to life?" Eric asked David and Viola.

Maya hadn't realized how nervous she would be about this elimination. She could tell herself she wanted Alice and Shannon to go head-to-head because they were both on her team. But was that really true? Or was she really only concerned with seeing Shannon succeed? Had she lost her objectivity? She was just glad she wouldn't have any judging responsibilities from this point forward.

"We like all the designs," Viola said.

"They were all creative, and we'd be proud to have any one of them at our wedding," David added. "So for us it came down to the interviews."

Maya's stomach clenched with nerves. She hadn't been privy to the interviews. But she knew Shannon's track record with them.

"Alice was super friendly and very down-to-earth. We felt like she really wanted to please us. And we liked Shannon, too. She asked great questions. Her attention to detail is evident in her design, because it's very specific to us. But Ned seemed like he might have a checklist of questions he asked every client. His cake looks great, but it also looks like it could fit a lot of different couples, not just us." Viola grasped David's hand and smiled at him. "So for that reason, we would like to see cakes made by Shannon and Alice."

Ned's face turned red and contorted with anger. Alice grabbed Shannon and hugged her tight, squeaking with pleasure. Shannon turned her head as she struggled to get free. But when her eyes met Maya's she seemed to calm down. Maya smiled, proud of both women, but especially of Shannon.

"This is bullshit," Ned exclaimed.

"Ned—"

"No. I deserve this more than either of these two—"

"Enough," Jacques barked before he could finish his insult. "The decision has been made. You will leave the kitchen now."

He scowled but didn't say anymore. As he stepped out of camera range, Hugh moved to his side and escorted him the rest of the way.

After they finished for the afternoon, Hugh reviewed their schedule for the following day. They would have the morning off, then would report to the set two hours before the finale. After hair and makeup, they would be allowed to do much of the prep work for their designs. Some shots from that activity would be aired during the live portion, while they continued to work. Then they and the beginnings of their cakes would be transported to the Ryman Auditorium, where they would finish working onstage at the mother church in front of a live audience.

❖

Sitting in a makeup chair, Shannon stared at herself in the mirror. She was less than two hours from a moment that could change her career. Despite her impatience to get her hands on some cake, she tried not to fidget while her makeup was applied. She tried to force herself to relax. Her life had changed the moment she accepted her place on this show, and she'd grown with each challenge, each win, and each loss since then. She didn't need to worry about the finale because the steps toward her future had already been set in motion. All she had to do was be patient and enjoy the ride.

In two hours she would be on a stage, behind a worktable, in front of a live audience. Somewhere in those seats, Jori and Sawyer, and her daughter and son-in-law would be watching, though she probably wouldn't be able to pick them out from where she stood.

"Nervous?" At Maya's voice, Shannon jerked her eyes back to the mirror. Maya stood behind her, smiling. She hadn't been through hair or makeup yet, so her soft locks lay flat against her head. Shannon still hadn't decided if she liked her hair that way better than when it was styled and edgy. She looked comfortable in jeans and a plain black T-shirt. Later she'd trade the outfit for a freshly pressed chef's coat.

"A little."

"Don't be. You'll be great. They've already approved your design. All you have to do is bring it to life."

"Are you giving Alice the same pep talk?" Shannon gave her a wink.

Maya glanced at the guy doing her makeup. "Can we have a minute?"

"Almost done." He didn't look up from putting the finishing touches on her lips.

Shannon could care less whether she was wearing lipstick on that stage, but she waited patiently until he stepped back, scanned her face, and gave an approving nod.

"Good luck." He squeezed her arm before walking away.

Maya took a step forward, standing so close Shannon could smell the spicy scent of her perfume. She lifted her hands and let them hover over Shannon's shoulders for a moment, as if she wanted to touch her, but then dropped them to her side.

"I missed you last night," Shannon said, still holding Maya's gaze in the mirror. "I was tempted to go down to the fitness room and see if you were there."

"I wasn't." Maya touched her own lips with two fingers. "I missed you, too. But I didn't think we should chance getting caught. So I had to entertain myself."

"If that means what I think it does, I'm sorry I missed it." At the moment, she couldn't think of anything hotter.

Maya's answering smile was full of promise.

"What's going to happen after the show?" Shannon blurted before she could stop herself, then was sorry she'd ruined that moment. "We haven't really talked about it—not specifically. I mean, can we even date given our involvement in the show?"

"Don't worry about that right now. The only thing you should be thinking about is the finale. You go do that first, and then we'll figure out the rest."

"Oh, okay."

"Hey, I'm not blowing you off." Maya glanced toward the door, then moved around to stand between Shannon and the mirror. She met Shannon's eyes. "I love you. I don't say that lightly. I'm not going to just let this go because some producers won't like it. So don't worry—don't let what we are or might be distract you. This—

the finale, it's an awesome moment for you. Enjoy it to the absolute fullest, win or lose."

Shannon nodded. "I love you, too." She grinned, hoping Maya could see the longing in her eyes, but she just in case she didn't, she said, "Now get out of here so I can think about something besides my desire to sweep that makeup table clean, then grab you and throw you up on it."

"Oh my God," Maya whispered, desire infusing her expression. "If you'd told me that's what you wanted our first day on set, I would've had more time to figure out how to sneak you in here and make it happen."

"I'll admit, I pretty much wanted that from the first time I met you."

When Eric called time, Shannon raised her hands and stepped back. She pulled a bandana from her back pocket and mopped her forehead. She'd never worked so hard and fast as she just had, while still trying to maintain her quality. In addition to blinding her from seeing very far into the audience, the lights onstage felt hotter than any she'd encountered on set.

"Ladies, if you'll join me over here." Eric stood several feet away from their two worktables.

After she and Alice crossed to him, he invited David, Viola, and the mentors to look over their finished cakes. While they circled the tables, Shannon took a moment to scrutinize them as well. She'd executed her designs cleanly and accurately. She could pick apart her sculpting, but actually she was quite proud of the end result.

Alice's wedding cake contained five tiers, though only the top and bottom tiers had actually been constructed of cake. Those two layers featured a lot of texture and the deep-purple color Viola had chosen for her wedding. The middle three layers consisted of round platforms filled with cupcakes in complementary colors and three different flavors. It was a clever design, but risky. Brides would either love or hate the idea of cupcakes in place of a traditional wedding cake. Viola must have been intrigued since she chose Alice over Ned.

She'd selected a music theme in her groom's cake design, creating an exact replica of David's favorite guitar, with a string of flowers in the same deep purple draped over the neck.

When David and Viola crossed the stage to stand next to them, Alice grabbed Shannon's hand and squeezed. Shannon squeezed back.

"Jacques, what did you think of our contestants today?"

"They've both done excellent work," he said.

Shannon didn't hear much after that as her eyes locked on Maya's. In Maya's expression, she found pride and support. Maya was a winner either way, since she'd mentored them both. But, though she was probably trying to stay objective, secretly Shannon hoped a part of Maya rooted for her to win. She'd taken this incredible journey with Maya from the beginning, and she was thrilled to be standing on this stage with her now.

"Maya, what about you? Both women were on your team."

"And they've both made themselves very proud here today." Of course, she wouldn't give anything other than a safe answer.

"Well, our mentors are certainly being nicer than they were throughout the season, aren't they?" Eric played to the audience, all of whom Shannon presumed had already seen the full season.

Though she'd been uncertain whether she wanted to, Shannon had watched the episodes with Jori and Sawyer. She'd been as nervous as she was excited. With a few exceptions, she was pleased with how the show came out. The producers had done some creative editing to play up the feud between her and Ned, when really there had only been the one confrontation when he ran his mouth about Maya.

"David, Viola, it's time to hear your decision. Which set of cakes will be featured at your nuptials this weekend?"

"Clearly, I'm going to defer to my lovely bride-to-be in this case."

"Oh, no, you're not putting all the pressure on me." Viola grabbed his lapel and jerked him across the stage to the far side.

"Seems our couple would like some privacy," Eric said with an exaggerated wink. He made a slashing motion across his throat. "Cut their mics, please." The audience protested when David and Viola huddled close together and whispered, but Eric waved them off. "Sorry, folks, one drawback of a live finale is that we can't reveal it to you in editing later."

The conference seemed like it lasted an hour, but Shannon knew it was probably less than a minute. When they rejoined the rest of the group, Eric signaled for their mics to be turned back on.

"So, who's going to do the honors?" he asked, glancing between David and Viola.

"I suppose I am." Viola spoke up. "Girls, we just loved both of your cakes. And I so wish we didn't have to choose." She looked at Eric as if he was going to suddenly agree with her. But he shook his head. "Oh, look at their hopeful faces. I don't think I can break one of their hearts."

David took her hand. "I guess it's up to me then. I'm no stranger to breaking women's hearts." He paused for a round of laughter. "Shannon, your poker cake is amazing. The little figures even look like us. But since the wedding cake will be the focal point of the evening, that's what we based our decision on. And while both were beautiful, we've decided that for our wedding we'd like the cupcake cake."

Alice squealed and threw her arms around Shannon. Shannon stood stiffly in her grasp, too stunned to move. As her shock started to wear off, a wave of disappointment swamped her. She didn't realize until that moment that she'd actually been expecting to win. Finally, she shook herself out of it and gave Alice a quick hug before graciously stepping back to let Alice receive her accolades.

She schooled her features into as polite an expression as she could manage. She nodded as the others onstage congratulated her on her efforts as well. She didn't trust herself to speak without getting emotional.

She'd just spun away from a bone-crushing hug from Wayne, when she was caught up in another embrace, this one softer and much more intimate.

"I'm sorry," Maya whispered.

Shannon thought she felt Maya press her lips to her temple, but the touch was fleeting, and when Maya released her quickly she was still reeling.

"It's—no, it's fine." She smoothed her hands over the front of her chef coat, trying to control her conflicting emotions regarding the outcome of the show and the feel of Maya so close. "She earned it. You told me after the first challenge it's all about pleasing your client. She bested me in that area today. I just can't believe I lost to some damn cupcakes. I'll never live that down."

Maya laughed. "Your sculpting was incredible."

"Not as good as yours."

"Well, that's a pretty high bar," Maya said with a wink, and then her expression turned sheepish. "I have to—Alice is on my team. I have to be over there for a while." She waved in Alice's direction.

"Sure." Shannon nodded. *That's just perfect. Not only did I lose, but now I get to watch the woman I love gush over the woman who beat me.*

"I'll catch you at the after party?"

"Of course." The producers were throwing a cocktail party back at a local club for the crew, the contestants, and their families.

"And maybe an *after* after party?" Maya raised her pierced brow in that sexy little way that had gotten to her since the beginning.

Shannon warmed at the reminder that there was life after the show. "As soon as we can."

❖

Maya slid the Cardkey into the hotel door, then pushed it open when the light turned green. As she entered, she set the Cardkey on the table by the door. She'd been pleasantly surprised when Shannon had slipped it to her during the after party earlier in the night.

The room appeared empty, but she heard the shower running through the partially open bathroom door. She pushed open the door slowly and leaned against the door frame. Shannon's soapy body was clearly visible through the glass shower-stall door.

"Hey," she called over the sound of the spray. "Do you want some company?"

"I'm getting out." Shannon twisted off the water and opened the door.

Maya grabbed a towel and held it out for her. Shannon stepped close, and she wrapped the towel around her.

"I thought you might want to go home tonight." She rubbed her hands over Shannon's back.

Shannon shrugged. "The room was paid for. Might as well live the dream for one more night."

Maya simply smiled at the edge of bitterness to Shannon's words. "Maybe we should enjoy every inch of this room on Hugh's dime."

"Absolutely." Shannon grabbed her waist and tugged her close, their lips finding each other.

Maya dropped the towel and slipped her hands over Shannon's bare back. "Speaking of Hugh—"

"Okay, new rule. No talking about Hugh while one of us is naked."

Maya laughed. "Noted. But, seriously, are you sure you want to sign up for this? I know what a whirlwind it can be after the show wraps. You're going to be crazy busy and inundated with offers for interviews and jobs and promotional gigs."

"It sounds like I should be asking you if you're sure you want to sign up for this? I know how you like to be all low-profile and private."

"I do. But for you—look, I don't want to hold you back. This is going to be a very exciting time in your life. You should be able to enjoy it to the fullest." She shouldn't have brought this up now. But historically, they didn't have the best timing when it came to serious discussions anyway.

Shannon cupped her face in both hands. "Don't you know how I feel? How much I want—" She kissed Maya. "You started your journey with the show when you were in your twenties, with no responsibilities and, if you're anything like the twenty-somethings I know, very few long-term goals."

"I still have no responsibilities and very few long-term goals."

Shannon smiled. "I began in a different place. I spent nine years in a marriage I probably never should have been in. For over ten years, I worked jobs I didn't care about so I could be home nights and weekends with my daughter. I finally went to culinary school because I wanted a career I could love. But I didn't come on the show for fame and fortune. I did it to prove something to myself, to find something for me. And all the work—all of these weeks—I did that."

Maya nodded.

"I found you."

"What?"

"Yes, this show taught me that I'm stronger than I thought and that I deserve to go after what I want. And I want to be the best pastry chef I can be. I don't ever want to *have* to take a job. And I certainly don't want anyone to ever tell me what I can and can't do. So if being connected to this show means they own me, then I'm out."

"You don't know what you're giving up."

"Maybe not. But I don't have to. Through everything else in my life, the one thing I've never had is a real partner—someone to truly share the journey with. And if that person is you, then that matters more to me than fame, or money, or whatever else comes along with it."

Maya nodded. "*If* that person is me?"

"I didn't scare you, did I? Are you freaking out?"

Maya pulled Shannon close, pressing against her. She buried her hand in the back of Shannon's hair and breathed in the scent of her shampoo. "I'm not freaking out one bit."

"You sound surprised."

"I've never felt this way before." Maya kissed her neck, getting distracted by the combination of Shannon's warm skin and the glow spreading through her from Shannon's declarations. "I've never been anyone's *real partner* before."

Shannon smiled and kissed her. "Do you need some time to get used to it?"

"Possibly. I'm thinking immersion therapy." Maya led her back to the bedroom. "The more time we spend together, the more accustomed I'll get."

Shannon threw back the covers. "I'm willing to try. Why don't you take off all those clothes and get in here?"

While Maya undressed, she said, "Since we're discussing spending more time together, I've been thinking about a change of pace."

"Yeah?"

Maya nodded. "I'll keep my place in New York. But there's no reason we can't spend as much time as you want to here, as well."

"I'm so glad to hear you say that."

"Why?" She slid into bed next to Shannon and drew her close. Shannon's arm came around her waist, and Maya wondered if she'd ever felt anything more perfect.

"Because Jori's pregnant."

"Really? That's great."

"I figure she might need some help at the bakery when she gets further along. I don't want her to worry about anything but having a healthy, happy pregnancy." She caressed Maya's chest, then rested her hand over her breast. Maya's nipple tightened and Shannon smiled, as if enjoying the sensation against her palm.

"So we have time for me to show you New York first?"

"Absolutely."

"And we should tell Hugh."

Shannon glared at her. "You're already breaking the rules."

❖

"He's going to flip out." Shannon paced the hallway outside Hugh's office.

"We won't know until we go in." Maya stepped in front of her and grabbed her shoulders. "You didn't come all the way to New York just to go sightseeing, did you?"

"No." Shannon met her eyes. "No. Let's get this over with so I can enjoy the rest of my trip with you."

Maya opened the door and held it for her. Inside, she gave her name to Hugh's administrative assistant, and soon they were escorted back to his office and left to wait. Maya took a seat in one of the chairs opposite Hugh's large glass-topped desk.

"Come sit." She caught Shannon's wrist as she ventured close and pulled her into the neighboring chair. She didn't release her hand, instead resting their joined hands on her own thigh.

The door opened and Hugh strode in, looking down at a stack of papers he carried. "I'm sorry, Maya, I'm swamped today. But I've always got time for—" He stopped when he saw Shannon.

"Hello, Hugh," Shannon said.

"Shannon, nice to see you." As he looked at Maya, his gaze visibly snagged on their clasped hands, and he began shaking his head. "No. Maya, no."

She managed a contrite expression. "I'm sorry if this complicates things for you—"

"Now? It's only been three weeks since the show wrapped. And you're really going to do this?" Before they could answer, Hugh went on. "I guess I should be glad you gave me a heads up first."

Maya chuckled. "It's not going to be a big announcement or anything." She squeezed Shannon's hand and smiled at her. "But we're not going to hide it either. We'll be seen together and it will come out."

He nodded slowly. "Okay, we play the whole thing like it happened after the show ended—while you were doing the press tour together." He gave them both a stern look. "It did start after the show ended, right?"

"Whatever you say, Hugh."

"Maya."

"Nothing we did impacted the judging of the show," Maya said. "She didn't even win."

"I'll have to discuss this with the other producers, but presumably our official stance is that nothing happened until the show was over."

"Understood." Maya stood up. "You can take whatever official stance you wish. My contract has been fulfilled and my affiliation with the show is *officially* over."

She strode to the door without looking back. Shannon followed. They rode the elevator to the ground floor in silence, and as they stepped onto the sidewalk, Maya asked, "So, what's next?" wondering if Shannon knew she was asking about more than just their itinerary.

"The Statue of Liberty," Shannon suggested. She took Maya's hand and squeezed it, providing all the answers Maya needed.

"Seriously?"

"Hey, I'm a tourist. It's my first time in New York City."

"Okay. You can be a tourist today." Maya wrapped her arm around Shannon's waist and pulled her closer. "But get it out of your system, because we're going to make a New Yorker out of you."

Shannon smiled and kissed Maya's cheek. "I don't even know what that means."

"It means, only one trip to the statue."

"Until my daughter comes to visit."

"Are you sure I can't interest you in a tour of my apartment instead, specifically the bedroom?"

"Is it a private tour?"

"Very private."

"I'm in." Shannon strode to the curb and stuck her hand out to hail a passing cab. When one stopped, she jerked the door open and said, "Get in."

Maya complied. And when Shannon slid in beside her, she murmured, "That was hot. I'll make a city girl out of you, yet."

"Just don't think I'm forgetting about the statue, or the Empire State Building, or Times Square."

"We'll see it all. Don't worry. We can do anything we want to." For the first time in Maya's life she truly understood what those words meant. She'd had the means to be free for years, and now she finally had a reason.

About the Author

Erin Dutton is the author of eight romance novels: *Sequestered Hearts, Fully Involved, A Place to Rest, Designed for Love, Point of Ignition, A Perfect Match, Reluctant Hope,* and *More Than Friends.* She is also a contributor to *Erotic Interludes 5: Road Games* and *Romantic Interludes 1 & 2* and revisited two characters from one of her novels in *Breathless: Tales of Celebration.* She is a 2011 recipient of the Alice B. Readers' Appreciation Award for her body of work.

When not working or writing, she enjoys playing golf and spending time with friends and family.

Books Available from Bold Strokes Books

Pedal to the Metal by Jesse J. Thoma. When unreformed thief Dubs Williams is released from prison to help Max Winters bust a car theft ring, Max learns that to catch a thief, get in bed with one. (978-1-62639-239-7)

Dragon Horse War by D. Jackson Leigh. A priestess of peace and a fiery warrior must defeat a vicious uprising that entwines their destinies and ultimately their hearts. (978-1-62639-240-3)

For the Love of Cake by Erin Dutton. When everything is on the line, and one taste can break a heart, will pastry chefs Maya and Shannon take a chance on reality? (978-1-62639-241-0)

Betting on Love by Alyssa Linn Palmer. A quiet country-girl-at-heart and a live-life-to-the-fullest biker take a risk at offering each other their hearts. (978-1-62639-242-7)

The Deadening by Yvonne Heidt. The lines between good and evil, right and wrong, have always been blurry for Shade. When Raven's actions force her to choose, which side will she come out on? (978-1-62639-243-4)

Ordinary Mayhem by Victoria A. Brownworth. Faye Blakemore has been taking photographs since she was ten, but those same photographs threaten to destroy everything she knows and everything she loves. (978-1-62639-315-8)

One Last Thing by Kim Baldwin & Xenia Alexiou. Blood is thicker than pride. The final book in the Elite Operative Series brings together foes, family, and friends to start a new order. (978-1-62639-230-4)

Songs Unfinished by Holly Stratimore. Two aspiring rock stars learn that falling in love while pursuing their dreams can be harmonious—if they can only keep their pasts from throwing them out of tune. (978-1-62639-231-1)

Beyond the Ridge by L.T. Marie. Will a contractor and a horse rancher overcome their family differences and find common ground to build a life together? (978-1-62639-232-8)

Swordfish by Andrea Bramhall. Four women battle the demons from their pasts. Will they learn to let go, or will happiness be forever beyond their grasp? (978-1-62639-233-5)

The Fiend Queen by Barbara Ann Wright. Princess Katya and her consort Starbride must turn evil against evil in order to banish Fiendish power from their kingdom, and only love will pull them back from the brink. (978-1-62639-234-2)

Up the Ante by PJ Trebelhorn. When Jordan Stryker and Ashley Noble meet again fifteen years after a short-lived affair, are either of them prepared to gamble on a chance at love? (978-1-62639-237-3)

Speakeasy by MJ Williamz. When mob leader Helen Byrne sets her sights on the girlfriend of Al Capone's right-hand man, passion and tempers flare on the streets of Chicago. (978-1-62639-238-0)

Venus in Love by Tina Michele. Morgan Blake can't afford any distractions and Ainsley Dencourt can't afford to lose control—but the beauty of life and art usually lies in the unpredictable strokes of the artist's brush. (978-1-62639-220-5)

Rules of Revenge by AJ Quinn. When a lethal operative on a collision course with her past agrees to help a CIA analyst on a critical assignment, the encounter proves explosive in ways neither woman anticipated. (978-1-62639-221-2)

The Romance Vote by Ali Vali. Chili Alexander is a sought-after campaign consultant who isn't prepared when her boss's daughter, Samantha Pellegrin, comes to work at the firm and shakes up Chili's life from the first day. (978-1-62639-222-9)

Advance: Exodus Book One by Gun Brooke. Admiral Dael Caydoc's mission to find a new homeworld for the Oconodian people is hazardous, but working with the infuriating Commander Aniwyn "Spinner" Seclan endangers her heart and soul. (978-1-62639-224-3)

UnCatholic Conduct by Stevie Mikayne. Jil Kidd goes undercover to investigate fraud at St. Marguerite's Catholic School, but life gets complicated when her student is killed—and she begins to fall for her prime target. (978-1-62639-304-2)

Season's Meetings by Amy Dunne. Catherine Birch reluctantly ventures on the festive road trip from hell with beautiful stranger Holly Daniels only to discover the road to true love has its own obstacles to maneuver. (978-1-62639-227-4)

Myth and Magic: Queer Fairy Tales edited by Radclyffe and Stacia Seaman. Myth, magic, and monsters—the stuff of childhood dreams (or nightmares) and adult fantasies. (978-1-62639-225-0)

Nine Nights on the Windy Tree by Martha Miller. Recovering drug addict, Bertha Brannon, is an attorney who is trying to stay clean when a murder sends her back to the bad end of town. (978-1-62639-179-6)

Driving Lessons by Annameekee Hesik. Dive into Abbey Brooks's sophomore year as she attempts to figure out the amazing, but sometimes complicated, life of a you-know-who girl at Gila High School. (978-1-62639-228-1)

Asher's Shot by Elizabeth Wheeler. Asher Price's candid photographs capture the truth, but when his success requires exposing an enemy, Asher discovers his only shot at happiness involves revealing secrets of his own. (978-1-62639-229-8)

Courtship by Carsen Taite. Love and justice—a lethal mix or a perfect match? (978-1-62639-210-6)

Against Doctor's Orders by Radclyffe. Corporate financier Presley Worth wants to shut down Argyle Community Hospital, but Dr. Harper Rivers will fight her every step of the way, if she can also fight their growing attraction. (978-1-62639-211-3)

A Spark of Heavenly Fire by Kathleen Knowles. Kerry and Beth are building their life together, but unexpected circumstances could destroy their happiness. (978-1-62639-212-0)

Never Too Late by Julie Blair. When Dr. Jamie Hammond is forced to hire a new office manager, she's shocked to come face to face with Carla Grant and memories from her past. (978-1-62639-213-7)

Widow by Martha Miller. Judge Bertha Brannon must solve the murder of her lover, a policewoman she thought she'd grow old with. As more bodies pile up, the murderer starts coming for her. (978-1-62639-214-4)

Twisted Echoes by Sheri Lewis Wohl. What's a woman to do when she realizes the voices in her head are real? (978-1-62639-215-1)

Criminal Gold by Ann Aptaker. Through a dangerous night in New York in 1949, Cantor Gold, dapper dyke-about-town, smuggler of fine art, is forced by a crime lord to be his instrument of vengeance. (978-1-62639-216-8)

The Melody of Light by M.L. Rice. After surviving abuse and loss, will Riley Gordon be able to navigate her first year of college and accept true love and family? (978-1-62639-219-9)

Because of You by Julie Cannon. What would you do for the woman you were forced to leave behind? (978-1-62639-199-4)

The Job by Jove Belle. Sera always dreamed that she would one day reunite with Tor. She just didn't think it would involve terrorists, firearms, and hostages. (978-1-62639-200-7)

Making Time by C.J. Harte. Two women going in different directions meet after fifteen years and struggle to reconnect in spite of the past that separated them. (978-1-62639-201-4)

Once The Clouds Have Gone by KE Payne. Overwhelmed by the dark clouds of her past, Tag Grainger is lost until the intriguing and spirited Freddie Metcalfe unexpectedly forces her to reevaluate her life. (978-1-62639-202-1)

The Acquittal by Anne Laughlin. Chicago private investigator Josie Harper searches for the real killer of a woman whose lover has been acquitted of the crime. (978-1-62639-203-8)

An American Queer: The Amazon Trail by Lee Lynch. Lee Lynch's heartening and heart-rending history of gay life from the turbulence of the late 1900s to the triumphs of the early 2000s are recorded in this selection of her columns. (978-1-62639-204-5)

Stick McLaughlin: The Prohibition Years by CF Frizzell. Corruption in 1918 cost Stick her lover, her freedom, and her identity, but a very special flapper and the family bond of her own gang could help win them back—even if it means outwitting the Boston Mob. (978-1-62639-205-2)

Edge of Awareness by C.A. Popovich. When Maria, a woman in the middle of her third divorce, meets Dana, an out lesbian, awareness of her feelings brings up reservations about the teachings of her church. (978-1-62639-188-8)

Taken by Storm by Kim Baldwin. Lives depend on two women when a train derails high in the remote Alps, but an unforgiving mountain, avalanches, crevasses, and other perils stand between them and safety. (978-1-62639-189-5)

The Common Thread by Jaime Maddox. Dr. Nicole Coussart's life is falling apart, but fortunately, DEA Attorney Rae Rhodes is there to pick up the pieces and help Nic put them back together. (978-1-62639-190-1)

Jolt by Kris Bryant. Mystery writer Bethany Lange wasn't prepared for the twisting emotions that left her breathless the moment she laid eyes on folk singer sensation Ali Hart. (978-1-62639-191-8)

Searching For Forever by Emily Smith. Dr. Natalie Jenner's life has always been about saving others, until young paramedic Charlie Thompson comes along and shows her maybe she's the one who needs saving. (978-1-62639-186-4)

A Queer Sort of Justice: Prison Tales Across Time by Rebecca S. Buck. When liberty is only a memory, and all seems lost, what freedoms and hopes can be found within us? (978-1-62639-195-6E)

Blue Water Dreams by Dena Hankins. Lania Marchiol keeps her wary sailor's gaze trained on the horizon until Oly Rassmussen, a wickedly handsome trans man, sends her trusty compass spinning off course. (978-1-62639-192-5)

Rest Home Runaways by Clifford Henderson. Baby boomer Morgan Ronzio's troubled marriage is the least of her worries when she gets the call that her addled, eighty-six-year-old, half-blind dad has escaped the rest home. (978-1-62639-169-7)

Charm City by Mason Dixon. Raq Overstreet's loyalty to her drug kingpin boss is put to the test when she begins to fall for Bathsheba Morris, the undercover cop assigned to bring him down. (978-1-62639-198-7)